EDGE OF REASON

AN E.D.G.E. SECURITY NOVEL

TRISH LOYE

ACKNOWLEDGMENTS

There are so many people who have helped in some way in the journey to becoming an author. I belong to an amazing critique group, where I have learned so much from some incredibly talented writers. In particular, Leanne Shirtliffe, an amazingly funny writer, teacher and superwoman, has taught me that I can do it all, but sometimes the kids eat cereal. Brad Somer is an inspiration to me, he writes with a dark humor that epitomizes who he is. From him I'm still learning how to craft killer sentences and how not to be afraid of the raw topics. Nancy Hayes is an extraordinary woman, traveling the world and helping others, while most women her age are just looking after their grandkids. She has shown me who I want to be when I grow up. Thank you all.

I also want to thank a good friend of mine, Will.
I feel privileged to have him in my life. As former special operations and current soldier, his help with the military aspects of this book have been invaluable.
Any mistakes are solely mine. Thanks, buddy.

And last but never least. To a woman who raised four kids while working nights as an emergency room nurse. Thanks for showing me how to work hard and for too much to say here.
This book is for you, Mom.

PROLOGUE

SOMEWHERE IN THE HINDU KUSH, AFGHANISTAN

Petty Officer Rhys "Lucky" Lafayette's legs burned as he raced to the mountaintop with the dead weight of an unconscious man over his shoulder. His lungs labored to gasp in enough air. Fifty yards to the plateau.

He and the rest of his team had just snatched the kidnapped journalist from the Taliban, who now gave chase. Somewhere at the top of the plateau a helicopter was on its way. He hoped.

His two other teammates already lay in wait at the top, their sniper rifles taking out any Taliban getting too close to him, while his best friend stayed at the bottom and also covered his ass. He pushed harder, knowing the longer he took, the longer Lieutenant Jake "College" Harrison was under heavy fire below him.

Sweat dripped into his eyes. Fucking mountains. Give him a flat beach or, hell, even surf torture any day over this scree-covered shit.

He crested the ridge and spotted his teammates Roddy and Scat aiming their rifles downhill. He lowered the haggard man to the ground behind a boulder to protect him from stray bullets, grateful to be rid of the dead weight. "At the top, College," Rhys said into the comm. "Haul ass."

"Wilco."

Rhys dropped to the ground and sighted along his rifle downhill as Jake did a last spray of bullets into the trees, switched out his mags, and sprinted up the slope.

Rhys breathed deep to slow his heart rate. The butt of his FN SCAR Mk 17 dug into his shoulder as he fired round after round into the Taliban assholes chasing Jake.

The thumping of helicopter rotors sounded close behind him, but he didn't look. It was friendly.

"Run faster, College," he said into his mic.

"Roger," came Jake's panting reply. Sure enough, Rhys watched him speed up.

But it wasn't fast enough. Rhys fired again and again.

A large dark-skinned man in unfamiliar fatigues dropped down beside Rhys with an M249 SAW light machine gun, and started strafing the Taliban soldiers who climbed behind Jake.

"Don't hit my guy," Rhys growled.

"Never," the man answered.

"What unit are you guys?" Rhys asked while still firing.

"E.D.G.E." he replied.

"Edge? What the hell is that?"

"The unit saving your asses."

Rhys would have replied but below him, Jake stumbled and clutched his leg. Rhys's chest tightened as Jake went down to one knee. It looked like he'd taken a hit to the thigh.

Rhys didn't even realize he'd gone to a crouched position. "Get up, Jake!" he screamed.

"Dude, where're you going?" the soldier beside him yelled.

Rhys didn't answer. He ran downslope, slipping in the scree, counting on the rest of his team and the new guy to keep him alive.

Jake was moving again—slower than before, but still upslope. It was a testament to his willpower that he kept going at all. Blood drenched his pant leg.

Rhys slid to a stop by Jake and tucked his shoulder under the shorter man's arm. "Come on, College. You're slower than molasses running uphill."

The new soldier had followed Rhys and took Jake's other arm. Together they got him to the top. More men from the new unit lay down covering fire for them. Rhys breathed a sigh of relief when he saw the helicopter sitting just behind the ridge. Jake would need an immediate evac.

Having crested the ridge, they stood in a relative calm on higher ground, protected from enemy fire by their location and the soldiers firing downhill keeping the Taliban back. A soldier from this Edge unit carried the journalist to the helicopter.

A tall woman strode toward them, shouldering her rifle. Her blazing blue eyes held his attention. "I'm Valkyrie," she said. "The team leader." She waved at the dark-skinned soldier holding Jake's other arm. "Doc's our medic, he'll see to your leg."

Rhys couldn't help but stare at the woman. What was she doing here? She turned to him, her face stone cold. "Do you have a problem, sailor?"

That stopped him. She knew they were SEALs, even without identifying insignia. "No, sir," he said and then corrected himself, feeling like a heel. "I mean, ma'am."

She rolled her eyes and faced Jake again. "My team can handle this from here. Get on the bird."

Jake didn't move, just stared at Valkyrie. "You're a woman."

Rhys snorted. No shit.

Valkyrie's voice took on an uncompromising edge. "I'm a captain, and you're done here, sailor. This is now my mission."

But Jake, stubborn as always, just kept going. "You're not spec ops."

Rhys almost grinned at the sparks of temper in Valkyrie's eyes. Whoever she was, she wasn't backing down from confronting a SEAL.

"No," she said. "We're E.D.G.E. operators. Now get your

ass onboard."

She marched off.

Rhys stared after her. "I think I'm in love."

"Edge?" Jake asked the soldier nicknamed Doc.

"E.D.G.E.," he said, as they helped Jake to the waiting helicopter. "Elite Digital and Global Enforcement unit."

"Never heard of it," Jake muttered.

The soldier grinned. "That's the idea."

Rhys knew that secrets lived within secrets in most governments and military units. But it was unusual they hadn't heard even a whisper of this group before. He helped get Jake settled in the MH-60 Black Hawk. Doc knelt beside him and unzipped a medical kit.

The unconscious journalist had already been strapped down and another soldier lifted his eyelids and shone a light in them.

"Thanks for your help, Doc," Rhys said.

"No worries." He applied clotting powder and bandages to Jake's wound, while the other soldier on board turned and immediately got a tourniquet wrapped around Jake's upper thigh, before pulling a saline drip out of a medical kit.

"We'll take care of your friend," Doc said.

An explosion thundered on the slope behind them. Rhys hoped that these E.D.G.E. guys had set that off and not the tangos.

Doc touched his PTT button on his headset and spoke into the mic. "Roger, Valkyrie." Then he nodded at Rhys.

"She needs another set of hands outside."

"I'm on it." Rhys jumped out of the helicopter. Valkyrie crouched behind a boulder with two other men. Gunfire had escalated in the area. He raced over to them and hunkered down.

"We need to get out of here," he said.

She scowled at him. "The Taliban just got reinforcements."

"Let me guess. They've got RPGs." Rocket-propelled grenades could shoot their helicopter out of the sky.

She nodded. "But don't worry, I've got something better." She pulled out six small metal balls from one of the pouches on her webbing.

"You gonna play marbles?" Rhys asked.

She handed three to one of the soldiers and then pointed down one side of the slope in front of them. "Position them there."

"Wilco," the guy said, and he and his buddy took off, staying low.

She watched them for a moment. "Okay. Cover me while I set these little guys."

Valkyrie took off—Rhys had no choice but to follow her. She ran down the mountain straight toward the tangos.

"Are you fucking crazy?" Rhys yelled.

She slid to a stop next to another boulder and crouched behind it. "We can't let the tangos hide in these rocks. They'll be able to take down our bird with those RPGs before we reach altitude." She pulled a strip of plastic off the back of one and stuck it to the rock face in the direction of the tangos.

"What are those things?" Rhys asked.

"Motion-sensor explosives. I designed them myself," she said with a grin.

He wanted to grin back, but this was serious stuff. "But will they work?" She scowled at him. "I just meant they're kinda tiny."

"It's not the size that matters," she said. Her lips quirked in a small smile. "I'm sure you've heard that before. Now cover me."

Before Rhys could think of a reply, she started setting her charges and he went to work firing at any tangos that popped their heads out of the woods below.

As soon as they left, the tangos would rush this slope and land right in the motion sensor's path. He prayed this woman knew what she was doing. He wasn't sure he fully trusted her yet, but she seemed confident about her little bombs.

"They're coming closer," he said. "You done yet?"

"Almost." She moved further downslope to another set of rocks, closer to the tangos.

"Woman, you are driving me insane," he muttered as he followed her, firing as he went.

She hunched down and set the last explosive. A bullet pinged off the rock near her head. Rhys waited for a reaction, but she didn't flinch, just continued working with steady hands. He picked off the tango who'd gotten too close.

"Done. Let's move, sailor," she said. She grabbed her rifle and laid down covering fire. "Run!" she barked at him.

He scowled. "I'm not leaving you."

She looked at him like he was crazy. "Of course you're not. But you must be almost out. Change your mag while you're on the move and then cover me."

"No way," he said, changing his mag while he crouched beside her behind the boulder. "We go together."

Her eyes blazed with anger. She shot more rounds at the encroaching enemy, swore, and then ran up the mountain.

He sprayed another burst and then followed her, pumping his legs, expecting to catch her within a few steps. He planned to run right behind her to protect her back with his body.

But he never got the chance. She raced up the mountain like some kind of deer. He pushed hard, not wanting to be hit by the gunfire that followed them, and he gained on her, but he didn't catch her.

He made the top and ducked behind the ridge, laying flat out beside her to watch the tangos enter their trap.

"Three little bombs might not be enough," he said. "Why don't you get on the bird? My guys and I can cover you and then haul ass to the next ridge where you can circle back for us."

"Shut the fuck up," she said.

"Listen, woman—"

She turned to him. "Call me Valkyrie, or don't call me anything. Now stay on target." She watched down the mountain. The tangos started running full bore up toward them.

Rhys swore to himself. There were too many of them. If they didn't get out of here they'd be slaughtered. He signaled his two other teammates to fall back to the helicopter.

He grit his teeth. He would get this woman, this Valkyrie, out of here even if he had to throw her over his shoulder and carry her to the helicopter. He'd started to rise when she grabbed his shoulder and hauled him back down.

"Three, two, one," she said.

The tangos had crossed into whatever kill zone she'd set up. The explosion boomed across the valley, followed by two more in quick succession. Pulverized rocks and dust covered the area, making it impossible to see.

A vibrating rumble shook the ground under them. The dust began to clear, and he saw Taliban soldiers bracing themselves where they stood or had fallen.

A deafening crack stopped the vibrations. A new mushroom cloud of dust surged up and over the area. At the same time, the thunderous crashing of rocks slid down the mountain in an avalanche, the men screaming as they fell under the wave of it.

"Shit," Rhys breathed. "Remind me never to piss you off."

She stood up and walked over to the waiting helicopter without replying.

Now *that* was a woman. Rhys grinned.

On the bird flying back to safety, she pretended to ignore him, but he could see her glancing at him from the corner of her eye every once in a while.

This wasn't over.

He would find out what E.D.G.E. was, because he planned to meet Valkyrie again.

CHAPTER 1

EIGHTEEN MONTHS LATER...

Cat 'Valkyrie' Richards shouldn't have come. She scanned the fancy-pants wine bar Liam had insisted on. The downtown after-work crowd filled the place. Men in suits and slicked-back hair chatted with women in spiky heels and silk blouses.

Cat played with her wine glass on the table, not listening to whatever legal issue Liam spoke about with his lawyer buddies. She'd only had a few sips, but her tolerance for wine had always been low and she avoided drinking more than one glass in public.

She'd just gotten back from a particularly nasty mission,

and she could still feel the grit of sand in her eyes. Her body ached from the remembered weight of her body armor. She just wanted to go home, throw on her PJs, crack a beer, and catch up on *The Bachelor*.

She shifted the material of her clingy, black blouse. It was ridiculous, with its plunging neckline and low back. A single tie at the back of her neck held the thing up. She wished she hadn't let Dani, her friend from E.D.G.E., talk her into buying it. It showed off her muscular shoulders and back. Dani had said she looked sexy, but from the sidelong glances of the men and women around her she wasn't so sure. Muscles like hers weren't often found on a woman. She twirled her wine again, the red color deep and almost absorbing the light. White wine had always been her preference, if she had to choose.

"Catherine? Earth to Catherine?" Liam said, his pale blue eyes focused on her.

With his expertly styled brown hair and lean, gym-fit body, he was attractive enough. He was no Bachelor, though. Last month he'd hit on her at the Chien Noir, the bar near E.D.G.E. headquarters, and on a whim she'd exchanged numbers with him. This was their second date.

"Yes?" she said.

"Geez, didn't you used to be a soldier? Always on alert? I think you wouldn't notice a terrorist right now if he were sitting next to you."

Not likely. She frowned. "Did you have a question?"

"Relax, Kitty-Cat," he said. "I didn't mean it."

"I've asked you not to call me that."

His two friends smirked, so she pretended they were Taliban fighters and planned out the best way to kill them without a gun. She let her thoughts show in her eyes.

The friends blanched and turned away.

"What is with you tonight, Catherine?" Liam said, scowling. "Why are you pulling this tough-guy shit? You're just a marketing peon now, remember?"

Her cover was a marketing job at E.D.G.E. Securities, a small security company that catered to clients both in North America and abroad. She couldn't tell anyone what she really did—not even her own family.

"I told you, Liam, I just got back from a work trip and I'm tired," she said. "I'm going to the restroom." She picked up her black clutch and headed for the back of the bar, where the washrooms were.

In the ladies' room, two women stood gossiping while a third leaned toward the mirror and applied bright red lipstick. Their conversation stopped. Lipstick woman straightened and gave a small shriek. Cat tensed, scanning the bathroom for a threat.

The woman put her hand over her heart and gave a little laugh. "Omigod, you're so…tall. I thought you were a man." All three women laughed embarrassedly before leaving the bathroom. Cat stood silent while they did. Responding never helped—she'd learned that in high school. She couldn't fight them physically, and she had never been good with words.

She wished Dani were here; her friend could out-snark anyone. Instead, Cat just grit her teeth and did her business.

She washed her hands and eyed herself in the mirror. She stood taller than most women—and most men—at six feet, and had lean muscular arms and shoulders from doing pull-ups and carrying rucksacks. With her short blonde hair, it was probably easy for people to mistake her for a man. And she wore heels tonight. That made her even taller.

More of a freak show.

She blew her bangs out of her eyes. What was she doing here? Why did she even bother to try? She didn't fit in with these dressed-up dolls.

But she didn't exactly fit in with the soldiers, either.

She shook her head. She was getting melancholy. It was time to go home.

Cat made her way back to Liam who, by the look of the bottle of wine, was on his third glass. His voice was loud and too exuberant for whatever story he told. She tapped him on the shoulder.

"Liam, I'm tired and I'd like to go home," she said.

"What? No way, Kitty-Cat. Come on, you can stay out a bit later."

"I asked you not to call me that."

"Kitty-Cat? But you like it." He reached out and stroked her hair. "You should really grow your hair long. It'd be amazing."

She pulled her head away from his hand. "So I can look

like Barbie? No thanks." What had she seen in this guy? Or had she just been tempted because some civilian actually wanted to date her? "I'm heading home. I'll see you around, Liam."

He grabbed her arm. "Wait, Kitty-Cat—I mean Catherine. Why don't you let me finish my wine and I'll see you home?"

His friends Dumb and Dumber stood behind Liam grinning over their glasses. She shook off his hand. "No, thanks. I can take care of myself."

Liam frowned. "You know what, Catherine? That's your problem. You're too much of a man to accept help from one."

She'd had enough. She was aware of someone tall standing at the edge of her vision. Her instinct told her to look, but she needed to finish this. "You mean I should pretend I need you to protect me?"

His lip curled. "No wonder you're single." He turned to his friends. "That bet is not worth it. It'd be like taking a guy to bed."

Her insides froze to ice with his words. The sounds of muted conversations and tinkling glasses rushed away. "What did you say?"

Liam turned to her and put his face close to hers. "I only went out with you on a bet. Seriously, you've got more muscles than most men. You're barely a woman."

The ice inside her cracked and split. She wanted to run, but her temper had other ideas. "You were going to sleep with me on a bet?"

"Yes," he said, straightening to his full height. "I hit on you that night because I was dared to. It's been interesting, if nothing else." He flicked his fingers as if to brush her away.

She didn't really recall snatching his hand, twisting it, and digging her strong fingers into the pressure point at the wrist, but suddenly Liam was on his knees before her, leaning forward trying to ease the pain in his wrist and shoulder. She twisted harder and he writhed.

"Fuck," he said. "Let me go, you crazy bitch."

She applied more pressure and he shrieked. His friends shifted their feet, but did nothing to help their buddy. No worries there. The rest of the crowd had edged back from the confrontation.

The tall figure in her periphery moved toward her main line of sight. Her stomach dropped. What was he doing here? This was so not her night.

Petty Officer Second Class Rhys 'Lucky' Lafayette didn't wear his uniform tonight, just a pair of low-slung jeans, a black t-shirt, and a battered leather jacket. He should have looked out of place among all the suits, but instead he radiated such a bad-boy vibe that every woman in the place followed him with her eyes.

"Hey, Cat," he said. His eyes flicked over Liam before catching hers again. "Whatcha doing, chère?"

His Louisiana drawl wrapped around her, just like his strong arms had six months before.

She swallowed, pushing away the memories of that one explosive night.

"Just teaching someone some manners," she said. How much had he heard? Crap. She could feel her face heat. With her pale skin, it would burn bright red. She looked away from those whiskey-colored eyes and down at the man still cursing her. She tightened her grip and he writhed again, but at least he'd shut up.

Rhys leaned on the table and sipped the beer he carried. "You know, chère, there's going to be a lot of paperwork if you break his arm."

She shrugged. It might be worth it. "What are you doing here? You're supposed to be deployed."

"I was," he said. "I did my tour and now I've got a new one. I'll be an E.D.G.E. operator starting tomorrow."

Crap.

Liam squealed, and she realized she'd twisted too hard. She eased off a bit. "You're assigned to E.D.G.E.? But you're a SEAL. What about your team?"

A grin eased onto his lips and lit his eyes, as if he could barely control his laughter. "E.D.G.E. is my team now."

This couldn't be happening.

Cat saw two male waiters hovering nearby, whispering furiously and gesturing toward her. She yanked Liam's head back by his hair and leaned in, speaking softly. "If I ever hear of you betting about sleeping with a woman again, I will find you and cut your balls off before you even see me coming. It's not like they ever got any use before–you'll hardly miss them."

She flung him to the ground and watched for a moment to make sure he wouldn't attack her when she walked away. Then she picked up her clutch and strode toward the front of the bar. People parted for her. Her heels clicked on the concrete floor in the silence. Everyone watched, but she refused to look around and kept her chin high, though her insides writhed in humiliation.

Outside, she breathed deep of the crisp late-August air, so different from the heat of the desert where she'd been yesterday. A cool wind from the river blew over her skin and she shivered.

She knew Rhys had followed her. He stood behind her right now, not speaking. She liked that. He somehow knew to give her space. She took another deep breath, watching the street traffic. "How much did you hear?" she asked.

"The guy was an ass, Cat."

"So…all of it, then." She closed her eyes. Crap. She did not need the rumor going around the unit that she couldn't get a date. It was true, of course, but she hated people talking about her. She turned to him. "Look, I appreciate you not interfering in there."

He shrugged. "Why would I interfere? You had everything under control."

"Right. Just not my temper."

He laughed. "I repeat, the guy was an ass and needed to be taken down. He's lucky it was you. I wouldn't have let him off so easy."

A warmth spread through her at his words, but she ignored it and stifled the urge to smile back at him.

"Thanks." Then her mind latched onto the last words he'd spoken in the bar.

E.D.G.E. Securities, the top-secret, international government unit where she loved working, now also employed Rhys. Her stomach fluttered with nerves. She wasn't sure if they were from Rhys standing too close to her, or the fact that he could destroy her reputation and even her career with a few well-chosen remarks.

She lifted her chin. "I'd appreciate you not telling anyone about this." She waved her hand at the bar and then waved it between them. "Or anything about…that night."

His head tilted as he studied her. She wanted to squirm under that intense gaze, but she held still. A slow smile lit his face and his eyes. "I don't kiss and tell, chère."

She blew her bangs out of her eyes. She was too tired to deal with Rhys. "I'll see you tomorrow at work." She pretended that thought didn't make her queasy and started walking home, leaving the temptation of his smile behind.

What the hell? Rhys stared after Cat as she walked away. He let her go for a moment and just appreciated the view. The top she wore exposed her back and narrow waist. The tight jeans showed off an excellent ass and long legs. The woman didn't need heels, but he wasn't complaining. They did something to the way she walked, giving more sway to her stride, focusing his attention there. It brought back memories of their night together.

He and his buddy Jake had just finished working an op with E.D.G.E., the Elite Digital and Global Enforcement unit. It had been a test run to see if he fit with the E.D.G.E. team. Cat had joined him in the elevator on the way out of HQ. He'd smiled a welcome.

"Looks like your friend, Jake, found a reason to join E.D.G.E.," she'd said. "Dani seems like a nice girl."

"She's not the only reason," he said. "Jake doesn't make emotional decisions." At least he never had before. Rhys shrugged. "Either way, I think this assignment will be good for him."

She'd watched him a moment. "But not you?"

"My SEAL team is deploying in two weeks, they're counting on me." He didn't add that he'd already decided it would be his last deployment with them. He wanted to work at E.D.G.E. He loved the idea of what they did, and was ready for something new. He eyed the tall blonde captain in front of him.

And the scenery wasn't too shabby, either.

She'd smiled then and, as his grand-mère would say, he'd seen the devil in her eyes. "Want to grab a drink, sailor?"

That was an invitation he couldn't refuse.

They hadn't even made it to the bar. He'd snagged her hand once they were outside and the current between them at the simple touch had stopped them both. The vivid blue of her eyes turned darker. He tugged lightly on her hand

and she'd come to him willingly. He'd loved her height and how he hadn't had to lean down to kiss her. But he'd loved the sounds she made even more. Her apartment had only been a few blocks away from E.D.G.E. HQ and they'd run there, laughing, as if they were doing something illicit.

And technically, an officer fraternizing with an enlisted man was a good way to get court-martialed, but she'd obviously thought he was leaving for good. He hadn't told her he was coming back, because he suspected she'd put an end to the heaven of that night. And hell, he wanted that piece of heaven. He'd dreamed of it throughout his whole deployment. She was strong and soft at the same time, a combination he couldn't stop thinking about.

One he wanted again.

It had been pure fluke running into her tonight. He happened to be staying in the hotel next to the bar. It wasn't his usual type of place, but the concierge had recommended it. When he'd seen her there, his gut had tightened and memories of that night had washed over him. It had taken him a long moment to see the tightness around her eyes and mouth, and the stiffness of her body. That's when he'd seen the asshole speaking to her, obviously giving her some kind of crap. He'd started toward her, but had stopped as soon as she'd put the guy in a wrist lock. Laughter bubbled up inside him even now as he remembered the look on the guy's face.

Cat's face, on the other hand, still had that pinched look as she walked away.

He shook his head. Maybe she needed a distraction.

He quickly caught up to her. "Where are we going, chère?"

She sighed and stopped. "*We* are not going anywhere. *I'm* going home. You can go anywhere you want."

He grinned when she held up her hand and amended herself. "Anywhere but my place. We had fun one night. But it was only one night. Leave it in the past. We'll be working together. It's not appropriate for…" Her hand waved back and forth between them.

"For?" His grin got wider when she narrowed her eyes at him.

Then she stepped close. "I will not have you jeopardizing my career. You will keep your mouth shut at E.D.G.E. or I will see your deployment here cut short, Petty Officer."

"Yes, ma'am," he said without hesitation. But he held her gaze for a moment before replying. "And I've already told you, I won't say anything."

"Good." She turned and strode away.

He let her get a bit ahead of him before he followed discreetly. Cat could take care of herself, but he'd been taught by his grand-mère to never let a woman walk home alone in the dark.

After a block, she turned and stared straight at him. He gave a little salute and smiled at the glare she gave him.

He'd known this would be an interesting assignment.

Cat scowled at Rhys as he smiled at her, even though the sight of him made her mouth water. Memories of their time together surfaced. Visions of his sculpted muscles and strong hands made her ache.

Stop that!

She whirled and stomped away, cursing the man. Did he think she needed protection? She was a highly trained soldier, dammit. She walked faster. Tonight had been a disaster from start to finish, she just wanted it over with.

Her phone chimed. A small groan escaped her when she saw the caller. Apparently the disaster was still in progress.

"Who's calling, chère?" Rhys asked from behind her.

She walked faster. A glance back showed he kept pace, his eyes glowing with amusement.

She debated not answering for a moment, but knew that she wouldn't be able to dodge the caller long. And it would only make the conversation worse when it finally happened.

She answered. "Hey, Mom." Her stomach plummeted when she heard Rhys snort softly behind her.

"Catherine," her mother chirped. "I've been trying to get hold of you for days. Haven't you gotten my voicemails?"

"Yes, Mom, but—"

"Do they keep you so busy at your company that you can't call your mother?"

"No, Mom. I mean yes, I've been busy. I was away on business." She hated lying to her mom, but no one, not even her brothers or father in the military, could know what she did.

"Away?" her mother sounded disappointed. "I thought you agreed to tell that company you didn't want to travel so much anymore."

Her shoulders tensed. She knew where this was going. Rhys was only five feet away as he kept pace with her, listening intently, a devilish gleam in his eye.

"Mom, I never agreed to that. You're the one who wants me to stop traveling."

Her mother's long drawn-out sigh made Cat pull the phone away from her ear and curse softly. Rhys chuckled. She scowled at him before putting the phone back to her ear. Her mother was still speaking.

"...ever meet a nice man?"

Someone shoot me.

"I meet plenty of nice men at work," Cat said.

Now Rhys sounded like he was choking.

"But," her mother said, "are they eligible men?"

She coughed. "Do we have to talk about this now, Mom?"

"Between you and your brother Dylan, I don't know who's worse."

Dylan was only her senior by two years. She'd followed him into CSOR, the Canadian Special Operations Regiment, and he'd been just as proud as her father when she'd earned a spot beside him. Dylan had taken her leaving CSOR hard and it had torn a rift between them.

"How is Dylan? Have you spoken to him?" Between her

schedule and Dylan's, and him being based in Petawawa and her in Montreal, she hadn't seen him in a year and hadn't spoken to him in months.

"Not recently. You know how busy the regiment is. But I called to talk about you, Catherine."

Cat tensed. "About me?"

"Well, I think you're working too hard. You're traveling too much. You should be enjoying life, having fun while you're young-"

"You mean dating," Cat said in a low voice. She could almost feel Rhys's interest perk up.

"Sweetie, you know I only have your best interests at heart."

"Look, Mom, I'm fine. In fact I was just on a date."

Rhys laughed. Cat stopped walking and punched him in the arm. That only made him laugh louder.

"I hear a man laughing," her mother said, sounding excited. "Are you still on your date?"

"No, Mom—"

Rhys continued to snicker.

"No, dear. I'm going to let you go. You can tell me all about him later." Her mother hung up.

Cat wanted to scream, knowing her mother would call tomorrow and want to hear all about her *date*. She slid her phone away and pointed at Rhys. "You are annoying." She strode away and yelled over her shoulder. "And stop following me!"

He didn't, of course. He chuckled and followed her to

her apartment building door two blocks later.

"Goodnight, chère," he said, his voice warm and low. "I'll see you tomorrow."

She hated that his voice made her insides melt, and it took a moment for his words to sink in.

Tomorrow.

She ground her teeth together. "You will not speak to anyone about this evening."

A little spark of anger lit his eyes and he moved closer, until she swore she could feel the heat from his body. "I've already told you, I won't say anything."

She refused to move back. "Good." She swallowed, trying to get herself under control. "We probably won't see much of each other anyway. My team is full."

He moved away, his eyes unreadable. "That's a damn shame, chère. I think we'd work well together." He nodded at her and sauntered off into the night. She cursed her luck and went up to her apartment, wondering what else could go wrong.

CHAPTER 2

The next morning, Cat yawned as she rode the elevator to the seventh floor and wondered whose team Rhys would be assigned to. E.D.G.E. operators usually worked in teams of four. At least she knew Rhys wouldn't be on hers. She, Lieutenant Colonel Derrick Blackwell, Sergeant Zach Grayson, and former CSIS agent Marc Koven made up Alpha team. They'd all swapped stories of what they'd do with their two weeks off when they made it home.

Once she filed her report, she was on R and R. Maybe she'd head to her parent's ranch outside Calgary. But then she'd have to defend herself from her father's guilt trips about leaving the Army and her mother's matchmaking attempts. According to her mother, Cat's biological clock was ticking. How she wished she could tell both of them—well, at least her father—what she was doing. She hated seeing the disappointment on his face.

She rolled her neck, trying to loosen the tight muscles. Maybe she'd just hang around Montreal and catch up on training. She must be due to re-qualify on something. And the longer she could put off seeing Rhys again the better—even if he had been sweet last night when he'd followed her home. It hadn't felt like an overprotective boyfriend, but more of a teammate who had her back. She just needed a bit of space and time to bury the feelings he stirred in her. The night they'd shared together had heated her dreams for months afterwards.

Just as it had last night.

The elevator door pinged open and she stepped out. Rhys stood in E.D.G.E.'s main reception area on the seventh floor. His jeans hung just a bit loose on him and a blue long-sleeved t-shirt hugged his chest and powerful arms. Her heart leapt at the sight of him, until she noticed who he was with.

Cat froze for a moment, assessing the scene in front of her. A splash of cold reality doused any lingering warmth she had for him.

He smiled down at cute, petite Ashley-who worked in the civilian side of the company, as an actual marketing exec to keep up its cover. Cat was pretty sure Ashley had no idea of what E.D.G.E. actually did. She seemed to be one of those people who was happy not to question the status quo, unlike Cat's friend Dani, who questioned everything, and consequently worked for the military side of E.D.G.E.

Ashley flung her blonde hair back as she laughed and placed a possessive hand on Rhys's bicep. Cat recognized the look on his face as he gazed at the girl.

'Lucky' Lafayette knew he could have her. Obviously, he was a player… Now she knew just where his handle had come from. A guy who liked women, and lots of them.

Ashley looked over at Cat and smiled, but Cat saw the warning in her eyes and the way her hand rubbed Rhys's arm, staking her territory.

Well, that was fine by her. It had been fun with Rhys, but it never could have continued. They worked together, and sooner or later, Rhys would have become resentful of her.

Her experience had taught her that through hard work and going beyond what was called for, she could convince men in the military that she not only belonged, but that she was their equal. Unfortunately, she'd also learned that all that hard work went out the window if you slept with one of them.

Time to put the memories of Rhys and that night away for good. She kept her face professional as she strode to Estelle Waters's desk. She was the steel-haired dragon lady who guarded Commander Knight from intruders. Cat had long ago learned to come bearing gifts. At the moment, Ms. Waters watched Rhys and Ashley as if they were trespassers not fit to be in her territory.

"Hey, Estelle," she said. "I brought you a book." She dug

out the latest Jeaniene Frost book and handed it over. She and Estelle both loved romance with a kick-butt heroine, though Cat wasn't quite as open about it as Estelle was. "Is the big guy in?"

Estelle nodded and took the book. "Was it as good as the last one?"

"Better," Cat said.

Rhys turned toward them and smiled at her. He opened his mouth to say something, but she walked away before he could.

She rapped once on Commander Adam Knight's office door. When a deep voice called out, she entered.

Commander Knight looked up from the papers spread out on the conference table on one side of the room. Alpha team leader Derrick Blackwell stood with him, as did Marc Koven.

"I'm sorry to interrupt, sir." She lifted the file folder she carried. "I just wanted to drop off my report on the last mission."

"No worries, Cat," Commander Knight said. "I'm glad you're here. We were going to call you in anyway."

That didn't sound good for her downtime, but she shrugged off the disappointment. This is what she'd signed up for when she'd agreed to be an E.D.G.E. operator, always ready for the next mission. She nodded and joined them at the table.

"Have you heard of Boko Haram?"

She nodded. "Militant Islamic group based in Nigeria.

They're terrorizing the country and the surrounding area. They kidnapped those schoolgirls last spring." It had been all over the news for weeks.

Commander Knight nodded. "Boko Haram means 'Western Education is forbidden.' The U.S. designated the group as a terrorist organization in November, 2013. They've abducted over five hundred women and children and killed more than five thousand civilians, including a large number of school-aged boys. They like to use suicide bombers and will kill anyone to achieve their goals—children, the elderly, and even other Muslims at prayer."

Anger swirled in her gut at the ruthlessness. "Do we get to go do something about them?"

"Not yet," Commander Knight said. "I'm just giving you some background. The rest of the intel is in the brief."

"Why are we involved then, sir?"

"A U.S. senator's son might be missing in the area. He's with Doctors Without Borders."

"*Might* be missing?"

"He's missed his check-in. I know the senator and he's asked us to be on standby. Which means your leave is cancelled, since I need you to bring on a new team member and get them up to speed."

She glanced at Blackwell. "But we've got four already."

Blackwell's lips compressed for a moment. "Sorry, Cat. I have personal business I have to attend to. I'm signing the team over to you. We'd like to eventually have you as a team leader, so this will be a good test."

Warmth spread through her. The fact that Blackwell and Knight thought she could lead the team better than anyone else made her stand straighter.

"Of course, sir. Who's the fourth member?" Even as she finished asking the question, she knew. Her stomach dropped and all the pride drained from her. She envisioned her hard-won career exploding like C-4 on a mud-hut wall.

Commander Knight answered, "Petty Officer Lafayette." He handed her a file folder. "Here's his information. I'm going to speak with him first, and then he's all yours."

There was nothing she could do but nod. "Very good, sir."

After speaking with Commander Knight, Rhys made his way to the sixth floor via the circular interior stairs that led down into the operator's lounge. The team leaders' offices sat on the other end of the building, past the workout room and a couple of conference rooms. He'd just learned of his new assignment, to Alpha team. According to his briefing, they'd just come back from the Middle East and were now on standby for a new mission in West Africa.

A busy life without a lot of time for training. Not like in the SEAL teams, where you deployed for six months and then trained extensively for twelve to eighteen months before deploying again. It's not like SEALs were home a lot, though. Like most spec ops warriors, their training took them all over the world.

But here at E.D.G.E., the operators fit in small bursts of training or re-qualifying between missions. It's why they only took on the elite of the elite. In Commander Knight's words, the operators had to know their shit before they got here. There was no time to play catch-up.

And that was just fine with him. He loved the adrenaline rush of missions. He knew he was dangerously close to becoming addicted, but he'd hidden that from his brothers-at-arms under his easygoing 'Lucky' persona.

He found the Alpha team's office and knocked. At the muffled "come in," he opened the door and came to attention, saluting sharply.

"At ease, Petty Officer," the husky female voice said.

He snapped his gaze toward the woman sitting behind the wooden desk and almost groaned aloud. Cat was his superior officer?

Fuck.

She nodded at the seat across from her, her face calm and professional, no hint of softness anywhere. Just like he'd expect from his superior. Damn. He slid into the chair.

"You're Alpha team leader, ma'am?" He had to be sure. Maybe it was a mistake.

She nodded and steel entered her voice. "You gonna have a problem with that, sailor?"

He shoved all images of her writhing naked beneath him into a box in his mind and locked it. Could he take orders from a woman? He never had before. She'd seemed competent enough the two times he'd worked with her, and she'd been cool and focused in the thick of it. As long as she was capable, then he could take her orders.

He hoped.

She still waited for his answer, her eyebrows drawing together.

"No, ma'am," he said. He was so fucked.

She kept up her stare for another minute, as if daring him to bring up either that one glorious night, or the fact that she was a woman. He just stared back, game face on. He'd see how she did. He was totally capable of handling a woman if she got stressed or scared, though he had a feeling Cat would be tougher than most.

She nodded once and then opened a file on her desk. "I'll keep this brief, since I know you're more than qualified to be here. All E.D.G.E. operators are." She flipped through a few pages. "What's your specialty?"

"Specialty? I'm a SEAL, ma'am. We're trained to do it all."

She rolled her eyes. "Yes, but what are you the best at? What do you like most of all?"

"I love it all, ma'am. Hand-to-hand, weapons, sniper, you name it. I'm a Jack-of-all-trades."

She studied him some more. "You realize that we are even more secretive than most special ops units. That only the highest branches of governments and the militaries we work for even know about us. And it has to stay that way."

What was she getting at? "Like I told you before: I don't tell my secrets."

She raised one slender brow at that. "This is more than

not telling anyone about the latest mission. This is about not telling anyone about your life. You will have a cover here that includes leaving the military."

He nodded. "The commander said as much."

She pressed her lips together, something he was beginning to recognize as the first pricking of her temper. "Let me say this a different way, *Lucky*. You won't be able to pick up women by telling them you're in the military."

He scowled. Was she seriously going there? "Excuse me, ma'am. But my personal life is none of your concern." He leaned back in his chair and put on a cocky smile. "I really won't have a problem, though. I've never had to rely on it before. Most women jump me without me even having to say a word. In fact, one time, in an elevator right here at E.D.G.E.—"

"You've made your point, Lafayette."

"Roger that, ma'am. Anything else?"

Her lips stayed pressed tightly together. "What about your friends and family? Can you live with them thinking you're no longer a vaunted SEAL?"

"Wow," he drawled sarcastically. "You really have a low estimation of my character."

"These are standard questions."

"Are they now?" Before she could say anything more, he answered her first question. "My friends know not to ask questions of my work."

"Meaning they're all SEALs."

He gave a sharp nod, feeling somehow not up to par

because he didn't have friends in the civilian world. But who had time for that in their lifestyle?

"And your family?"

He grit his teeth. "If you'd bothered to read that file in front of you, you would have seen that I have no family."

She had the grace to look embarrassed. She closed the file. "I'm sorry," she said. "There's no excuse."

The softly spoken apology made up for whatever criticism she had directed at him. "It's fine."

"Good. We're on call for a mission in West Africa. Introduce yourself to the rest of Alpha team and get settled in today. IT will need to see you as well. Briefing at 0500 tomorrow."

"Yes, ma'am." He stood.

She leaned back in the chair and sighed. "We're not so formal here, Lucky. Lose the ma'am."

"Yes, ma-" He raised his eyebrows, waiting.

"The team calls me Valkyrie."

He couldn't help his grin widening. "I remember. It suits you."

CHAPTER 3

"A senator's son has gone missing," Blackwell told Cat and her team the next morning. "His father has asked us to find him and bring him home."

Blackwell tapped some buttons and the virtual monitor appeared on the plexi-wall behind him, made for that purpose. He stood and pulled on a special glove with nano-circuitry that allowed him to flick through the files of the computer as if he touched the virtual screen. Soon a map appeared. He made an expanding motion with his hand and the map zoomed in.

Nigeria.

"Senator Warren Hutchins's son is a doctor who went to Nigeria with Doctors Without Borders. He's been there for three months. Last week, he traveled to a small village south of Hadejia with another man, Dr. Samuel Botman." With a flick of his fingers, Blackwell brought up two photos—one of a smiling man in his mid-twenties with long hair pulled back in a ponytail, and the other of an older gentleman with a graying close-clipped beard.

"Neither of them returned," he continued. "I don't need to remind any of you that Northeastern Nigeria is Boko Haram's territory. I've had IT scour the Black Net for any new uploaded videos, but they've come up empty. If the Boko Haram have them then they're not saying."

Doc leaned his large frame back in the chair. "Could these guys just be lost?"

Blackwell sighed. "It's a possibility, and the best one we've got at the moment. Either way, you'll insert with a HAHO night jump from a C-130 Hercules at thirty thousand feet. You'll have forty kilometers to navigate to get to the village. An intelligence asset will make contact south of the village. This is a fact-finding mission, but if you get an actual lead on the young doctor then grab him if you can."

"Roger that, sir," Cat said.

"Further details are in the brief."

She frowned. "What do we know of the asset? Are they one of ours?"

Blackwell shook his head. "CIA's."

"So that means they're only trustworthy until the money runs out," Marc said cynically.

Blackwell looked at Cat. "You up for this?"

"Of course, sir." As if she would say anything else. "But like Marc, I've always got reservations about an unknown asset."

"Don't we all. Keep your eyes sharp over there," Blackwell said. "The rest of the info is in the brief. Wheels up in four hours."

They filed out and headed for the locker room where they began kitting up-double checking their weapons, ammo, rucksacks, and parachutes.

Everything needed to be meticulously packed and the weight evenly distributed. With a high-altitude, high-opening jump, each member of the team needed to weigh the same. This meant Cat had to carry more weight than Zach, who outweighed her by at least fifty pounds. She considered HAHO jumps to be the most exhilarating, but they were also damned uncomfortable.

Three hours and forty-five minutes later, Cat waited on the roof for her team to arrive. The high walls hid the two CH-146 Griffon helicopters from the sight of other buildings. Their pilot already waited in the bird with most of their gear, and would take them to the jet that would fly them the rest of the way.

Marc and Zach nodded at her as they came up onto the roof. They both wore their BDUs like she did and had their FN SCAR rifles packed in special carry cases slung over their shoulders. The sight of them would make any civilian in downtown Montreal pause, which was why all of their equipment was kept onsite and out of view.

Now, Rhys followed Zach and Marc. He grinned as he passed her. "Valkyrie."

Why when he said her call sign did it sound like a term of endearment from one lover to another? The last thing she needed was for him to see her that way. Today she would begin to prove to him that she was more than capable of leading this team. It was also time to see whether he had what it took to work with Alpha team.

She climbed aboard the Griffon and gave the pilot the all-clear. Within moments they lifted off, having already gained clearance from Montreal air traffic control.

"Did you read the brief on the asset?" she asked Marc once they'd all donned their ear protection and mics.

"Yes," Marc said. "He seems legit, but there're too many variables."

"Where's the fun in knowing everything, eh, Spooky?" she said, and couldn't stop her grin.

"Fuck, you know I hate that name."

"We know it," she and Zach said together.

"CIA?" Rhys asked him.

If anything, Koven's scowl deepened. "CSIS," he said, naming the Canadian spy agency.

Rhys nodded and looked to Zach. "Doc. So you're a medic?"

"Well, he's not a dwarf," Cat said.

Zach laughed and stretched his six-foot frame. "18-Delta." It was all Zach needed to say. 18-Delta was the forty-six-week Special Operations Combat Medic course that said he was the best of the best.

"But that's not the real reason we call him that," Cat said.

Rhys looked at her. She shrugged. "Zach takes care of everyone."

"Whether they want him to or not," Marc muttered.

"So says our resident cynic," Cat said.

"Better cynic than a fucking optimist."

"Children, please," Zach said. "Not in front of the FNG."

Rhys snorted. "I haven't been called the fucking new guy in years."

"Then tell me," Zach said, "why do they call you Lucky?"

Rhys shrugged and leaned back. "I had a close call at BUD/S. The petty officer in charge said I was the luckiest sonuvabitch he'd met."

"Huh," Marc said. "I would have thought it was for other reasons."

Cat tried to pretend she wasn't listening to every word, but Rhys caught her gaze when he answered, his Louisiana drawl deepening. "Well, others have thought the same for some reason. And I confess, I do have other skills…like I'm a badass poker player."

Zach laughed while Cat busied herself checking her gear. No matter what he said, Rhys 'Lucky' Lafayette had player written all over him.

The guys began chatting and getting to know each other, but Cat withdrew from the conversation. Time to focus on the mission. She pulled out her maps to study while they flew.

Cat and the rest of her team slept as much as they could on the way to the staging area at a Niger airbase friendly to the West. Once they were downrange, sleep and food were luxuries that weren't always possible.

Many hours later, after a jet and a stop in Germany to switch to a C-160 Transall transport plane, the team finally landed at the Niger airbase where they switched to a C-130 Hercules.

The bare-bones interior of a Herc wasn't a comfy place to sleep, with its webbing jump seats and the noise of the aircraft throbbing in Cat's teeth. The cold at this altitude sank into her bones, making sleep even more difficult. They also all wore oxygen masks to prevent hypoxia and carried supplemental oxygen on the jump. She was still able to doze a bit, having learned long ago to sleep when and where she could.

She was confident she knew the mission. The HAHO night drop was possibly the hardest part. A hop and pop always held dangers. Frostbite, life-threatening hypoxia, and chute failure were only some of them. Once in theatre they'd meet the asset, get his info, and hump it out to their exfil thirty klicks north to the border, where a Black Hawk would pick them up. Hopefully, they'd even have the young doctor in tow.

The jump master—a squat, square man—shook her out of her doze. "Twenty minutes. Oxygen check."

She checked her oxygen flow through her mask and gave a thumbs up. Time to start preparing. She stood, stretching her arms high and cracking her neck. "Any new weather systems, chief?" she asked over the comm system.

"Skies are clear, ma'am," the jump master replied.

In the air, the jump master ruled. He could abort their mission if he felt the jump unsafe in any way. But according to him, the weather was holding clear—good news, since it was wet season in Nigeria.

Cat already wore her protective jumpsuit to shield her from the cold. Now was the time to double check each other's packs, chutes, and lines.

She tapped Marc and Zach's shoulders where they sat slumped against the cabin wall of the Herc. Rhys's eyes opened before she even touched him.

"Twenty minutes," she said.

Marc and Zac paired up checking each other while she as team leader took the new guy. She checked Rhys's harnesses and his attached drop bag, being thorough as she tugged at the shoulder, leg, and waist straps. She made sure his weapon was tied against his side out of the way of his oxygen tank, before checking the drop bag attached to his front and strapped in front of his thighs.

She gave him a thumbs up and then he did the same for her, double and triple checking her harnesses. She stepped back when he went to check her parachute for a fourth time. "I think I'm good, Lucky."

"Just wanted to be sure," he said, and his hands flexed.

She stared hard at him. He was feeling protective, and that wasn't a good thing. Teammates had to have each other's backs, but they also had to trust each other to get the job done. If Rhys felt too protective then he might second-guess her or her orders. It had happened to her in the past, when men she'd been assigned to work with hadn't been able to overcome the desire to protect a woman. It caused strife among the team and she now knew the warning signs.

This was a simple mission, and a seasoned SEAL shouldn't be tense. Cat looked at Rhys, whose hands still flexed and clenched. He kept sneaking peeks at her and his mouth would open like he wanted to say something, but he never did.

Her gut twisted and the skin at the back of her neck prickled. Marc and Zach noticed Rhys's preoccupation, too. If they started watching each other instead of paying attention to the mission, this was going to end up as a shit show.

She growled into her mask. Not her mission.

She stood in front of Rhys. "Channel two, sailor." She wanted him on a private comm link.

As soon as he flipped the switch, she let him have it. "Whiskey tango foxtrot, Lucky?"

"What do you mean, what the fuck?" he asked, his eyes widening behind his goggles.

"You're acting like this is your first jump. What. The. Fuck?"

"I'm fine."

She shook her head. "Don't give me that shit. We're about to go into the mission. We can all see you're tense.

And unless you're the only SEAL to never do a covert night jump, then you're worried about working with me."

"Fuck," he said, anger lighting his eyes. "Fine. Have you led missions before? Have you done HAHOs?"

"You're asking me now for my fucking resume?" she said. "Just curious, but do you trust Marc and Zach? Do you want their resumes too?"

He hesitated, and that told her everything. He did trust Marc and Zach. And he didn't trust her. Obviously he was trying to spare her feelings, or some shit like that.

"If you trust the men," she snapped, "then trust me. I have the same experience level, but I've led more missions than either of them. How the fuck do you think I became team leader?"

He didn't answer, but his angry eyes told her everything. She sucked in a breath, feeling almost as if he'd punched her.

"I earned this position," she growled. "I am *not* a fucking quota and I certainly didn't sleep my way here."

"I didn't sa—"

"Shut the fuck up," she said, rage boiling. "You listen to me and you do exactly what I say down there. Or I swear, I'll leave you to guard the DZ."

She switched back to the main channel. Marc and Zach watched her. "You good, Valkyrie?" asked Zach, his compassionate gaze at odds with the sight of his large frame kitted out with 150 pounds of weapons and gear. He stood as if he didn't carry any extra weight at all.

Zach had been with her the longest. They'd met in the Canadian Special Operations Regiment. He'd been one of the first to treat her fairly, and for that he'd always be one of her closest friends.

She took a deep breath and released it slowly, willing her emotions away. A mission was no time to have a temper tantrum. As much as she wanted to pound the shit out of something, that would have to wait.

"I'm good," she replied, her voice steady. "Let's fly."

The jump master gave the signal and they made their way back to the ramp as it lowered, moving awkwardly under the weight of all the gear and the packing necessary for a balanced jump. Red lights lined the ramp on either side.

Freezing air rushed around them, biting at any exposed skin. The ground was lost in the dark. With no illumination below, it looked like they were jumping into a black oblivion lit only by the flashing lights on their plane's wings. It was truly a leap of faith.

She shivered in anticipation. Nothing was better than a night jump, and she wasn't going to let Rhys's caveman attitude get to her or this mission.

"Radio check." While this wasn't a complicated mission, she needed to stay vigilant and not lose focus again.

"Five by five, Valkyrie," Rhys said, his voice sounding clear in her ear bud inside her helmet. She let the bit of edge in his voice pass.

Zach and Marc checked in and the team lined up behind

her. She checked her heading in her GPS and the wind speed, doing some mental calculations-trying to enjoy the howling wind, knowing she would be steaming in the heat very soon.

"Fifteen seconds," the jump master said.

Cat balanced her weight on her toes, ready to jump.

The ramp lights turned green. The jump master extended his arm, pointing at the ramp. "Go. Go. Go."

"Time to fly," she said.

She leapt, arching her back, thrusting out her arms and legs, almost spread-eagled. Speed and turbulence hit. The wind tore at her as she rushed toward the ground, letting the darkness swallow her.

CHAPTER 4

R hys watched Cat leap from the plane and disappear into the night. He jumped right after her, Marc and Zach on his heels. They each had an infrared light attached to their helmets so they could track each other in the darkness with their NVGs on.

The wind tore into every crevice in his jumpsuit and pack, cutting with an icy blade into his skin and roaring its fury. Frostbite was a real danger at this altitude. Even so, the rush of falling at 120 miles per hour set his heart thumping. He loved jumping and usually grinned his whole way down.

Not this time.

His gut twisted with worry. Not for himself—his rucksack felt balanced and so did he, which meant no uncontrolled spinning. He glanced at Cat and resisted the urge to streamline his body to get closer to her. That would be suicide if their chutes opened too close. Below him, she pulled her chute. It filled perfectly and something inside him eased.

He looked at his altimeter, attached to his left forearm like a giant watch. Twenty-seven thousand feet. They only had a little more than ten seconds of free fall on this jump before they'd glide the twenty-five miles to the DZ, near the village. Cat had chosen a small clearing for the drop zone, one that shouldn't pose problems as long as the weather held.

He brought his right hand to the ripcord and put his left behind his head to balance. Then he spread both arms wide again, pulling his chute at the same time.

The jolt of the chute opening threw him hard and even though he'd been expecting it, the harness wrapped around his legs still dug into his groin. He'd be sore through his shoulders tomorrow, but he'd still take the thrill of a hop and pop over a regular jump any day.

The release tugged him upward and the roaring sound of the wind lessened as his chute opened fully and he began to glide. Not that he could hear much with his helmet and oxygen mask. He used the waist toggles to steer and followed Cat's lead. A quick glance over his shoulder and he spotted both Marc and Zach's chutes open above him. Then he checked his GPS and heading, making sure they were on course. That wasn't him not trusting Cat—every special ops soldier checked their own altimeter and GPS on a HAHO.

But he had to stop himself from verbally checking in with her. He wondered if she'd done many of these jumps. Would she release her drop bag on time?

He growled. What the fuck was wrong with him? He hadn't been this stressed about a jump since the first time he'd done one. He had to stop thinking of her as someone breakable, someone who needed help. She was his fucking team leader, and he'd better get his head screwed on right or he could fuck up this whole mission.

Ten minutes into the glide, Rhys checked his GPS. "Valkyrie, we need to correct our bearing by two degrees."

A long, drawn-out sigh came through his earpiece. Definitely Cat.

Then he heard Zach's deep chuckle. "Boy, you are in for it."

"Lucky," Cat said, using his call sign now that the mission had started. "I have the GPS coordinates for the DZ. There is also a ten-kilometer-per-hour wind from the south, hence my bearing is altered slightly to accommodate it. Do you have any other questions?"

By the time she'd finished speaking, a dangerous edge had grown in her voice. "Negative, Valkyrie." He wasn't stupid.

They didn't speak much after that. And that was okay. He loved the quiet tranquility of a jump before a mission. At twelve thousand feet, he pulled his oxygen mask off and relished breathing fresh crisp air.

He managed to stay quiet until he spotted the clearing. Two thousand feet and dropping fast. The wind shifted and the words came out before he could stop them. "Watch the wind, Valkyrie," he said over the radio. "It's shifted to the west. It'll add to your landing speed."

"Shut the fuck up, Lucky."

Marc snickered over the comms.

At five hundred feet he toggled and trimmed his chute, turning into the wind to help reduce his speed. His teammates did the same. He spared a quick glance and saw Cat already on the ground disengaging from her chute.

He lowered his drop bag so he could release it before he landed and it wouldn't tangle his legs. At sixty feet he braked.

The ground rushed up at him. He hit, rolled, and bounced up. The chute dragged him a couple of steps before he controlled it. He shook out his legs-numb from hanging in a harness for thirty minutes-as he unhooked himself and started hauling in his chute. His drop bag waited about thirty yards away. He pulled his ruck out and stuffed his parachute and jumpsuit inside.

When he looked up, Cat stood in front of him, her drop bag already buried under dirt and brush at the edge of the clearing. "Can you do this, Lucky?" she asked.

He frowned. "What do you mean?"

"I mean, can you trust my judgment and skills?"

He couldn't see much of her expression in the dark, but

there was no anger there, just a calm focus. "I can do this," Rhys said. "I've got your back."

Now she scowled as if he'd said the wrong thing. But he did have her back. He'd protect her from whatever came their way.

Cat shook off her frustration. It would probably just take time for Rhys to learn to trust her skills as a soldier and leader. She just hoped they had that time.

They buried their drop bags with their chutes on the north side of the small clearing. It was a clear night, but the moon was only a sliver, which worked to their benefit. She pointed east. "Doc and Spooky, head to the village and give me a sitrep."

They nodded and took off into the growth of stunted trees that passed for woods in Northern Nigeria.

"You're with me," she told Lucky. It'd be best if she kept him close so she could keep an eye on him and rein him in if needed.

She ran southeast, her rifle ready and her eyes clear behind her NVGs. After three kilometers, they approached the target location and she slowed to a silent walk. A small red light in the distance caught her eye before it disappeared. She directed Rhys's attention to it. One hundred meters. She crept forward, Rhys right behind her. She stopped beside a tree and held up a fist. Rhys stopped too.

Ahead of them, the trees thinned. A two-rut road wound from the north where the village would be. A jeep had stopped on it and a man leaned against it. Smoking.

The flare of the cigarette shone red like a beacon when he inhaled.

Was he stupid or arrogant?

This had to be the CIA asset that Blackwell had spoken about. While most assets never received training, they usually had more sense than this. Her head tilted as she studied him and the area from the dubious safety of the trees.

The skin down her back twitched. Rhys had a matching frown on his face as he scanned the road and watched the way they'd come.

The man had no weapon that she could see—though anything could be hidden in the jeep. He looked back up the road, toward the village.

She keyed her throat mic and barely breathed her words. "Doc, this is Valkyrie. Sitrep, over."

"Valkyrie," Doc responded. "Something's not right. Almost at location. No lights. And the smell."

"The smell?"

"Smoke and...death. I don't have a good feeling."

"Sitrep when you reach location."

"Copy that."

"Valkyrie, out."

She took a deep breath. Something was very wrong. But would it affect her fact finding? With no further information, someone had to check this guy out and it would have to be her. She gestured to Rhys to stay and he shook his head, grabbing her arm.

He gestured. *Not safe.*

Show me. Did he see something she didn't?

His frustrated grimace told her everything. He had the same feeling she did: something was off. But they couldn't just abort the mission because they had a bad feeling.

She shook his hand off and signaled for him to cross the road further down, to come up behind the man, while Cat approached from their position.

Rhys nodded and took off.

Cat waited, counting her breaths. A shadow flitted across the road in the distance. Even though she'd been looking for him, she'd barely seen Rhys. The man by the jeep didn't change position. She gave Rhys another minute to get to his new location before she crouched down and leopard-crawled through the tall grass.

She moved silently, stalking the man, holding motionless whenever he glanced her way. Within moments, she was close enough to see the beads of sweat at his temples. Rhys should be in position now. She studied the man, trying to pinpoint what made her uneasy.

The intel said his name was Madu Okeke, a local school teacher who worked with resistance against the Boko Haram. He was the right height, and a thick scar ran down his left cheek—given to him by one of the group's enthusiasts, according to the dossier Cat had been given.

Based on the number of cigarette butts on the ground beside him, either he was a chain smoker or he was very nervous.

Cat stood up slowly about ten feet from him. "Madu," she whispered. She kept her gaze on him, feeling too exposed on this road, glad that Rhys was close and had her back.

He started, lowering the cigarette. "You are American?" His whisper was too loud on this quiet night.

"Yes. Do you have information for me?"

"You're a woman?" He frowned. "You've come alone?"

She didn't let irritation shift her focus. "Do you have information for me?"

He stepped back and raised the hand with the cigarette.

Every one of Cat's instincts went on high alert.

"I'm sorry," Madu whispered. He flung the cigarette off to the far side of the jeep.

A signal.

Shadowed figures surged from the trees on the far side of the road, north of the jeep.

"Ambush," she shouted, diving for Madu. He was their only link to the senator's son. Bullets ripped through the night. Something heavy hit her on the side, taking her to the ground before she could reach Madu.

Rhys.

"What are you doing?" she yelled over the barrage of gunfire.

"Saving your life," Rhys said. "You're welcome."

"Get the fuck off me," she snarled. "Where's Madu?"

Rhys had his rifle in his hands firing back at the men running toward them. "By the jeep."

"Warn Doc and Spooky." She ran to the man who'd signaled the start of the ambush.

"Valkyrie!"

She ignored Rhys and slid in beside Madu. He groaned when she grabbed his shoulder. "Where's Dr. Hutchins?"

Madu moaned. He'd been shot in the chest—there was no saving him, she knew. She shook his shoulder. "Answer me."

"I'm…sorry," he said. "Took…my family…"

He stopped speaking and his head lolled.

"Fuck."

"Valkyrie. Time to go," Rhys said.

"Roger." She pulled a surprise from a pocket on her webbing and threw it into the jeep. Then, she sprinted back to Rhys while he covered her, keeping the ambushers back until she dropped beside him.

Zach's voice came over her earbud. "Valkyrie, we hear gunshots."

"Enemy contact," she said. "We need you. Our location."

"On our way. Keep the party going."

"Copy that." She turned to Rhys. "Go. I'll cover."

He hesitated a fraction of a second too long.

"Now, sailor!"

"Roger." He took off while she lay down, suppressing fire.

Twenty meters away, he dropped to a prone position

and began shooting.

She sprinted to him, careful to stay out of his line of fire. She dropped and shot the tangos who'd almost made it to the jeep.

"Reloading," Rhys shouted.

"Copy," she said. She pressed her mic. "Doc. ETA."

"One minute." From Zach's breathing she knew he was running full-out. "A truck. A dozen tangos. Incoming."

Fuck. They had reinforcements.

"Copy that." Rhys had finished reloading and was keeping the enemy back. They had superior firepower, but limited ammo. "Let them get to the jeep," she told him.

He frowned, but stopped firing. The men scrambled up from where they'd been huddled on the ground and ran toward Cat and Rhys, screaming death.

"Valkyrie?" he asked.

"Three, two, one," she said. An explosion rocked the jeep and thundered against their ears. A second explosion, louder than the first, lit the night with fire and shrapnel as the gas tank blew.

Rhys grinned at her. She grinned back.

"We're on your six, Valkyrie," Doc's voice said in her ear. "Looks like you're having fun, but company's on its way."

"Party's over," she said. "Provide cover, Doc."

"Roger that."

She and Rhys stood and raced for the trees, where Marc and Zach waited shooting at their pursuers. The truck couldn't follow them into the trees. She signaled for silence, and they ran north and west. Their NVGs allowed them to dodge trees and brush, and to see their pursuers stumbling in the dark with just a few flashlights.

It wasn't long before they'd lost all pursuers. The team slowed but still continued to jog as they made their way north. With the slower pace, they each caught their breath and sipped water as they ran. When they'd put five kilometers between them and the last sighting of the enemy, Cat let them rest.

"So what the fuck?" Marc asked, after sucking hard on the hydration tube attached to his ruck.

Cat scowled. "It was a trap. The asset was compromised."

"Did you get any information?" Marc asked.

"No," she forced herself not to look at Rhys. "He was shot before he could tell us anything. What about the village? Anything?"

"It was a fucking slaughterhouse," Marc said.

"What?"

"The village is gone," Zach said softly. "If anyone survived they've run off."

"Tell me more."

Zach looked at his feet and swallowed. "It was…"

"It was a massacre," Marc said bitterly. "Mostly men and old women…and kids, all shot or hacked. The houses burned."

She looked at Zach. "Women and girls?"

Zach nodded. "From what we saw, it looks like they took them."

Fuck. She turned away to try to control her rage at the thought of what had happened to those innocent people, the families destroyed, and what the women and girls taken were going through right now. And she couldn't do a damn thing about it.

She swung back. Rhys stood next to her, his hand outstretched as if he had been about to pat her back. Did he think she needed comfort? She scowled at him and stepped away.

"We'll add it to the report when we get back." She brought out her GPS and oriented herself. "Time for a ruck march, boys."

CHAPTER 5

The Griffon helicopter circled the roof of the E.D.G.E. building in Montreal. Cat could see Blackwell waiting for them on the roof. This would not be good. Neither she nor Rhys had spoken much since they'd made the exfil yesterday. They'd been flying almost nonstop to get back to Montreal. Usually after a mission the team would be rowdy, ribbing each other, and after cleaning their gear, they'd head to the operator's lounge for a quick debrief and beer.

Instead, her team sat silent and sullen. The simple mission that should have built camaraderie with their newest member had instead splintered the unit. She needed to get a handle on this fast or she'd be pulled as leader—and maybe even from E.D.G.E. itself.

That wasn't an option. She grit her teeth. She would make this work. Somehow.

As soon as the chopper landed, before the rotors had even started to slow, she jumped off with a wave to the crew chief and went to meet Lieutenant Colonel Blackwell, whose dark eyes scoured her. He jerked his head behind him, indicating she should follow. He turned without a word and strode inside.

Cat handed her rifle to Zach before following him to E.D.G.E.'s private elevator, where there was no chance of a civilian seeing her in her BDUs, and down to his office. He didn't say a word or in any way indicate what he was thinking. Blackwell was stone faced at the best of times, but somehow this was worse. Inside his office, he sat behind his desk and she came to attention. She stared at a spot over his head and waited.

He let her stew in the silence for a moment. "At ease, Captain," he said. "Report."

She relaxed her stance, placed her hands behind her back, and told him what had happened without any excuses.

"What went wrong?" Blackwell asked. "How did the asset get killed?"

"I failed to protect him from the militants, sir."

"I'm sure you did your best, Valkyrie."

She could just leave it at that, but she felt she needed to own the whole debacle. "Sir, I think we could have saved the asset and gotten information if I'd been a better leader."

His eyes narrowed as he studied her. "How so?"

"I let Petty Officer Lafayette get distracted, sir."

"Distracted? By what?"

Her muscles tensed as she decided how to answer this, and then went with the truth. She sighed. "By protecting me, sir."

"Explain."

She shrugged. "He obviously hasn't worked with women in such situations, sir."

"That shouldn't compromise his training, Captain." He sighed. "Do you think you can handle him?"

Her hands curled into fists behind her back. This was her challenge to overcome.

"Yes, sir. I'll work with him."

"You realize as soon as we have more information we'll need to send a team back to rescue Dr. Hutchins. Should I brief Bravo team?"

"No, sir," she said. "I can handle this. My team will be ready."

Someone coughed behind her. "Excuse me, sir. May I say something?"

Cat stiffened. Out of the corner of her eye she saw Rhys stand at attention beside her. What was he doing here? Had he come to report on her? Shit. Maybe she should have left him back in Nigeria.

"At ease. Both of you," Blackwell said with a sigh. "Tell me, Petty Officer Lafayette, what happened on this mission. Why was the asset killed?"

Cat waited for Rhys to throw her under the bus. It's what

any number of soldiers had done in similar situations. It hadn't happened as often once she'd made it into special operations, and not at all at E.D.G.E., but it was a pattern she was used to. Some men just couldn't handle a woman on their team, and they made their issues her problem— one she had to figure out in order to make things work. Was Rhys one of those men?

"It was completely my fault, sir," Rhys said. "I take full responsibility."

"What happened?" Blackwell growled.

Rhys hesitated. "Captain Richards is right. I haven't worked with women before. I need to adjust my thinking. I let my doubts get in the way of the mission."

Blackwell waited a long moment before speaking. "I'm very disappointed. The captain is a valued member of E.D.G.E. You need to remember that, or this might not be the place for you. I'd hate to think we made a mistake recruiting you. Dismissed."

"Sir." Rhys caught Cat's gaze. She could read the concern there and frowned at him. She didn't need his protection. He turned and left the room.

"Valkyrie," Blackwell said. "You are an excellent operator. I believe you can also be an excellent leader, but I need you to get a grip on your team. If you can't handle them, then I'll find someone who can."

The rest of the team waited in the staging room.

Cat dumped her gear before snagging a chair at the long table. She disassembled her rifle alongside the others, bending her head over it as she cleaned the barrel. Zach and Marc spoke quietly about their plans for the night.

She lost herself in the intricacy of the detailed cleaning, inspecting each piece before rubbing it down with gun oil and cloths. The work soothed her, and she let her mind wander.

"I'm sorry."

Cat looked up. Zach and Marc had left and Rhys sat across from her, his rifle in one piece, his cleaning complete. She cocked her head. "What exactly are you sorry for?"

Like her, he'd stripped off the outer layer of his BDUs and sat in an olive green t-shirt. His biceps flexed when he ran his hand through his overly long, sandy-blond hair.

"For not trusting you," he said. He sighed. "I'm not sure what I was thinking, but when you stepped forward into the gunfire I couldn't help but stop you."

"I'm not some helpless civilian," she said. "I've got just as much training as you. I've been in many nasty situations. If you're on my team, you'll need to trust me. You'll have to follow where I lead. Can you do that?"

He studied her face. She wondered if he could see beyond her blonde hair and blue eyes, to the soldier underneath.

Finally he nodded. "Yes, ma'am."

"Good." She smiled grimly. "Then you and I start training together tomorrow."

"Training?"

"Meet me in front of the building at 0530. We'll start with a run."

Rhys yawned and swung his arms to warm them up, before jogging a bit in place. The streetlights still lit the road, though the gray predawn light made everything visible. Five twenty-five a.m. Cat came out of the building's front doors wearing only running shorts that showed off her long, muscular legs, and a tank top. He swallowed.

No inappropriate thoughts, Rhys. He grit his teeth, but couldn't help envisioning what he'd like to do with her. Those long legs featured a starring role wrapped around his waist.

No. She was his team leader.

It didn't help that memories of that night six months ago resurged with palpable ferocity. He pushed them away and managed to keep his eyes up and on her face, rather than on that delectable body.

"You ready?" she asked.

He was more than ready.

Don't smile, he ordered himself. "Yes, ma'am."

She shook her head. "Lose the ma'am."

"Okay, Valkyrie. Let's go."

This would be torture, he thought, trying not to watch her for however long she decided to run. He figured it wouldn't be that bad, maybe thirty minutes at most. He could avoid looking at her for that long.

They started off at a loping pace, nothing too strenuous. She took them east for the first couple of miles. Once they'd left downtown, she lengthened her stride. Their feet hit the pavement in unison, the cool morning air refreshing against his heated skin. Montreal was not a flat city. She led him up and down hills as they continued to work their way east, before she turned north.

Within half a mile she'd turned back west so they ran toward the Mountain, the name Montrealers gave the elevated park in the middle of their city. It seemed to loom over downtown, and Valkyrie headed straight for it.

So she was going to prove how tough she was to him? He almost rolled his eyes, but decided to play along.

"So," Cat said, sounding barely out of breath. "Tell me about yourself. Something not in your file. Like why you would want to join E.D.G.E.?"

He studied the side of her face for a moment. She wasn't sweating that much, and didn't seem to be breathing hard as she kept pace. This could get interesting.

"Something not in my file?" He let his drawl thicken. "I love Creole food." He waited to see what she'd do with that info.

"Why?"

"Because of the spiciness."

"Indian food is spicy. Why do you like Creole?"

"Because I'm from N'Awlins," he said, his accent as thick

as any time he spoke.

"So you like reminders of home?"

"Are you trying to play amateur psychologist?"

"Don't you like talking about your home?"

He decided he didn't like her games anymore and lengthened his stride—time to see if she could keep up. She kept pace and didn't acknowledge what he'd done.

"You know I don't have a home," he said.

"I know no such thing," she said. "I know you said you have no family. That doesn't mean you don't think of New Orleans as your home."

He didn't say anything, but increased the pace again. They neared the mountain and the incline increased. He wanted to leave her behind.

"Why did you join E.D.G.E.?" she asked.

"Why did you?"

This time, she did look at him. An eyebrow cocked, but she didn't reprimand him for his snapped question. "I want to be the best soldier I can be," she said. "When E.D.G.E. asked me to join, I leapt at the opportunity."

"Why?" He made his voice softer this time. "Why did you want to be a soldier?"

"To help people. To make a difference."

"Why not a doctor?"

She snorted. "You sound like my mother. Do you believe like she does, that a woman is too delicate to be in a war zone?"

He wasn't sure how to answer that. Sure, he'd seen some

tough women in his time. He knew logically that women were already in wars all over the world, but he just couldn't believe they could do the types of jobs he could do.

She shook her head slightly. "Men," she muttered, and increased the pace again. He frowned but didn't say anything, just stretched his long legs. They were in the park now, racing up the hilly path toward the top. He could feel his quads burning as he plowed up the hill beside her. Sweat ran down his back and he breathed deeply. More runners were out and they dodged them as they ran the circuitous path.

They'd been running for about thirty minutes, and he figured they'd covered a good four miles. The woman beside him seemed to be going faster the steeper the incline. He grinned and pushed himself to go a bit faster, just to see if she could keep up.

She bared her teeth in a fierce grin and kept up stride for stride with him. They pounded up the slope, breathing hard. Sweat dripped down his back and his muscles loosened and warmed. He pushed harder, faster. The top was in sight. The woman beside him flew beside him like the fierce warrior woman she was nicknamed for.

Within moments they'd hit the top, an area cleared of trees with a view of the city below. Montreal lay before them. The morning sun with its orange-red light struck the mirrored buildings of downtown, creating shadows and silhouettes that demanded he pause.

He slowed. Cat did too, once she noticed him looking.

They jogged in place. "It's beautiful, isn't it?" she said. "A melding of manmade and natural beauty."

"Beautiful," he agreed, but he watched Cat and not the view anymore. Her long limbs were covered in a slight sheen of sweat. She pushed her blonde bangs out of those incredible blue eyes. She froze when she caught his gaze, her mouth parting slightly. He could tell she wasn't as indifferent to him as she'd like him to believe. It made him smile.

Careful, Rhys. Time to get his thoughts back on track.

"Let me guess," he said. "Track star?"

She nodded carefully. "I did some track. We should head back. We'll take a more direct route. You ready?"

"Anytime," he said.

The run back was almost lazy. It wasn't slow by any means, but it wasn't the fierce, driving pace they'd come up the hill with. Cat kept it steady and strong, but he couldn't help being disappointed. She didn't look winded, but maybe she'd used all she had already.

The exhilaration he'd been feeling drained away, leaving his body itchy to do more, press harder. Maybe he'd do another loop of the route they'd just done and then hit that gym Jake had told him about. Would she come with him?

They ran up to the doors of the E.D.G.E. building and he jogged in place. "Well, thanks for the run," he said. "I think I'm going to do another loop. Do you want to join me?"

She smirked at him. "We're not finished yet, Lucky. That was only the warmup. We're hitting the Beast now."

CHAPTER 6

C at wanted to laugh at the look on Rhys's face.

"The Beast?" he asked.

"Follow me." She entered the building, waved at the security personnel at the front desk—who were civilians but still under E.D.G.E. employment—and went to the E.D.G.E. private elevator. Inside, she pressed her thumb against the scanner and typed B3 on the keypad.

"How many sub levels are there?" Rhys asked.

"Below the parking? Seven, as far as I know," she said. "Research, weapons and ranges, and training takes three floors. The Beast takes two."

The elevator doors slid silently open. Lights flickered on, revealing a large two-story room filled with an inclined rock wall for climbing, four hanging ropes for the same, a two-lane lap pool, and a massive obstacle course that would impress the best of athletes. Rhys didn't disappoint in his reaction.

He whistled and walked straight toward the ten-foot wall, the first obstacle, and ran his hands over the smooth polished wood. "This is the Beast?"

Cat nodded. "You've got five minutes to look over the obstacles."

"And then?"

She smiled. "And then we have some fun."

She turned her back and began stretching her legs from the run, then swung her arms in circles, warming them up. There was a lot of upper-body work required to get through the Beast and she needed to be ready if she was going to prove her point to Rhys.

After the designated five minutes, she turned back to see Rhys studying her. "How are we doing this?" he asked.

She knew what he was asking. "A race. You against me."

He huffed a breath. "You want to race me?"

"Not particularly," she said. "The Beast is made to instill teamwork. It's very tricky to do alone, but I need to prove a point to you."

He frowned. "What's that?"

"That I am just as capable as you physically." She could tell by his eyes that he didn't believe her, but that was okay. He would soon.

"On three," she said, her blood already starting to pump at the thought of the race. "Two. One."

They both ran at the ten-foot wall. Cat remembered her first obstacle course in basic training. Then, it had only been a six-foot wall and she'd only made it over because she was taller than the average girl. Most of the recruits had been left behind that first day, until the directing staff had taken pity on them and shown them how to get over it.

Getting over a wall was more technique than brute force. It helped that Cat kept up her strength, both upper and lower, by working out religiously when she wasn't on a mission—and sometimes even when she was, depending on what it was. Rock climbing was one of the things she loved to do, and it helped her keep up her strength more than most things.

She sprinted toward the wall. A step away, she leapt and placed her foot on the wall and kicked off as hard as she could, reaching for the top edge. Her fingers grazed the lip and she gripped it hard, pulling herself up.

Rhys already straddled the wall, watching her. He grinned. "This is gonna be fun."

"Only if you like losing," she said, and dropped down to the other side.

The other side was a misnomer, though. Two narrow planks, six feet apart and held up by chains, ran perpendicular to the wall. She dropped to the one in front of her, her arms out as it wobbled underneath her feet. After Rhys landed on his, he had to take a moment to steady himself against the wall.

She used that second to get ahead of him, walking

quickly along the plank to the other side. Jumping off the end, she faced the under-and-over obstacle. She dropped and wiggled under a thick pole placed horizontally, only eight inches from the ground. Rhys grunted behind her and she grinned as she took a running step at the six-foot wall in front of her, swinging up and over easily, dropping again to go under the next pole. She had the advantage when going under, being more slender than Rhys. Thank god she didn't have big boobs or she'd be in trouble.

As it was, Rhys almost caught up to her. She needed some distance between them and pushed herself harder, not thinking, just moving fast and sure. Down, roll, up, leap and push over the wall. Two more times and then she was through.

Hanging rings were the next obstacle. She jumped and grabbed the first one, swinging her way through them in a rhythm. She could just see Rhys in her peripheral vision, a look of determination on his face. He so didn't want her to win. She laughed as she grabbed the next ring.

His gaze snapped to her and his outstretched hand missed the ring he needed. She didn't look back, but took advantage of his mistake, keeping her eyes focused on what lay ahead of her. She needed that extra second for what was coming next.

She swung hard with the last ring to make it across the line on the floor, bending her knees to take the shock of the landing. Ahead of her was a metal tunnel, only two feet wide, that snaked along the floor and ended in a twenty-five meter, covered pool. Being a SEAL, Rhys would probably kick her butt swimming underwater, so she needed as much time ahead of him as she could get.

She dove into the tunnel, the cold metal of it banging her knees. She moved as fast as she could, now unable to check on Rhys's progress. Darkness grew as she crawled and water began to cover her hands and knees as the tunnel sloped downwards into the dark pool. She slowed fractionally and mentally kicked herself.

This is just the tunnel, Cat. You've done it hundreds of times. It's a pool, not a river.

This obstacle posed more of a mental challenge than a physical one. Especially for her. She splashed her way further into the dark. The cold water rose past her elbows now. It was a gradual incline into the pool, with the last five meters completely submerged in the narrow confines of the darkened tube. She turned her head to the side to get her last breath of air before plunging in fully. Her legs kicked powerfully, while her arms pulled her along gripping the sides of the tunnel. Her lungs began to burn and her heartrate climbed too high, but there wasn't much she could do about that. The tunnel was too narrow to turn around. She had to keep going forward.

Almost done. Keep going.

Within seconds she was at the end and out into open water. Here, some light shone down around the edges of the pool cover and her heartrate steadied. Then, she mentally cursed.

Rhys waited ahead of her, watching her tunnel. She glared as much as she could while holding her breath like a puffer fish. She didn't need his help.

He grinned and let some air bubbles out before turning and swimming like a freaking fish to the other end. She was a decent swimmer, but Rhys was something else entirely. She pulled through the water as hard as she could, but he was at least three body lengths ahead of her before she reached the end.

She pulled herself up and out, dragging in a huge breath while still moving toward the final obstacle. A fifteen-foot rope net.

Rhys was halfway up. She ran and leapt as high as she could, the ropes slipping a little in her wet hands, but she held firm. She used her upper body as much as her lower, pushing herself hard. Her panting breaths competed with her heartbeat thundering in her ears. Everything burned— her arms, her legs, her lungs.

She couldn't seem to gain on Rhys, but he wasn't pulling ahead. He looked back at one point and his eyes widened.

That's right, she thought. *I'm almost on you.*

His hand touched the bar at the top and in an incredible athletic feat he pulled himself up and swung over. His eyes tracked her for a second before he started his descent.

Showoff.

She reached the top bar and pulled herself up with both hands and swung her legs over. She didn't use her legs on the way down, hoping to gain some time. It was a bit dangerous because it was trickier, but she'd done it before. She dropped from rung to rung, making up time on Rhys. He was almost at the bottom.

"Gotta touch the wall," she called out.

He dropped the last few feet and sprinted to the wall.

She let go. It was about eight feet and her knees complained, but she didn't listen and leapt after him. He slapped the far wall a mere second before she did.

They both stood there panting, hands on hips, grinning with the adrenaline rush of the race.

"Damn," Rhys said. "I haven't had that much fun in a long time."

Cat snorted. "Well, be prepared for some more."

"More?"

Cat's grin widened. "Now that you're familiar with the Beast, it's time to do it again."

Rhys pulled off his wet t-shirt. "Are you sure you want to go up against me again?"

Cat swallowed and pulled her eyes away from Rhys's sculpted chest. *Keep it professional.*

"Anytime, Lucky," she said. "But that's not the objective this time around."

He frowned, but she turned away and led him back to the start line. This way, she didn't have to see the water drip down the muscles of his chest—muscles that begged for her hands to caress them.

"This time we work as a team," she said. Behind the start line against the wall was a mini fridge. She bent and snagged two water bottles from it.

"A team?"

She turned and his gaze snapped up to hers from where it had been...eyeing her ass? He'd said that night how much he loved it.

Professional, Cat!

She nodded and tossed him a water bottle. "We do it together, carrying that." She pointed behind her to a weighted stretcher lying against the wall. Six feet long, it only weighed a hundred pounds, not the actual weight of a person if someone had been strapped to it, but it served its purpose in the Beast.

He twisted the lid off the bottle and gulped down some water. She did the same. He was watching her again when she looked up.

"What?" she said, arching an eyebrow. Did he not think she could handle her end?

He shook his head a little without breaking eye contact. "It's just...I never knew you were so tough."

She opened her mouth to defend herself and he held up his hands. "Wait. I mean I knew you were in special operations. Hell, you saved our asses that time in Afghanistan, but still... You almost beat me."

"If you weren't such a fish, I would have."

"We've all got our strengths." He crossed his arms, his biceps flexing. Cat took a step back, away from temptation, and toward the stretcher hanging on the wall.

"What's yours?" he asked.

She heaved the stretcher off the wall and carried it over to him. "What?"

"What's your strength? It's the question you asked me before. What's your specialty? What do you bring to the team?"

"You can't guess?" She couldn't help the smile that crossed her face. "I'm a demolitions expert. I like to blow shit up."

CHAPTER 7

They did the Beast three more times carrying the stretcher. With each run-through, Rhys's admiration of the woman working beside him grew. She never gave up, pushed them both hard, and asked just as much of herself as she did of him—if not more. He could see why her other team members respected her.

They both carried the stretcher back to the wall, breathing hard.

"Is it the water you don't like?" he asked. "Or the tunnel?"

She blew out a breath and shook her head. "Both. Was it that obvious?"

"Not really," he said. And it hadn't been, but those first couple of runs he'd been watching her closely to see if she could keep up with him. Now he knew she could, but he'd seen a hesitation in her each time they'd approached the tunnel.

"It's why I couldn't figure out exactly what it was that threw you off. Claustrophobic?"

"Nothing so extreme. I just..." She shrugged. "I hate small, dark spaces filled with water."

"So does everyone," he said. "It seems like more."

She didn't say anything. In a normal situation he'd drop it, but they were going to be on a team together. He had to know everything, to trust her implicitly. "I need to know," he said.

She expelled a deep breath. "You're right. It was a mission that almost went sideways. A car chase at night that ended in us going over a bridge."

"What happened?"

Her hands fisted while she stared at a spot over his shoulder. He ached to hold her in his arms, but knew a stupid move like that would end with him in traction. Instead, he waited.

"I think I went unconscious when we hit the water. I woke up in the dark. We were fully submerged already. Icy water covered my legs and stole my breath. It climbed rapidly. My partner, who'd been driving, didn't answer me."

Her breathing picked up. Rhys pressed his arms to his sides so he wouldn't touch her.

"He had a heartbeat. I had to get us out of there. I used my gun to break the window. Freezing water poured in with massive pressure. There was no pushing past it. It felt like a death sentence sitting there, waiting for the water to fill the car past the broken window so we could swim out."

Her eyes met his and he saw the nightmare in them.

"I'd made a stupid mistake," she whispered. "I'd forgotten to get his seatbelt off before the water came in. I couldn't undo it. My hands were numb from the cold." She shook her head.

"Hell," he muttered and he reached for her, wrapping her tight in his arms, surprised when she didn't protest. She just rested her head on his shoulder and shivered. He stroked her hair and gave her the comfort she sought. He tried hard not to think about her lithe body against his and just focused on being what she needed—a shoulder to lean on, if only for a moment.

"What happened?" he asked gently when she stopped shivering.

"I managed to get him out," she said. "Barely. I was so close to leaving him behind. We almost didn't make it even after I got him out of the car. The current was strong. It pulled us back under more than once." She lifted her head and he lost himself in her striking blue eyes, but it didn't surprise him that this woman had been able to rescue her partner.

"Thank you," she said, stepping back out of his arms. "It was a dark moment that still gives me nightmares."

He nodded solemnly. "I know about nightmares." Anyone in special ops had seen and done things that chased them in their dreams. It was a consequence of what they did. "I'm surprised that tunnel doesn't have more of an effect on you."

She gave a short, humorless laugh. "I spent hours going through the Beast, and sitting at the bottom of the pool in the dark."

"So you're a woman who likes to torture herself."

She grabbed a towel from the table beside the fridge and threw it at his head. "Dry off, sailor. We've got a full day planned."

He used the towel on his hair and noticed how she averted her gaze from his chest. He smiled. Nice to know that she was as affected by him as he was by her. But now wasn't the time to explore that. They were teammates. He had to put aside his memories of their night together. He could do that.

He hoped.

He watched out of the corner of his eye as Cat ran excess water from her short hair. The water darkened it to a golden color that made her blue eyes brilliant against her lightly tanned skin. Water dripped down her neck and a drop ran down over her collarbone and toward...

"Lafayette?"

Shit. His gaze snapped to hers and he thankfully saw a twinkle there. "Yes?"

"I asked if you have full clearance yet?"

He nodded. They'd given it to him on his first day, and they already had his fingerprints on file from the last time he'd been to E.D.G.E.

"Good. Meet me on level B4 in an hour. That should be enough time to clean up and have breakfast."

"What's on B4?"

"The range." She smiled, and the look of mischief in her eyes made those inappropriate thoughts hard not to think. It was the same look she'd gotten when she'd first approached him in the elevator so long ago. "I'm going to put you through your paces."

"Yes, ma'am," he said, and almost growled with desire.

No. He had to get it together. They were just teammates. He could do this.

Cat sat at her desk at the end of the day going over reports. At a knock on her door, she glanced up. "Dani, when'd you get back?"

"Last night," Dani said. She walked into the office, her t-shirt declaring 'What the Frak?' and her dark hair swept up in a ponytail.

"Success?"

"Close," Dani said, flopping down into a chair. "We've got most of the Rusakov trafficking contacts rounded up, but there's still more to be found."

Cat nodded and then grinned. "Been in any shootouts lately?"

"Hell, no!" Dani said. "I'm staying right where I'm supposed to, in front of my laptop."

"Yeah, right," Cat said with a snort. "You couldn't follow a rule if you tried."

"And you, my friend, follow them too closely." Dani stood up. "Come on, you're coming for dinner tonight."

"I've got reports," Cat said. After the Beast, she'd spent the morning on the range with Rhys. In the afternoon, she'd shown him some of the explosives she'd designed in the lab. They'd had fun, blowing things up together—in fact, she'd never had so much fun with a man before. He made her laugh, and that had made her linger longer than she should have, but now she was behind on her paperwork.

"We all have reports," Dani said.

She sighed, knowing Dani wouldn't give up. Cat hadn't had a girlfriend in a long time, and she treasured her friendship with Dani. Besides, maybe she'd have some advice on how to keep it professional with Rhys.

"Fine," she said. "Let me finish these up and I'll meet you at your place. What are we ordering tonight?"

"We're cooking," Dani said.

"Seriously?" Cat shook her head. "I'm not sure I can handle another experiment. I barely survived the indigestion from the last one."

"Where's your sense of adventure?" Dani laughed and left the office before Cat could reply.

An hour later, Cat felt she'd caught up enough to head to her friend's place. She took her E.D.G.E. military-encrypted phone and shoved it into her pocket. She didn't need to change since she'd dressed casually today, in jeans and a light sweater.

The drive to Dani's apartment took only minutes, since rush-hour traffic had eased. When she stepped off the elevator onto Dani's floor, the scent of chicken, onions, and hot peppers surrounded her. Her stomach was growling by the time she knocked on the door.

Jake answered. "We almost ate without you."

"I can't believe what I'm smelling," Cat said, shrugging out of her leather jacket. "Which one of you is creating that divine smell?"

"I am," Rhys said.

He stood in Dani's small kitchen, a dish towel tucked into the waist of his low-slung jeans, stirring a large pot on the stove.

Surprise immobilized her for a moment. She hadn't expected to see him so soon after the tests of today, but she obviously hadn't realized the extent of his friendship with Jake. She'd wanted to keep their relationship purely business for her own peace of mind, but many of the E.D.G.E operators were friends and hung out together outside of work. There was no reason she and Rhys couldn't do that, as well.

Only the fact that you keep lusting after him, her inner voice taunted.

Well, she wouldn't anymore. They were teammates now. She wouldn't let anything interfere with that.

Her inner voice laughed.

So she cursed it and smiled at Rhys. A friendly,

professional smile. "What are you making?"

"Gumbo."

"Gumbo? I've heard of it, but never had it."

"Well then, chère," he said, letting his accent thicken. "You're in for a treat. Chicken and andouille sausage gumbo is pure N'Awlins dee-light." He waved his hand toward a tray holding a short golden loaf resting on the countertop. "And cornbread, of course."

She inhaled the delicious scents and her stomach growled again. "Where did you learn to cook?"

"My grandmother," Rhys said, looking back at the gumbo he stirred.

Cat sensed a story there, but didn't pursue it since Dani called out from the living room. "I just can't get it, Rhys. Come show me again."

A grin lit Rhys's face as he left the kitchen, and Cat had to follow that smile. In the living room, Dani stood with part of a deck of cards in one hand and the other part all over the room. A bulletin board had been set up on a chair. "Show me again," Dani demanded.

"You've created a monster, Rhys," Jake said with a laugh. He lazed on the couch watching his girlfriend. "We're going to have a mess of cards in here until she figures it out."

Rhys laughed and took the cards Dani offered him. "The trick is to hold them lightly. You're not throwing them, they're flying out of your hands when you flick your wrist." He threw a card in a quick motion and it thunked into the bulletin board edgewise and stuck there, quivering slightly.

"Holy crap," Cat said. "Should we call you Gambit instead?"

Rhys scowled while Jake laughed. "It was close," Jake said. "But Lucky had already stuck."

She spent the next few minutes alongside Dani, trying to get a card even close to the board.

"Let me show you," Rhys said and stepped in behind her, placing one arm alongside hers, the front of his body almost, but not quite, touching her back. She bit her lip as tension tightened her muscles.

"Relax," Rhys said in her ear. She fought the shiver that raced through her at the sound of his low voice so close. She swallowed, conscious of Jake and Dani in the room. She went to flick the card just to get it done, but Rhys's hand enclosed hers, stopping her.

"Easy," he said, his voice lower still. She glanced at him. That was a mistake. His eyes glowed with amusement. Her heart skipped a beat. He looked down at their joined hands and her gaze followed.

"Like this," he said. He curled their combined hands toward them and then snapped them out.

The card shot from her fingers and straight to the board. It didn't stick, but it had flown true. All thought of Rhys standing too close vanished. "Cool!" She immediately took another card.

Rhys stepped away from her, a small smile on his face as he watched her fling two more cards. "Addictive, isn't it?"

Jake groaned. "Seriously, Lucky. Now you've got both of

them making a mess."

Rhys just laughed. "I think the gumbo's ready. Let's eat."

After a few more cards, only one of which flew straight, Cat filed into the kitchen after the others and filled her dish with rice, then layered the rich gumbo on top. No one spoke much through the first bowls, but eventually Cat's curiosity got the better of her.

"Your grandmother taught you well," Cat said. "Did she live in New Orleans with you?"

Rhys averted his gaze. "Yes."

He didn't elaborate and Cat could tell by his face that the woman had meant a lot to him. "You must miss her."

Jake stood up. "I'm getting a beer. Any takers?"

"I'd love one," Dani said, standing too. "Cat?"

Cat wasn't fooled. Jake and Dani were trying to redirect the conversation. She arched an eyebrow at them. "I'm on call and so is Rhys." Dani shook her head at Cat as she and Jake went into the kitchen.

Cat turned to Rhys. "I'm sorry if I'm prying. It's just that your grandmother seems to have had a big influence on you. She must have been a wonderful woman."

Rhys's lips twisted in a half-smile. "She was. And my life isn't a secret, I just don't talk about it much." He shrugged. "I was raised by my grand-mère. When she died, I was on my own until I joined the Navy at seventeen."

Cat couldn't comprehend such a life. Her family was big, boisterous, and too much in her business at times, but she couldn't imagine being without them.

His word choice struck her. "What do you mean, on your own?"

Rhys toyed with his spoon. "Foster care sucks when you're sixteen. I spent that year on the street instead."

She frowned, trying to picture the confident, skilled operator before her as a street kid.

"Stop it," Rhys said.

She sat back. "What?"

"Stop pitying me," he said. "I love my life and I turned out fine. I don't need anyone to look down on me." He grabbed his bowl and followed Jake and Dani into the kitchen.

"Nice work, Cat," she muttered. "Alienate him, just as he's beginning to trust you." She stood too. She'd have to talk to him.

Her phone vibrated from her back pocket. She checked it: a text from E.D.G.E. Her team had been called in.

"Rhys?" she called.

"I got the message," he said, coming back to the table with his phone in hand. "Let me get my stuff. You can drive."

CHAPTER 8

C at gripped the steering wheel too hard as she drove back to E.D.G.E. HQ. Rhys sat silent and still beside her. The awkwardness was her fault. She couldn't let it continue.

"I'm sorry," Cat said. "I—"

"Don't worry about it," Rhys said. "It's nothing."

But it wasn't—she could tell by the tone of his voice and the way he stared straight ahead. She took a breath and tried again.

"I've got a big family. Three older brothers, one helo pilot, one doctor, and one lawyer. Two of them in the military. My Dad's a retired Colonel—"

"Why are you telling me this? To rub in the fact that you've got a family?"

"And a busybody, stay-at-home mom."

Rhys snorted. "You really suck at making people feel better about their lives."

She blew out a long breath. "I'm telling you so you realize that yes, I did feel sorry for you. I come from a crazy family. But we love and mostly support each other."

"Mostly?"

She waved a hand. "Long story and not the point."

He arched an eyebrow. "There is one?"

"There would be if you'd let me finish."

"Please," he said. "I'm your captive audience." He waved at the car. "Literally."

She sighed. "I'm making a mess of this, but I wanted to let you know why I felt sorry for you." She shook her head. "Not you, but your situation. I can't imagine not having my family behind me. So while I have no understanding of what you went through, I am here if you need anything. The team and I are your family now."

The silence from Rhys made her gut tighten. Had she blown it again? Maybe she should have just let it drop. "Did I go too far?"

"No. It's good." Rhys's voice came out gruff. "We're good." Then he gave her a smile. "Thank god you didn't become a counsellor though. You suck at it."

She laughed.

They drove in silence for a bit before she spoke again. "What was it like?" she asked quietly. "When I was sixteen, my biggest worry was being too tall to get a date. It seems self-indulgent now."

He didn't say anything for a moment. When he started to speak, it was slow—as if he weighed his words before choosing them.

"I slept in the backroom of a pool hall. The owner liked my cooking, so I'd help out on weekends, cooking or hustling the customers."

She raised her eyebrows in question.

"I'm very good at poker and pool," he answered. "I gave the owner eighty percent of my winnings."

"Eighty?"

"Room and board. It was crappy, but better than joining a gang." His lips twisted and he stared straight ahead.

She gripped the steering wheel, thinking about what he'd been through as a teenager. The silence soothed her for a moment before she spoke again, needing to lighten the air between them. "Just so you know, after tasting that gumbo, you might be the official chef of the team. Dani and Jake have tried hosting all of us over the holidays and their cooking is only one step above poisoning."

He looked at her quizzically. "I thought you said you had a big family?"

She realized her mistake too late. "I do," she said in a light tone. "Sometimes it's just easier to spend the holidays here."

"How come?"

Why had she started this heart to heart? But if he'd shared with her, then she felt she had to share in return.

She sighed softly. "Expectations. I've let my family down. My father and brothers think I've sold out by working at a civilian company after all the hard work I put into my Army career."

"And your mother?"

Cat could feel her face heat. "My mom wants to know why I'm not married." *Or even dating.*

Rhys laughed. And laughed some more. She tapped her fingers on the steering wheel while he muffled more chuckles. "You done now?"

"I'm sorry," he said. "It's just so…" He laughed again.

"Enough, Rhys. Don't make me regret telling you."

He sobered. "I'm sorry, Cat." His hand reached out and patted her knee. Tingles shot through her body and she stiffened. He withdrew his hand.

"I'm sorry," he said again. "I didn't mean to offend you. It's just so crazy. I honestly can't imagine how your family could be disappointed with you. You're an amazing woman."

Cat was glad of the darkness as her face heated again. "Thanks. Maybe you should come for the next family dinner and tell them that." She swallowed hard. Had she really just invited him to meet her family? She stopped herself from squirming in her seat. "I meant that as a joke. Well…not a joke. Of course, you could come for dinner. I meant that I wasn't asking you because I like you. I mean I like you as a friend, just not…oh, crap." If she could bang her head on the steering wheel and still drive safely she would.

Rhys laughed again. "You seriously suck at people skills, don't you?"

She sighed. "It's my worst trait. And it's why…"

"Why what?"

She'd already made a fool of herself, so why not tell him everything? He'd figure it out sooner or later. "It's why I don't have many dates," she said. Or any, if she was honest. But Rhys didn't need to know that. "I'm a bit too direct for most men. My mother thinks I need to soften myself somehow."

"It's not your directness, chère," he said softly. "It's because you've been dating losers."

She couldn't really argue with that. Liam had definitely been a loser, and so had her long-term boyfriends before that. She gave a little self-deprecating laugh. "You might be right. I probably just need to stay away from men in general."

"Not all men, chère. Not all."

She didn't touch that, and just focused on driving to the briefing. She needed her head in the game, not distraction from the tall, gorgeous, smooth-as-silk man beside her. Besides, he wasn't offering her anything.

Was he?

Cat sat at the conference table less than twenty minutes later. Rhys took a seat across from her, while Blackwell worked on a laptop. Behind him on the virtual screen were the same photos of the senator's son, Dr. Hutchins, and the other missing man, Dr. Botman. Marc and Zach came in within minutes.

"What do we have, sir?" she asked.

"This hit the internet two hours ago."

A few quick hand movements and Blackwell replaced the photos with a grainy video. Cat grimaced, since she knew where this would lead. Men dressed in black turbans, fatigues, and combat boots held rifles and crowded around a prisoner. Dr. Botman knelt on the ground, his hands tied behind his back, one eye swollen and his gray beard darkened with blood. He swayed with his eyes closed, as if unaware of what was happening. One man stood in front of the others, beside Botman.

Blackwell stopped the video and pointed to the man Cat had noticed. "That is Jameel Ichanga, one of Abubakar Shekau's lieutenants. He runs the Boko Haram in this region." He flicked his fingers and the video played again.

Ichanga began to speak in broken English. "The West and its people are evil. Allah says we must kill infidels…" The man continued on for two minutes about the evils of the West, while the prisoner continued to sway where he knelt. Cat's stomach twisted at what was coming. "Allahu Akbar," the man said. Another man behind the prisoner drew a glittering machete. Ichanga nodded at him.

Cat forced herself to watch as the man swung the machete and took the prisoner's head.

She took a deep cleansing breath, let it out, and forced the anger into a calm focus.

"Dr. Hutchins?" Cat asked.

Blackwell nodded. "As far as we know, the senator's son is still alive and being held at Ichanga's base of operations. We need to extract him before the press gets hold of this news."

"Is there a particular reason, sir?" Rhys asked.

Blackwell grimaced as if he tasted something sour. "Apparently, the senator—a Democrat—is against sending more troops overseas, and this incident would make his stance hypocritical. He wants us to save his son, but he doesn't want anyone to know anything about it."

"I'm fine with working under the radar," Rhys said, "but that's rather cold on the senator's part."

"It doesn't matter why we're getting him out," Cat said. "Just that we do."

Rhys nodded. "Agreed."

Blackwell continued his brief. "We've arranged transport tomorrow morning at 0500 hours to Germany, and from there to a new staging area in Niger. A base more equipped to handle our needs."

"The drone airbase near Diffa and Lake Chad?" Cat asked.

Blackwell enlarged the map of Niger and pointed to a location north of where the Yobe River became the border between Niger and Nigeria. "Yes, it's right across the border from the heart of the Boko Haram's territory. You'll have full access to weapons and supplies. The base CO knows you're coming and will brief you on what intel they have."

She straightened her fingers, which had clenched into fists. "Is Colonel Harris still working with the drones there?" She'd spent a few weeks stationed at this particular base the previous year for a mission. Colonel Harris had had a hate-on for her from the start.

She felt the focus of her team and Blackwell's gaze as he answered. "Actually, he's the base CO now. Is there a problem, Valkyrie?"

Crap. This would make things awkward, but she had a mission and would work around Harris and his old-fashioned prejudices. "No, sir. I've had a few run-ins with him, that's all. Nothing I can't handle."

"Good. Does everyone speak Hausa?"

"No," both Zach and Rhys said.

"Enough to get by," Cat said, while Marc just nodded.

If they had two speakers of the most prominent language of Nigeria on their small team, then they'd be in good stead for the mission.

Blackwell shut off the virtual screen with a swipe of his hand, signaling the end of the briefing. "Good luck, and keep me informed."

At 0455 hours, Rhys waited with his teammates in the dark on the rooftop of the E.D.G.E. building. The high walls protected them from sight, but not from the cold air that whipped toward them from the Griffon helicopter that would transport them to the jet flying them to Germany.

With his kit at his feet and his rifle slung over his shoulder, Rhys watched Cat speak quietly with Blackwell, who'd come to see them off. In the last week, he'd come to respect the woman as a soldier and as a leader, and nothing proved leadership skills more than actual combat. Cat had already shown she was competent and fierce in battle.

He'd seen more than one officer lose it when the bullets started to fly. Admittedly, he hadn't seen it since he'd become a SEAL, because weak officers never made it through training in any of the spec ops forces.

It was because she was a woman that he still doubted her ability, he acknowledged to himself. Even though he'd seen her in Nigeria and on that mountaintop in Afghanistan, he still worried. Her other teammates accepted her and he could see their trust in her, but he had to admit he still needed further proof. Damn. He hadn't thought he was a chauvinist.

Even so, he just couldn't get over the feeling. He was going to have to do something about it. No way could he go on a mission with doubts about his team leader.

"Time to go," Cat yelled over the noise of the rotors.

He lowered his head and stared at his boots. Could he go?

Black boots stepped into his view. "Lafayette?" Cat said.

He met her gaze and saw the steel there.

Her chin raised. "If you can't follow my orders," she said, "you know you don't belong."

He struggled to view her as just another soldier. She was physically competent, intelligent, and calm under pressure. He had to believe she could do this. He wouldn't let his prejudices harm the mission. And he refused to let himself treat her differently than he would any other leader. Time to shut off his small brain and only think with his big one, as his grand-mère used to say.

He nodded. "Copy that, Valkyrie," he said. "I'm good to go."

Her shoulders relaxed subtly. "Then let's do this."

CHAPTER 9

The Black Hawk helicopter's rotors threw up a mini dust storm as it settled to the ground at the airbase in Niger. Just before they'd landed, Cat had caught a glimpse of the Yobe River in the distance.

It had been a long trip. Cat's BDU shirt clung to her back with sweat. Dirt grimed her face, and her eyes begged to close, but her stomach complained most loudly of all. The rest of her team looked like she felt, though Rhys grinned like a kid on his birthday as he flicked through the deck of cards in his hand. He didn't look at them as he flipped them over and under his fingers, the suits flashing by too quickly to see.

The Black Hawk barely jostled her when it landed. The pilot wasn't part of SOAR, the 160th Special Operations

Aviation Regiment, but he still had some nice skills. She made a mental note to request him for their mission exfil.

She grabbed her pack and her weapons bag and jumped off the helicopter with a wave to the pilot. Her team followed.

The base wasn't large, just enough to house a couple of Black Hawks, two MH-6 Little Birds, and three Predators—the remote-controlled drones used for surveillance and sometimes a bit of extra firepower, since each of the MQ-1s carried two Hellfire missiles. Cat would rather the next-generation MQ-9 Reapers be here since they carried fifteen times the ordnance, but she knew they shouldn't need the backup. If they did, then something had gone drastically wrong with the mission.

It would be a quick in and out, she repeated to herself.

The MH-6 Little Birds were used by the U.S. special operations forces for insertion, so Cat knew there probably were a couple of SOAR pilots around and some operators. She made a mental note to find them to see about intel for the area.

The base HQ was a squat concrete building that looked like it might have once been a school. Around it were the sturdy temporary shelters the military deployed in situations like this. To the side of the small landing strip were the three thirty-foot trailers that housed the operating systems and pilots for each Predator.

The airbase was here to help the West African nations with surveillance of the Boko Haram and similar militant

Islamic groups. One of the activities the world knew them to be doing was trying to find the two hundred schoolgirls who had been kidnapped by the ruthless leader of Boko Haram.

They hadn't had any luck, and she knew how wearying such a defeat could be. The narrowed eyes and grim faces of the soldiers they passed attested to this. Too many of them gave her second glances, some appraising, some wary, and some lustful. She braced herself as she headed toward the HQ where she'd find Colonel Harris.

Rhys strode up beside her. "You've been here before."

She nodded. "A previous mission. Nothing hugely classified—the team helped search for those girls." They'd spent weeks following any lead, hoping to save some of the girls. They'd gotten a few out, but not enough. Not nearly enough.

She left her team in the admin section of HQ, where a sergeant briefed them for their short stay on the base. Then, she knocked on the CO's door.

"Enter," he barked.

Colonel Harris had the attitude of a Rottweiler in the body of a bull terrier. Lean and hard, his aggression seemed to increase in direct proportion to the height difference between him and whomever he was speaking with. It doubled when he spoke with a woman.

Cat grit her teeth, dropped her kit just inside the door, and walked into his office. It smelled of the cigarillos he favored. His gaze narrowed. "Well, look who Cat dragged in."

She stood at attention. "Nice to see you too, sir."

He sat silently, letting her stay at attention. She clenched her teeth harder.

"I'd heard you couldn't handle spec ops anymore and quit. So what are you doing here?"

She wondered if she'd have any teeth left when this conversation was over, she was grinding them so hard. "I'm sorry, sir, but that's classified."

"I may not be special operations, but I'm a colonel in the United States Air Force and I have top-secret clearance," he said.

"Sorry, sir." In a normal situation she'd have filled the base CO in on her mission as best she could, out of respect, but that wasn't happening here. "I'm sure you've been told what you need to know."

"That some spec ops unit which I'm not even allowed to know the name of is coming in, and that I have to give you what you ask for? That doesn't fly with me, young lady."

Young lady?

"I am still a captain in the Canadian Army," she said. "You will address me as such." She paused. "Sir."

He stood up, but even standing he couldn't meet her gaze with her standing at attention and looking straight ahead. "I'm sure you will find everything you need, *Captain*. But don't expect any special treatment. As far as I know your team is nothing special and you'll have to put in a requisition form for anything you need, just like everyone else on this godforsaken base."

Now she lowered her gaze and met him straight on. "You have orders not to hinder this mission in any way."

"I won't hinder you, Captain, but if you can't handle working without special treatment then maybe you shouldn't be in the Army." He sat back down. "Dismissed."

Cat grabbed her kit and left without another word, striding back to the others.

Zach took one look at her and shook his head. "So the colonel's still an ass?"

She didn't respond because she knew she'd start venting the anger that had built up, and they didn't have time for that. "Did they give you bunks?"

"Yes, and who to go to for basic intel," Zach said.

He pointed to one of the shelters and told her the officer in charge of intel. Hopefully, he'd be more accommodating than the colonel.

"And the nice sergeant also told us there are rumored to be some D-boys here," Marc said. "They should be able to help us with more intel, since they're probably here running black ops."

"Something else the colonel won't know about," Cat said. "And it's part of the reason why he's got such a freaking huge chip on his shoulder."

Cat shrugged off the colonel's tantrum. Time to work. She checked her watch. "Local time is 1100 hours. Let's grab some food, some rack time, and then meet at 1800 for mission brief. Barring any further issues, we head out at oh-dark-thirty."

Once Rhys and the guys dumped their kit on some spare bunks, they made their way to the chow hall. Cat stood inside waiting for them. The tent was fairly full as soldiers came in for lunch.

Almost like a high school cafeteria with its cliques, the soldiers sat with their units each in different areas. Raucous laughter and brash talk designated the regular-force Army unit sitting around most of the perimeter. Rhys figured they were posted here for base security. The air force personnel sat in the center talking quietly, unconcerned that they were surrounded.

A few hard-looking but quiet men in the corner had beards and longer hair. They moved with a controlled athleticism and faded into the background, trying not to be noticed. But in the midst of the soldiers, everyone noticed the Delta Force warriors.

The D-boys in the corner tracked E.D.G.E.'s movement to the chow line. Rhys nodded at them and they nodded back before turning back to their discussion.

Lunch turned out to be a chicken and plantain stew over rice, with enough spices to satisfy a New Orleans boy like himself. He sat beside Cat with his back to the tent wall, down the long table from the other spec ops guys.

None of them spoke as they ate, all of them focused on fuel before getting some sleep. Cat frowned at her stew, but ate quickly. Rhys could see the tightness around her eyes. Whatever the CO had said, she hadn't liked it.

He ate the flavorful stew and made a note to drink extra water before sleep. It tasted like the cooks used a lot of salt. Cat tensed beside him. He followed her gaze to see a Canadian Army major walking toward them, his eyes on Cat. A small curse escaped her.

"You good?" he asked.

She gave a sharp nod. "Fine."

"Catherine," the major said. "It's been a long time."

Cat stood up, her face stony. "Steve." She nodded at his epaulettes. "Congrats on making major."

He shrugged. "Bound to happen, right?" Rhys didn't like the way the guy's eyes moved to Cat's shoulders, free of any epaulettes denoting rank. "They attached me to an American unit when they promoted me. What are you doing here?" His eyes scanned the other three members of the team. "I thought you'd left CSOR."

"I did," Cat said. "If you'll excuse me, I've got to prep for a briefing."

Cat strode away without a glance back. Steve watched her go and Rhys had to bite back a smile at the frustration on his face. The guy didn't bother to look at them, and walked after her. He did stop by a few of the rowdy regular-force soldiers on the other side of the tent, and spoke with them for a few seconds before heading out. The soldiers followed him.

Zach took a last spoonful of stew and then stood up.

"This could be interesting."

"How so?" Rhys stood to follow, too.

"The major was an old flame of Cat's before she joined CSOR. Word has it that he tried out too, but failed. He couldn't handle that she got in and started spreading shit about her."

"What kind?"

"Said she'd slept her way into the job." Zach snorted. "Fucking prick got found out and hand-slapped, but the rumors had already done their damage."

Anger sparked inside Rhys. "Let's go see what the prick is up to then."

The three of them dumped their bowls in the bins at the end of the table and went out into the heat and sun. Rhys paused.

Cat was nowhere to be seen, but the soldiers, who'd followed the major out, stood speaking with each other in low tones near the latrines.

The major leaned against the wall of the CO's building, far enough away to not be associated with the soldiers, but close enough to watch what went on. Rhys's gut tightened. He did not like this.

"Seriously?" Marc said. "They're really going to do this? I don't know how she stands it."

Cat walked out of the washrooms and stopped, her gaze scanning the men before her. The soldiers faced her and spread out.

"Why?" Rhys asked as he jogged over, Marc and Zach

right beside him. No way were these guys going to ambush one of his teammates.

"They hear she's spec ops and they either think she screwed her way in, or they lowered the standards," Zach said. "Either way, they want their shot to prove she's not deserving."

"Dumb fucks," Marc muttered.

"What's going on?" Rhys called out as he shouldered his way to the front of the group.

"Oh, I see," the leader of the group, a young, muscled corporal said and snickered. "You've got your guys here to help you out. Tell me, boys," he said as he turned to Rhys, "is she a good fuck? Maybe me and the boys could borrow your combat Barbie."

Rhys got in the corporal's face. "Listen, asshole—"

"Stand down," Cat said.

But Rhys couldn't step aside and let Cat be insulted. "You're going to regret ever say—"

"Lucky, stand down!"

Cat's words penetrated and he shut up, but he didn't move from his position until Cat elbowed him aside and stepped in front of him, keeping her hands loose at her sides as she faced the muscled corporal in front of her. "You in charge of this group of idiots?"

The corporal snorted. "I'm their section commander."

"Okay, where do you want to do this?" Cat said in a bored voice, though Rhys could see the anger sparking her blue eyes.

The corporal's eyes narrowed. "Do what?" he asked as he looked around the group. It had grown from just his section and their team. The D-boys had joined the outer edges, watching quietly. "You offering me some special treatment, baby?"

Rhys clenched his fists. Marc touched his arm and motioned him to the side of the circle. "Trust her," he said quietly. "Our job is to make sure no one else jumps in."

"I'm going to teach you a lesson in hand-to-hand combat," Cat said to the corporal. "Now, do you want to do it here or do you have a place with mats so when I throw you down it won't hurt as much?"

He crossed his arms. "I'm not fighting a girl," he said.

"Scared?" Zach taunted.

Rhys clenched his teeth. The corporal had the thick muscle of a lifter, which didn't mean he wasn't also fast or a decent fighter. If he landed a good punch he could break Cat's jaw. Rhys stepped forward.

Zach pulled him back. "Seriously, man," he whispered. "She's got this."

"Look," Cat was saying. "I'm tired and have a lot to do, so I'll make this easy for you. We'll fight one-on-one, right here, right now. First one who yields wins." She unbuttoned the shirt of her BDUs. With each button, the section whistled and catcalled. Rhys's hands clenched into fists. He wanted to pound someone.

Cat had an olive green v-neck tee underneath, but that didn't stop the comments. She dropped her shirt at Rhys's feet.

Her face was calm and her eyes stony as she shook out her arms. "You and I will talk later about obeying orders," she said quietly.

She turned to the corporal.

The corporal smiled. "I'm not going easy on you, I don't care who you screwed in the past."

Cat didn't reply, she just sank into a fighting stance and waited. One of the D-boys nodded approvingly, but Cat looked only at the man in front of her. "Come on, asshole."

CHAPTER 10

The corporal swung a fist, faster than she'd expected, but not fast enough to hit her. She ducked and sank a fist into his gut, dancing back out of the way. The crowd around them roared at the first hit, but she ignored them and kept zoned in on her opponent.

"Lucky punch," the corporal said.

Cat didn't debate it. She feinted left and struck hard with a right cross. The corporal's head rocked back, blood spurting from his nose.

"Ready to yield, tough guy?" she said, deliberately taunting him. She could end this quickly, but the meeting with the CO had her fired up and she needed to vent. Beating the crap out of this idiot might alleviate her stress.

She almost smiled at the thought, and stepped out of range of another of his swings.

Then things got interesting. He barreled at her, striking hard with his hands and even throwing a kick in. The pattern had the clumsy feel of a newbie kickboxer. She ducked, dodged, and swatted his punches aside, not going on the offensive yet. She wanted to see what he had. He panted hard but grinned, thinking since she didn't hit back he must be winning.

Jab, jab, right. A fast left, right, left, right, before a roundhouse to the ribs. He did the combination once more and she let him tire himself out, but never let a punch land. Then on his next jab, she pushed his strike aside and stepped in close, striking hard with an elbow to his cheek. The skin split, but she didn't stop.

It was her turn now. She followed with two more elbows, stunning him enough that she could grab his head and yank it to her upcoming knee strike. She softened the blow a bit so she wouldn't damage the corporal too much. He went limp and thudded to the ground.

His section stared at her. "Any other takers?" she asked.

They shook their heads in unison. She would have laughed if she still didn't have anger surging through her system like a drug. The corporal's section picked him up and hauled him away.

The three watching D-Boys nodded—a rousing chorus of approval for them—and slipped away.

"Nice work as always, Valkyrie," Marc said.

"You going to deal with him?" Zach pointed to the major who walked toward them.

She lifted her chin. "Yes, he's definitely next."

"Come get us if you need anything." He and Marc walked toward the shelter where their bunks were located.

Cat snatched her shirt from the ground. The look of appreciation in Rhys's eyes stopped her for a moment. The anger could explode into heat if she let it. She wanted to explore what was between them—and she wanted to do it right now.

Dammit. She shook her head and forced her gaze from his tall, muscled form. This was not the time.

Steve stopped in front of her and she couldn't help but compare the two men. Rhys, with his lean muscles and chiseled cheekbones, appealed to her not just because he was gorgeous, but also because he physically challenged her. She had to work hard to beat him in a race, and even so she wasn't sure who'd win.

Beside him, Steve stood with his square face and looked almost squat, like a high school football player going to fat. His muscles bulked his body up to the point that she suspected it hampered his agility and speed. She wondered if he still took steroids. It had been one of the arguments that had broken them up. He'd used them after he'd failed to get into CSOR with her.

She had been so busy with the regiment that she hadn't noticed what he'd been doing. She'd only spent thirty-some-odd nights at home in that first year and they'd grown apart—and not just because of the lack of time spent together, but also because of Steve's jealousy.

He'd tried once more to make it into CSOR and failed. When she tried to console him, he told her the regiment was only filling a quota by letting her in. That remark had killed the last of her feelings for him and she'd ended the relationship.

By the glint in his eye as he stood in front of her, he'd seen her take down his corporal and he wasn't pleased, though that didn't stop him from letting his eyes wander to her chest. She gripped her shirt in her hands, refusing to give him the satisfaction of covering up.

Rhys was right. She did pick losers to date.

She put her hands on her hips. "Why'd you set your guy on me?" she asked. "If you want to fight me, then challenge me yourself, don't send your minions."

Out of the corner of her eye, she saw Rhys step back and cross his arms while a small smile played on his face. She would deal with him next. She wasn't here to amuse anyone.

Steve made a face. "Stop being so dramatic, Cat. Corporal Anderson was just seeing what you're made of. It's what guys do."

"You're so full of it." She turned away. He grabbed her arm, and without thinking she dug her fingers into the soft underside of his wrist and twisted. He let go quickly, but she didn't. She held his arm in a slight twist, not enough to bring him to his knees—something she wouldn't do when she knew his men watched discreetly from inside the buildings—but she put enough pressure into the grip that she had his attention.

"Don't touch me again," she said, releasing him.

His eyes narrowed and he opened his mouth, but Rhys stepped in front of him. "We have a mission to get ready for. If you'll excuse us." He turned his back on the major and quirked an eyebrow at her.

She nodded, and together they walked toward the HQ. He didn't say anything when she chose to alter their route and they walked past HQ and away from most of the other buildings on base. She veered away from the small airfield and made for the perimeter fence.

"How do you do it?" Rhys asked after they'd walked for a few minutes.

She frowned at him. "Do what?"

He jerked his chin back the way they'd come. "Do you have to deal with dickheads like that wherever you go?"

The question made her sigh. She stopped short of the chain-link fence, her fingers white on the shirt that was still gripped in her hand. "Not everywhere," she said. "But enough places that it sometimes makes me wonder if it's worth it." She stared into the stunted trees bordering one side of the base and spotted two sentries facing away from them.

"And is it?"

"Worth it?" She turned to Rhys. His brown eyes held questions and concern. She wanted neither. Her blood still pumped too fast from the confrontations. She wanted more fight, more fire. She wanted Rhys. "Hell, yes, it's worth it. I like knowing that what I do makes a difference in the world. A real difference." She bared her teeth in a fierce grin. "And besides, what other job is going to let me blow shit up?"

Rhys pursed his lips. "A construction worker?"

She laughed. "I will definitely consider that career when I retire."

Her smiled died. No matter how nice he was, she had to remember that he wasn't for her. She was his team leader. "We need to talk," she said.

"I figured this wasn't just a friendly walk."

"You have to treat me like an equal, Rhys. You can't try to protect me."

His head tilted as he studied her. "I have been treating you like an equal."

"You tried to stop the fight back there. You're no better than those dickheads, as you called them. How many times do I have to prove to you that I can take care of myself?"

His eyes glittered dangerously and he took a step toward her. "I was treating you like my teammate. I wouldn't have let those assholes treat Marc or Zach or anyone with that kind of disrespect. Of course I got in their faces. It's what teammates do for each other."

"That's not how it works with me," she said, not backing down. She lifted her chin. "If I'm seen taking any kind of help then that just fuels their rumors."

"Why the hell do you care so much about what they

think?"

Her blood pounded in her ears and she fought for control, but the anger of being forced to prove herself over and over again won. "Because I am *sick* of the whispers and the doubt about whether I can do my job. And *you* are not helping. So either get out of my way or request a new team."

She turned to head back when Rhys grabbed her arm. "You want me to trust you," he said, putting his face close to hers. "Then you've got to trust me, too. Trust that I'm not judging you and that I've got your back." He pulled back slightly, but his searing gaze never left hers. "You trusted me with everything once."

Heat flushed her body at the memories his low words stirred. "Don't bring that up."

"Why not?" he said, his hand no longer gripping her arm, but caressing it instead. "What we had was good."

She clenched her teeth. "You don't get it. We work together. If we hook up, then my reputation goes into the shitter and yours gets a boost."

Rhys pulled her closer and into the shadow of a building, out of sight of the HQ. "Who said anything about *hooking up*?"

She pushed her bangs off her forehead, frustration making her movements jerky. "You just did."

He sighed and pulled her closer, his hands loose on her hips. "You don't have to prove anything to me or anyone else. We're two consenting adults."

She opened her mouth to argue, but he overrode her.

"We're teammates. Colleagues," he said. "We're not in the reg force. I don't believe there are rules against us fraternizing."

He pulled her tighter against him. This time, she let him. The electric shock of his chest touching hers silenced her argument.

What was it about this man that sent her blood pressure shooting skyward? His hands caressed up her bare arms to her neck, sending shivers of need through her. He cupped her head with his large palms and his whiskey-colored gaze captured hers.

"I trust you," he whispered. "Now trust me back." He lowered his mouth to hers. His lips, warm and soft, pressed against hers and she melted into him, her hands gripping his shirt, pulling him closer.

Just one moment, she promised herself. Just one moment to enjoy, that's all she wanted. One moment to be a woman desired for who she was and not as a trophy by her peers.

She opened her mouth under his and moaned as his hands traveled down her back and dipped under the bottom of her t-shirt. His rough palms rubbed over her heated skin. One slid around to her front and up to her breasts. He cupped one and his thumb stroked over her nipple. She moaned as fire surged through her.

Rhys lifted her without breaking the kiss and she wrapped her legs around his waist. He took two steps and pushed her back against the concrete wall of the building. She used her legs to bring his body closer. His hard length pressed against her while their tongues teased and tormented each other. His hand found her breast again. She pulled back for a breath and he kissed his way down her neck. She barely stifled another moan when his hot mouth found the spot behind her ear. She dug her fingers into his shoulders, trying to anchor herself.

Footsteps sounded from nearby. She and Rhys froze.

"What are we doing out here, Mac?" a strange voice said.

The soldiers were headed straight for them. Rhys set her on the ground silently and motioned for her to follow him.

"The colonel just told me to grab somebody and head out this way," a gruff voice answered the first. "I don't know what the hell for. Maybe he thought he saw something."

Anger flashed through Cat as she followed Rhys around the corner of the building. A glance back showed a sergeant and a corporal striding toward the perimeter fence, right past where they'd been standing.

And kissing.

The colonel must have seen them walk out this way and suspected something. How could she have been such a fool? Dammit. One kiss was too much. She might be in E.D.G.E. now, but nothing said she would be there forever. She had a reputation to maintain.

Rhys stopped and looked at her, his eyes quiet. "That doesn't look good."

She glanced back at the soldiers behind them. They hadn't seen them. "What?"

"Your expression. You've decided what we have isn't worth going after."

Her lips pressed together. "It's not." The words *I'm sorry* hovered on her lips, but she bit them back. She would not be sorry for choosing her career over a night of passion. And she knew for a fact that that was all Rhys offered.

"You're serious, chère?" he asked, his voice gruff. "After that kiss?"

"Forget the kiss." She held up her hands as if to ward him off, though he hadn't moved. "And don't call me chère."

He scowled and opened his mouth. She cut him off. "I am your team leader. We are just teammates. Now, I've got to go grill an intel officer."

"I assume you want to do it alone. Like everything else you do," Rhys said.

"What is that supposed to mean?"

"You're smart," he said. "Figure it out, teammate."

He strode away. She clenched her jaw so she wouldn't call him back.

Cat spread the map on the table in the small room she'd been given for her team briefing. She'd just come from the female barracks where she'd grabbed some rack time, but had hardly been able to sleep.

Because of Rhys and his kiss.

Maybe they shouldn't be on the same team. She forced all thoughts of him away and locked them away in the back of her mind. She had a mission and a man's life to think about now.

Zach and Marc entered first, then Rhys. They all grabbed chairs.

"What do you have for us?" Marc said.

"I didn't get much from the intel guys here. But one of the D-boys offered up some information. They've been all over and know this area."

"Do we know what they're here for?" Zach said.

She shook her head. "No, but I don't think it'll affect our mission. The D-boy let me know the best route to Dr. Hutchins suspected location." She pointed at the map. "This area near Lake Chad is where our source says he's being held prisoner. Based on their typical pattern, we've got approximately forty-eight hours before they execute him. That means we fly out tonight."

She pointed to a new location on the map, about five kilometers from the river. "We'll insert here. Cross the Yobe River at this bridge. Then it's a quick ten-mile run." She grinned to show she knew it would be strenuous on them all. "Once at the location, we'll do a sneak-and-peek before the extraction. We'll get our guy out to the exfil at the same location."

"What if he's in bad shape?" Zach asked.

"We bring a portable stretcher, but the terrain won't permit a medevac until after that bridge."

"Grab and go," Rhys said.

She went over more details for the mission before breaking. "Meet on the airstrip at 2400 hours."

She went back to her bunk and checked her pack, her

weapon, and her gear. She smeared camouflage paint on her face, neck, hands, and any skin that might show pale in the dark, before heading to the airstrip.

The sun sank toward the horizon and turned the sky reddish orange.

She sighed when Steve fell into step with her.

"I saw you and your boy walk off together. So did lots of others."

"Go away, Steve."

"I know what you're doing," he said. "There's been rumors of an American hostage among the locals. You're going after him, aren't you?"

She didn't bother to acknowledge him.

"I can help," he said.

She snorted, but didn't say anything.

He went to grab her arm, but she shifted away without breaking her stride. "If you touch me, I will break something. That is your only warning."

"Why do you have to be like that?" he said. "I've got a company of men who could…"

She stopped and turned, cutting off his words. "This is a covert mission. You know what that means. You're not even supposed to be asking about it."

"Come on. You know I could do this. If you told your team you needed my help—"

"But I don't."

"What if you get captured, Cat? I'm just worried about you."

She stepped close to him and put her face in his. "Bullshit. You're a glory hound. You always want something for nothing." She sucked in a breath. "This posting is a punishment, isn't it? Who'd you piss off now, Steve? Wait— you know what? I don't care. I am not helping you."

"You think you're as good as a man," he snarled. "But you're not. You're just a bitch."

She shook her head, refusing to listen to any more of his insults. She strode away, taking deep breaths to shake off her rising anger. The mission called for a clear head.

A few minutes later, she found her team waiting at the end of the tarmac, where two pilots checked over a Little Bird. She nodded at the pilots and checked in with her guys. All had their game faces on, even Rhys; nothing about him betrayed the fact that they'd shared a wild kiss earlier. No leers or inappropriate comments. Tension left her shoulders.

Time to work.

CHAPTER 11

The MH-6 Little Bird only had room for the two pilots inside the helicopter. It carried its four passengers on external bench seats, two people per side. Rhys sat beside Cat, his FN SCAR rifle strapped across his front.

Full dark had fallen as the bird thumped its way to their infil location. Rhys mentally went over the plan as they rode the thirty minutes to the LZ.

Cat was silent beside him. A part of him was still pissed that she'd made the decision to end any relationship between them before she'd even given it a chance. She was a hell of a woman and one that suited him perfectly—they were explosive in bed, and had fun both in and out of it. He had no issues mixing work and pleasure, at least not with her.

He decided he had a new mission once they hit stateside again: to convince Cat to give them a shot. Tension left his neck and shoulders once he'd made the decision, and Rhys's mind went back to the mission at hand.

The ground was dark, his NVGs giving him glimpses of the landscape they flew over. He took a quick glance at the stars overhead. The glittering landscape revealed above was truly beautiful, and he never tired of looking at it.

"Infil five minutes." The pilot's voice came over his headset.

"Roger," Cat said.

Rhys went back to scanning the landscape below. In the distance, he saw more trees, and the river they had to cross.

The bird slowed and hovered over an open field near the tree line. "Let's do it," Cat said.

He threw out his thick rope, the line pinched between his feet to control his speed, and jumped off the bird with the rope in his gloved hands. He crouched as soon as his boots touched the ground, his rifle up, and scanned his field of fire. The others would be covering their own locations, so the full perimeter around the LZ would be protected.

Once the helicopter flew off and they no longer felt its beating wind, the oppressive heat and humidity hit Rhys. Sweat instantly dotted his face and made his skin slick under the weight of his armor and gear.

"Everyone down?" Cat's voice.

"Roger," they all replied.

"Let's move."

They went quiet after that. Moving fast, yet silent. Hand signals only. Running when the trees allowed.

It wasn't long before the bridge came in sight, maybe thirty minutes. Zach covered their rear while Cat, Marc, and Rhys surveyed the bridge. Made of wooden crossbeams and cement pillars, it was built wide enough for three men to walk abreast.

Two sentries smoked at the other end of the bridge, their cigarettes flaring in the NVGs with every inhalation. Rhys only prayed that every sentry they encountered would be as stupid.

"How do you want to play this?" Marc asked.

The sound of the dark rushing waters under the bridge covered their conversation. Cat stared at those waters a brief moment before looking at him and Marc. "We go under the bridge."

Rhys raised an eyebrow, but didn't say anything. If Cat didn't think her fear of water would be an issue, he had to trust his teammate on her choice. *Only teammates*, he reminded himself.

They slithered one by one down the bank. Cat signaled for him to follow her while Marc and Zach covered them. They slung their rifles and Cat grabbed a wooden crossbeam, tested her weight on it, and then swung out over the river. Her toes were only inches above the water. She swung hand over hand from crossbeam to crossbeam.

Rhys let her get about ten feet in front of him before he swung out after her. His shoulder and back muscles flexed to hold himself plus the extra fifty pounds of gear and ammo in his ruck and webbing, not including the twenty pounds of high-tech body armor, or his eight-pound FN SCAR MK 17. It made him proud at how effortless Cat made this crossing appear.

Halfway across, one of the sentries shouted. Rhys and Cat both froze. Sweat slithered down his back as a slender beam of light appeared and bobbed over the bridge.

Rhys shifted his grip and hung one-handed, making sure his rifle was easily accessible, before placing his hand back on the wooden plank he hung from. Otherwise he didn't move, taking his cue from Cat, who was closer to the situation.

The hiss and snowy crackle of a radio sounded loud even over the water. A man's voice shouted into the radio, while the other laughed. Rhys had no idea what was going on since they spoke Hausa and he had only the bare minimum of the language. The light from the flashlight still waved around.

Cat shifted her hands on the crossbeam she held. His shoulders burned, so he knew hers must, too. They needed to get across this river before they dropped into it. The waters were deep, the current fast, and if they weren't dragged down by their equipment, then they'd be pounded by the rocks.

It was time to do something. He shifted a hand to his rifle. Almost as if she sensed what he was doing, Cat turned her head to him and shook it.

Fine. He'd wait, but he wasn't going to let either of them drop into the river.

A full minute later, the light and the radio shut off. Cat waited another thirty seconds before moving. They quickly made it across from there, leaping to the ground and landing on the river's muddy edge silently. He unslung his rifle and aimed it upward, through the cracks between the boards to the two soldiers above. The acrid smoke from the guards' cigarettes had a sweetness to it, probably from some kind of drug mixed into the tobacco.

They murmured in Hausa to each other, the one's hands waving with whatever story he told. Rhys had never learned the multitude of African languages—most of his were either European or Middle Eastern. A quick glance showed Marc and Zach almost across.

Cat nodded at him when the rest of the team landed beside them. In a crouch, he crept along the riverbank away from the bridge. At twenty yards, he crawled up the bank and slid into the stunted trees. He aimed his rifle back toward the sentries, while keeping an eye on the others.

Cat came next. Her movements held the grace of a stalking predator. From there, the rest of the trek to the militant's base was a cakewalk. They ran the ten miles through the sparse woods, sipping water from their CamelBaks to stay hydrated, and detouring around sentries easily seen with their NVGs.

Once they arrived, Cat signaled Zach and Marc to do a quick outer perimeter recon of one side of the encampment while he and Cat did the other.

The encampment looked more like an occupied village, with its thatched roof huts scattered around five main concrete buildings. One dirt road ran through it. The acrid scent of urine and feces announced the location of the latrines on the west side of the encampment. Not far from that were three flatbed trucks, four pickups, and three jeeps. They crept around the vehicles, using them for cover.

Shouts and laughter came from one lit-up building not far from the vehicles. Sounded like a party of some sort. A gunshot cracked the night, but only laughter followed it so they kept moving.

They'd circled the entire camp and met up with Marc and Zach on the far side before they pulled back into the dark shadows of the trees.

"Any sign of the doctor?" Cat asked.

"Negative," Marc said.

Rhys pursed his lips. "Let's hope he's not at the party in that west building."

It was 0300 local time. Cat scanned the encampment before her, considering the options. She nodded to herself. "Okay. Lucky and I will take the south end. Doc and Spooky, you've got the other end. You see the doctor, then you hit the comm link twice. Let's find him fast and get the hell out of this shithole."

Tension thrummed through her. Something about this place made her back itch, like something bad was waiting to happen. She lifted her chin. She didn't have time to figure out what bothered her. They had to find that doctor or they had to find hidey holes to watch the encampment for the day. And she had no desire to watch these ignorant idiots play soldier all day.

She motioned to Rhys and they went back the way they'd come, moving closer to the buildings now. There were three in her area of operation. She and Rhys moved up to the first one. It was dark and quiet. She led the way to the doorway.

No door, just darkness beyond. Rhys tapped her shoulder, signaling he was ready for entry. She swooped inside, covering the right side. He came in a second behind her, his rifle up and pointed toward the left.

"Clear," Cat whispered. Rhys replied the same back.

Two doors led from the large room, empty except for a desk and a table with papers spread over it. Cat glanced at them as she went to the first door. Maps. She twisted the doorknob.

"Locked," she whispered.

Rhys tried the other one and shook his head. He came to her. "I got this," he whispered, and knelt. She kept her rifle trained back the way they'd come while he picked the lock. Outside, someone stumbled toward the building. She slung her rifle and pulled her knife, moving to the side of the door. Rhys never looked up, just concentrated on his task, leaving her to deal with any situation that might arise.

She waited, breathing slow as she focused her mind on her moves. If whoever it was came inside, she would grab them and stab them in the throat—a brutal but effective way to silence any scream.

The footsteps stopped and heavy breathing sounded. A zipper pulled down, loud in the night, and clothing shifted and rustled. Liquid splashed on the ground outside the door. The man was taking a piss.

She waited, muscles tense. Rhys had turned to her, still in a crouch by the door he'd unlocked. She met his calm eyes. They were riding a time limit, but this was only a minor delay.

Outside, the man mumbled something, zipped up, and stumbled on. She slid her knife away and unslung her rifle. She nodded at Rhys.

The first room held shelving with video equipment, files, and some desks with archaic computers. "Should we look for intel?" he asked.

"Negative," Cat said. "The doctor takes priority."

Rhys unlocked the second door and a stench wafted out of the pitch-black interior. Cat's NVGs helped her see the man lying prone facing the wall, his hands and feet bound with rope. She passed shelves filled with ammo and weapons. Kidnapping and ransoming must be lucrative for the group.

She knelt by the man on the floor and turned him to face her. Dark skin and a torn Nigerian Army uniform. Not the doctor. The man's eyes remained closed and his breathing shallow and rapid. Unconscious.

"He's not our guy," she whispered, standing up and turning away. Her gut clenched. She was leaving this man to face probable torture and death, but if they wanted to get the doctor out then they had to be ghosts. They couldn't help this man.

"Next building," she said.

The party in the main building seemed to be dying off. They crept past it to the dark cement building closest to the vehicles. Three large fire pits were in front. After listening for a few moments to the silence inside, they opened the door and slipped inside.

"Kitchen," Rhys said.

"And food storage," she said. Her hand trailed over the rough burlap sacks of grain piled in the corner. "Still doesn't seem like quite enough to feed two hundred men." She refused to call them soldiers.

"Maybe ransoming people isn't as profitable as it seems," Rhys said.

"Maybe they're not getting ransom because they keep beheading people." She glanced out the door. Clear. "Let's go check that main building."

"Roger that."

A few men patrolled the perimeter of the encampment, but they looked outwards. Cat and Rhys eased along the side of the rectangular building to one open window that spilled light onto the ground.

Laughter and slurred words in the Hausa language could

be heard, along with grunting and rhythmic squeaking. The skin along the back of her neck tightened. She wasn't going to like what she found. They inched closer. She now heard the men inside encouraging one of their own to go faster—they wanted a turn.

It was the small whimper that sharpened her focus. The same focus she had before every firefight. She quick-peeked inside and signaled to Rhys, fighting the bile that rose in her.

Eight men, she hand-signaled. Two girls.

She didn't need to tell him what the girls were doing there. And girls they were. Not women. They couldn't have been much into their teen years. She pushed her anger down.

The doctor wasn't in that room. They moved past to the next window.

It was shuttered closed and padlocked on the outside. Her heart leapt. Someone obviously wanted to keep the occupants inside from getting out. She signaled and Rhys brought out his tools again. Within moments he had the lock off and was easing the one shutter open a crack to peer inside.

He stepped back, his lips compressed, and shook his head.

Damn. Where the hell was their doctor? She stepped forward to peer inside when Rhys grabbed her arm.

"Don't," he whispered so quietly she could barely hear him. What was inside that would make him say that?

She swallowed against the rising premonition of what might be waiting in that room. "You know I have to," she said, just as quietly.

When she saw who lay inside, she had to force herself to remain still and not make a sound, though she wanted to cry out against the tragedy. About twenty girls lay inside, huddled against each other, most teenagers. Some whimpered or cried in their sleep. Bruises and cuts marred their skin. One young one near the door, who looked about thirteen, was obviously pregnant.

These were some of the Nigerian schoolgirls taken from their families so many months ago.

Her comm link clicked twice.

She stepped back from the window to answer. "Go ahead, over."

"Valkyrie," Marc's voice said in her ear. "We located the target, but there's a problem and you're not going to like it."

"Define problem."

"Just get here ASAP."

Fuck. "Copy that. En route to your location."

She swallowed hard and closed the shutter on the girls' room. She couldn't make herself relock it.

This wasn't over, she promised herself.

They took off running silently through the encampment. Zach stepped out from the shadows of a small building and waved them over. Inside, a small lantern with its wick set low showed Marc leaning against a large table in the center of the room, watching the man they'd come for.

The doctor was about her age, wiry, with wild dark hair. One of the lenses in his glasses was cracked. He sat on a rumpled pallet in a corner of the room. Boxes of bandages and medical supplies stood against the wall near him.

"They've got you treating people?" Cat said.

The doctor startled. "You're a woman! Thank god," he said. "You'll understand why I can't go."

"Can't go?" she asked. She looked to Marc.

He rolled his eyes. "The problem I mentioned."

The doctor stood up. "They've got schoolgirls here. It's horrific. You've got to rescue them, too. We can't leave them here."

"Is that true?" Zach asked, coming inside. "Are those girls here?"

She nodded. "There's about twenty of them in the main building."

"Can they travel?" Zach asked.

"Not all," Cat said, thinking of the pregnant girl.

"We can carry them," Zach said.

"We don't have the manpower," Marc said, "to carry them or to get that many out."

Zach shook his head. "The doctor's right. We can't leave little girls here."

"We'll get us and them killed trying to rescue them," Marc countered. "We have no medevac for them. We need more manpower."

"Enough," Cat said. It was her decision. She looked at Rhys. His brown eyes held pity for the decision that was hers to make.

She swallowed bile. "Marc's right, Doc, and you know it," she told Zach.

"Marc is a coldhearted bastard." He shook his head. "Fuck. Don't do this, Cat," he whispered. "It's not right."

She knew that better than him after what she'd seen earlier. It wasn't right to leave them behind, but she knew there was no choice. If she had some quality explosives or more men, then she would be able to think of a plan. But as it was, the four of them trying to protect twenty girls while outrunning two hundred armed men was a true suicide mission. It wasn't just her team's lives she had to consider—it was also the girls'.

Zach opened his mouth to say more, but she held up her hand to stop him. "We can't get them out. We don't have the manpower and we don't have an exfil strategy for them." She pushed past the urge to vomit at the thought of what she was consigning those girls to. "We'll come back," she said softly to him. "We'll get more men and a decent plan. We won't forget them."

Zach's eyes narrowed as if he didn't trust her words. That hurt, but she knew he was right. Who was she to say that their superiors would even let them return? Her lips firmed. They had to let her come back. They wouldn't be able to turn their backs on those girls.

Like she was doing.

Dr. Hutchins crossed his arms. "I'm not leaving without them."

Anger flared hot and bright, finding an outlet for her suppressed frustration and rage. "You are going to do exactly what I say, when I say, or I'll shoot you myself."

"You're worse than a man," he said. "I can't believe you don't care what those girls are going through."

She turned away, knowing it was futile to get in an argument with him. "Gather whatever you might want. We're leaving."

She blew out the lantern before stalking outside to wait in the hellish dark of the night, wondering for a moment if she was as bad a monster as the men who'd kidnapped those girls.

CHAPTER 12

Rhys wanted to punch something. He knew they all felt it—the anger of doing what was right for the mission and yet morally wrong for their consciences. Leaving those girls behind dug in his gut and stained his soul.

The trek back to the bridge was slower with Dr. Hutchins in tow. He was fit, just half-starved and indignant about leaving the girls behind.

"You'll come back for them, right?" His stage whisper seemed to echo through the trees.

Cat's fingers flickered, but she didn't look back from where she led the way. She wanted the doctor shut up or killed if Rhys read her signals right. It almost made him smile. Almost.

"No talking," Rhys said. "Not if you want to get out of here alive."

The doctor stopped walking. "Seriously. Will you go back?"

Rhys grit his teeth. All of them wanted to go back–that wasn't the question. You'd have to be beyond heartless to not want to save those girls. "It's not our decision," he said.

The doctor opened his mouth, so Rhys shoved him forward before he could speak. "No more talking."

They made it back to the bridge about an hour before dawn. He hunkered down beside Cat where she crouched behind a tree watching the lone sentry on the bridge.

He pointed at the sentry and then himself. Her lips firmed like she wanted to argue, but Rhys wasn't going to let her. She had enough on her shoulders with the weight of the decision she'd had to make back at the encampment. He pointed at himself again. She gave a sharp nod.

He stood and crept toward the sentry. There was no sign of the guy's partner. Maybe he'd left. It didn't matter—they no longer cared if the sentry missed any check-ins, so Rhys would take care of him permanently.

The guard never saw his death coming. Rhys slipped up to him from behind, got him in a chokehold, and held on until the man went limp. Then he held on for longer, until he knew the man was dead. He felt no remorse. This man had probably raped those girls on multiple occasions and killed little boys just because they were a different religion. He was Boko Haram, after all. Rhys threw the man's body from the bridge and into the river.

The team jogged up, passing him silently. Dr. Hutchins stared at him, his mouth open. Rhys just motioned him along, wanting this mission over with.

After crossing the bridge, Cat radioed in. "Alpha Charlie this is Bravo Zero, over."

After a moment she spoke quietly. "Five minutes to exfil, gentlemen. Let's hustle. I don't want to miss our ride."

They jogged through the stunted trees on this side of the river. Rhys kept his hand on the doctor's arm, steering him clear of obstacles since the man didn't have NVGs, and helping him keep up with the others. His wheezing breath interspersed with whimpers made him sound like a wounded dog trying to keep up with its owners.

Rhys couldn't seem to muster any sympathy for him, just kept dragging him along, taking more and more of the guy's weight as they went. They stayed in the trees when they hit the clearing, waiting for the bird that would take them back to base.

No one spoke. Usually he'd be cracking jokes at this point in the mission, but nothing struck him as funny. The thumping of the helicopter blades didn't bring the relief it usually did.

He probably just needed sleep. He turned his back to the incoming bird and looked back the way they'd come. No movement, but he didn't let up on his vigilance until Cat tapped him on the shoulder.

The bird had landed—a UH-60 Black Hawk. The nearest

gunner waved to them before going back to scanning the trees with his M134 Minigun.

Marc and Zach took off with the doctor between them. Rhys and Cat followed. Once onboard, they buckled in for the flight back. Again no one spoke. The young doctor lay his head on his knees. By the way his shoulders shook, Rhys knew he cried.

He looked away, forcing his own emotions down. They'd accomplished their mission with no loss of life, and yet it felt like they'd failed. Cat sat across from him, her gaze on her hands as she alternated between stretching the fingers out and clenching them into fists.

He turned from her and gazed out into the dark sky, searching for stars. Even with his NVGs, hardly any still glittered in the predawn light.

Cat left the crying Dr. Hutchins in Zach's capable hands. He'd see to him medically, and she wouldn't have to listen to the man complain about her decision to leave those girls behind. Her mind was already replaying the vision of what she'd seen in that room. Those eight men and the two girls.

Anger seethed inside her. It was time to do something about it.

She didn't bother cleaning off her camouflage paint, she just trotted across the landing strip, weapon still in hand, and headed for the HQ. The sun had risen and she knew the base CO would be up and working already.

One of the clerks jerked and spilled her coffee when Cat slammed inside.

"Is he in his office?" Cat asked, not stopping.

The clerk nodded. "I wouldn't—"

She rapped hard on his door, and at his gruff reply swung open the door and stepped inside. "Sir, I need a moment of your time."

"Casualties?" he barked.

"No, sir, but—"

"Did you complete your mission?"

"Yes, sir, but—"

"Then what's the problem?"

She was not going to take attitude from this man. She looked down her nose at him without speaking for a moment, staring him right in the eyes. She waited until he opened his mouth to speak and then she cut him off. "We found some of those missing girls."

He deflated in front of her eyes. His shoulders slumped and his gaze dropped from hers to the desk.

"Colonel? Did you hear me? We found some of them. We need to organize a mission to get them out."

He started shaking his head before he'd even raised his eyes to hers, and she prepared to fight. She wasn't going to let some old misogynist colonel keep little girls in danger just because he didn't like Cat being in spec ops. But when she saw his eyes, hopeless and tormented, any words of anger caught in her throat.

"We've been told to stand down in that matter," he said.

"You knew." Cat took a step back. "You knew they were there."

He held up a hand. "We suspected. Aw, hell. Yes, we knew. But there's nothing we can do about it. We don't have the manpower here for a major offensive. We only have a single infantry company. We're a drone base and that's it. Even if we did have the boots on the ground, we'd need both the U.S. Senate's permission and Nigeria's." He shook his head. "We haven't had any luck so far. The Nigerian government is corrupt and a pain in the ass to deal with. And the U.S. can't officially do anything without their permission." He sighed. "I have a teenage daughter. The thought of those girls gives me nightmares."

This couldn't be happening. "What about the Canadians?" she asked almost desperately. "Do they know?"

The colonel nodded. "I'm sure the major reported it up the line, but you know as well as I do, if the U.S. can't get access for a mission like this, then the Canadians won't be able to either. Go ask your major."

"He's not my major," she said automatically. "And I will."

She found Steve having breakfast. She strode up to him, still with weapon in hand. "I need to talk to you."

He raised his eyebrows. "Well, if it isn't GI Jane." No one sitting near him so much as smiled. A couple even shifted uncomfortably. Maybe they'd finally realized she was a serious operator. Not that she cared.

"Now, Steve." She turned and walked out, knowing he'd follow, but there was no satisfaction in making him do what she wanted. Her only thought was of those girls.

Outside, she only had to wait a minute before he showed.

"What's this all about, Cat? You can't pull that shit in front of my men—"

"Did you know some of the missing schoolgirls were in that encampment across the river?"

Steve stopped trying to talk. In fact, he froze as if she'd caught him in a lie. His gaze flicked around.

"So you did know," she said.

He puffed up his chest. "Yes, I did. We all know. But so what? We can't do anything about it."

"You have a company of men here."

He gave a short laugh. "Seriously, Cat? I'm a Canadian officer attached to an American company. I don't have any pull. And besides, no matter what I want to do, the fact of the matter is that I have my orders. It would mean my career and most likely the lives of some of the men to rescue those girls. We'd be going in without support. Just because they should be rescued doesn't mean they will be."

"How can you not fight for them? Don't you care?"

He ran a hand over his buzzed hair. "Of course I care. I'm not a monster. But the world doesn't, Cat."

"You mean the politicians."

"I mean the people in charge," he said. "Their own government knows where they are and doesn't give a shit about rescuing them. To the world, they're nobodies."

He'd given up. She could see that, in the slump of his shoulders and the shake of his head. Her hands fisted.

"These girls need someone to care." She took a breath, the next words costing her some of her pride. "Please, Steve. You begged me yesterday to help."

"Yesterday you were on a sanctioned mission to rescue an American citizen. Today you're asking me to commit career suicide. I'm sorry, Cat. I can't help you." He walked back inside.

The reality of what she'd done hit her. She'd left behind innocents. She wanted to fall to her knees and scream—anything to relieve the pressure of her failure to protect those who needed protecting the most.

Instead, she gazed into the cloudless blue of the morning sky, blinking fast against the welling of tears. She swallowed hard.

She wasn't completely out of options. E.D.G.E. and its resources were her last chance. She would deliver the senator's son home and then she and E.D.G.E. would organize another mission. They would come back.

She hoped.

Her team waited at the edge of the tarmac, ready to return. They wore stony looks, but Cat saw the stiffness in their stances. They felt betrayed. Zach turned away from her and her hands clenched. It had been her call. He'd wanted to stay.

Marc slapped Zach on the back and spoke a few words to him. Zach shrugged him off and stormed away to the barracks. Their flight home would be in two hours. Enough time to clean up their weapons and themselves.

She watched her team disperse, not moving from her spot. Only Rhys met her gaze. He captured hers with a weight that made it hard to breathe. She looked away first, away from the absolution he offered. She didn't deserve it.

When she finally looked back, he was gone and she was alone.

CHAPTER 13

"The senator's son is safe at home," Blackwell said. He sat at the head of the table in E.D.G.E. HQ, while Cat and the rest of the team sat around it. "Good work, Alpha team."

Everyone nodded, but no one spoke.

They'd gotten back this morning and had spent the day writing reports and thoroughly cleaning their weapons. Cat wore her jeans, boots, and a black t-shirt, all of which now had smears of gun oil on them. She sighed and ran a hand through her hair. She was looking forward to sleeping in her own bed tonight. Looking at the others, she could tell they felt the same. This mission had left a bad feeling in all their guts.

Blackwell studied them. Cat avoided his gaze and met

Rhys's instead. He had his game face on. None of them had said much as they'd handed over the senator's son to the CIA in Germany, nor on the transport home.

"What's wrong?" Blackwell said. "Valkyrie, report."

She grit her teeth, but then decided to lay it on the line. "It's about those Nigerian schoolgirls, sir. We found some and weren't able to extract them. It's in my report."

"Yes, I read that. I'll pass the info along to the appropriate people."

Her muscles tensed. "And nothing will happen, will it, sir?"

Blackwell sat back. "I can see how this has affected you all. Give me some time to see if I can nudge the right people into doing the right thing."

"From what I heard, you'd have to put a gun to their heads," Cat muttered.

Blackwell took another moment to look over each team member. "Alpha team is on leave till Monday. Go enjoy yourselves. Just don't go too far. There's another mission on the books. Training starts Monday."

"That's it?" Cat asked. "We're just supposed to forget about them?"

"I will do what I can, Valkyrie, but getting authorization for a mission like this takes time."

"You mean a mission where there's no Western interests at stake."

His eyes narrowed. "Yes, Valkyrie, that's exactly what I mean. Now be ready to train on Monday."

Blackwell left the room.

The team stayed sitting for a moment before Marc stood up. "I'm heading to the Chien Noir," he said. "I need a drink, or three. Anyone coming?"

"Hells yes," Rhys said. "I'm in."

Zach stood up, too. "You coming, Cat?"

"I'm just going to catch up on a bit of paperwork. I'll meet you guys there."

"Make sure you come," Zach said. "You need a break too."

Right, but those girls won't be getting a break.

She pushed away from the table and strode to her office. She didn't really have much paperwork, but she didn't feel like hanging out in a bar, nor did she feel like going to her apartment. It felt wrong to be able to go to her safe home when she knew those girls might never see theirs again.

She sighed and half-heartedly flipped through some case files on her desk. She was reading personnel files about potential recruits when Blackwell knocked on her open door.

"What are you doing here?" he asked.

"Just catching—"

"You hardly get any leave from this job. When you get some, you take it, or you will burn out. Are we clear?"

"Yes, sir," she said.

"Good." He stood at the door watching her. Then he shook his head. "Cat, I will push hard for this mission. Now go and relax." He left her in her office.

She stood and picked up her leather jacket, her movements slow. Fatigue dragged at her, but she couldn't face her apartment. She would go have that drink with her team. Maybe they'd forgiven her.

But could she forgive herself?

Rhys took a swallow of his beer. He stood at a high-top table in the Chien Noir. He'd been here once before and it seemed like a classier place than most bars that military folk chose, but that could be because it was a downtown Montreal bar far from any base. No one knew E.D.G.E. was military, and they kept up their covers by pretending to be normal businessmen and women.

The room was long and narrow, with a mirror behind the polished wooden bar that ran along one wall. High round tables, some with chairs, dotted the center of the room while dark booths lined the other wall.

He spotted the asshole Cat had put in a wrist lock at that fancy wine bar. The guy swayed where he stood, sloshing his martini on his business suit. Drunk on a Wednesday night. He grit his teeth. Cat would rather date an asshole like that than him?

He kept an eye on the prick. He didn't want him to make a sneak attack if Cat showed. Some men never knew when to quit, and this guy with his liquid courage definitely showed danger signs. Cat could handle herself, but she didn't need any bullshit after the mission.

He nursed his beer at the table they'd pulled closer to the wall, so they could stand with their backs to it. He, Marc, and Zach had attracted attention while he'd been musing. A group of four women stood not far away and eyed them discreetly. The leader of the group, tall and model-thin, pushed out her boob job when she saw him looking and fluffed the chestnut hair trailing down her back.

Exactly his type.

Cat had said no to him. More than once. He should probably leave her alone and start looking at other women. He sighed. What was wrong with him? It had been a long deployment and then he'd been shipped right away to E.D.G.E. He hadn't had downtime in too long.

The woman smiled at him, inviting him with her eyes. He looked away and took another slug of his beer. What was with him tonight?

She isn't Cat.

Dammit, he had it bad.

Marc met his gaze from across the small table and then looked behind Rhys's shoulder. His small smile let Rhys know the women had finally worked up their courage to approach them.

"Ladies," Marc said. "Care to join us?"

The tall chestnut-haired woman sidled up next to Rhys and laid a hand on his arm, just below where his t-shirt stopped. "Thank you," she purred, her eyes only on Rhys. "I'm Tania. And who are you?"

Rhys sipped his beer and didn't look at her. "Rhys."

The other women divided themselves around Marc and Zach. Marc looked like he was tossing a mental coin about whether to take the Asian woman or the redhead home. A petite and curvy brunette chatted up Zach, who looked like he'd just gotten an extra piece of pie.

Tania's fingers still trailed up and down his arm. He'd tried to move away, but they followed him. He didn't want to be rude, and so resigned himself to the feeling of ants crawling over his arm. She chatted with him about her work—she was in sales or something.

Rhys nodded every now and then as she spoke, but really he was trying to figure out why she bored the crap out of him. She was beautiful, smart, and she obviously wanted him. But it wasn't doing anything for him.

Someone walked in the door. His eyes snapped to her and his senses came alive.

Cat.

She stood out from the people around her. It wasn't that she was tall, or only wearing jeans and a leather jacket; she radiated confidence and strength. Add that to her brilliant blue eyes and she struck the core of him. Her eyes still held shadows, which added a touch of sadness to her. A sadness Rhys wanted to erase.

She shrugged off her jacket and he noted she still wore the tight, faded jeans that showed off that delicious ass, as well as a black v-neck t-shirt that hinted at cleavage and showed off her sculpted arms. She pushed her bangs out of her eyes and her gaze found his.

He couldn't help his smile and didn't care what it meant that it had come out for her. His got wider when she smiled back at him. It had been one of the only ones he'd seen from her in the last two days.

Tiny nips on his arm pulled his attention. Tania had dug her claws in.

Cat's smile dimmed, and then turned professionally friendly.

Rhys sighed. Probably for the best. *We're just teammates.* That word was driving him crazy. He watched her graceful stride as she came toward their table, her eyes scanning the crowd. He knew the moment she spotted the asshole. She stiffened but kept walking, another layer of shadows darkening her brilliant eyes.

"Hey, Cat," Rhys said. "Can I grab you a drink?"

Nails on his arm. He shook them off.

Cat's eyes slid to the woman beside him. "No, I'm good. I was just stopping in to say goodnight."

"Goodnight," Tania murmured beside him.

Cat's eyes narrowed and Rhys almost smiled. She didn't take shit from anyone.

"Stay," he said. "One beer."

Zach moved. "I'll get the next round. And one for our fearless leader," he said.

Cat opened her mouth, but Zach put up a hand. "You're staying, Valkyrie."

"Valkyrie?" Tania said. "What kind of name is that?"

"Fine. Just one." Cat said, ignoring Tania. "Then I'm

going home."

"Hot date?" Rhys asked before he could stop himself. She'd better not have.

Cat's lips twisted as she slid a glance at Tania. "Something like that."

Rhys's eyebrows raised. Cat obviously didn't want to say what she'd be doing in front of Tania. But from the look on her face, he'd bet it wasn't a date—or at least it wasn't one she was looking forward to.

Was she going out with another asshole like Liam? God, he hoped not. She deserved way better. His eyes sought out the guy who now stood alone at his table, his eyes focused balefully on Cat.

Just try something, buddy. Please.

Zach arrived with the beers, though Rhys was barely halfway through his first. Still, he pushed it aside for the cold one. He had no desire to drown his sorrows. He had one too many friends go down that path. He twisted the cold bottle in his grip.

"What's wrong?" Tania asked, her fingers again on his arm. "I'm pretty intuitive, you know. I can tell that something's bothering you."

"No shit?" Rhys said, an edge finally creeping into his voice. He moved his arm again. When would this woman get the hint?

"Lucky," Cat said in a warning voice. "Ease off."

Tania frowned as she looked at Cat and then back to Rhys. "Lucky? You have a nickname? Did she give it to you?" Her hand dropped from his arm.

Cat gave a small laugh and raised her hands. "It's a work thing. We work together," she said. "We're just friends."

Rhys pressed his lips together to stop the denial he wanted to shout. He took a swallow of beer. "Right, just friends."

Tania's hand came back onto his arm. "Well, *Rhys*, why don't you tell me what's bothering you?"

He shifted a few inches away and Tania followed. How was he supposed to get rid of this woman? Cat obviously didn't want him to be mean, but he'd had enough.

Cat lifted her beer and took a sip. The drink moistened her lips, and her eyes twinkled with suppressed laughter at his situation. She was gorgeous, and he ached with the need to kiss her.

No. Just friends.

So he narrowed his eyes slightly and mouthed. "I'll get you back."

Cat snorted and turned away. Now his smile came out.

Marc nudged him. He leaned away from Tania to hear what Marc had to say, his eyes still on Cat as she laughed at something Zach said to her.

"Be careful," Marc said.

His gaze jerked to Marc. "What'd you say?"

"You heard me," Marc said. He jerked his chin toward Cat. "I've seen how you look at her. We all have."

Rhys shrugged and focused on his beer. "So what? She's a beautiful woman."

"No," Marc said sharply. "She's your teammate. Don't think of her as anything else. She's not a player, not like you are. Don't mess with the team, man."

Rhys faced Marc, his anger snapping. "Back off. I know the score. I'm not messing with anything. Or anyone."

"Make sure it stays that way."

Cat leaned over to them across the table. "You two doing okay?"

Marc slung his arm around Rhys's shoulders and tightened hard, digging his fingers into his arm. "Fucking fantastic. Right, Lucky?"

Rhys saluted Cat with his beer bottle, shaking off Marc's arm. "Just awesome."

Cat watched them both for a moment more and then nodded. "Okay. If you need to work something out, then hit the gym tomorrow. I know—"

"Are you their mom or something?" Tania asked. "Cause you're certainly dressed the part."

The Asian woman beside Marc tittered. He straightened away from her. Both Rhys and Marc opened their mouths to speak, but Cat held up a hand. She looked at Tania, her eyes glittering like ice chips.

"You've been trying to get my attention since I walked in here. You've got it. What do you want?"

Tania stepped back, her eyes wide. Rhys had to smother his amusement. At least she'd finally stopped touching his arm.

"Nothing to say?" Cat said. "I find that's typical of women

like you. Petty behind a person's back, but as soon as you're confronted you act shocked."

"No… I… Well, yes," she finally said. "I am shocked. I don't know what you're talking about."

Cat tipped her beer back and swallowed the last of it before setting the bottle on the table. She stepped close to Tania and whispered something. Tania's eyes widened and her face drained of color.

Cat stepped back, tilted her head as if inspecting her work, then she nodded. Tania swallowed. Her eyes flicked from Cat to Rhys and then the other men as if searching for help, or maybe her backbone, before her eyes settled back on Cat.

"Crazy bitch," she whispered, and then stalked off.

Cat smiled. "Sorry about your date, Rhys."

"She wasn't my date, and you don't look sorry at all."

Cat laughed. "I'm not. Well, I'm off, guys. Goodnight."

She strode away from them and Rhys let himself watch her walk away. He didn't care what Marc said—a woman with a body like that was too much of a temptation for him not to look a little, even if they were teammates.

Then he saw Marc watching her too, and he almost growled. *Mine.*

They both stiffened when they saw the man walking out after her, his eyes focused on her like a target.

It was the asshole.

Rhys put his beer down and started to move to the door.

"Trouble?" Marc asked.

Zach perked up at the question.

"Nah," Rhys said. "It's her ex. I just want to make sure he's not hassling her. She's too nice to him."

Zach swung around and stared out the door. "That was the Liam guy?"

"She told you?" Rhys said, startled that Cat would mention what had happened.

Zach narrowed his eyes. "She only told me he was boring."

Both Marc and Zach straightened and put their drinks down. If they followed him out because Rhys had opened his big mouth, Cat would shoot him. She didn't need help with the asshole, and she'd just be embarrassed if the situation got out. He held up his hands. "Guys, it's good. If we all go out there, we'll make a scene and she'll hate that. She's probably already gone. I'm just gonna do a quick recce."

Zach and Marc relaxed only slightly. "Make sure it's just a quick recce on your *teammate*," Marc said.

"Of course," Rhys said with a smile. Then he strode out of there to find Cat before the asshole did.

CHAPTER 14

C at crossed her arms over her chest as she stared at the man who swayed under the streetlight in front of her. They stood on the blessedly empty sidewalk in front of the Chien Noir. "What planet are you from that makes you think I owe you an apology?" she asked.

"You embarrassed me."

"Good," Cat said. She didn't walk away because she didn't want this fool at her back.

"I could file an assault charge against you," he said, lisping slightly from too many drinks. "I have witnesses."

Cat sighed. This day really couldn't get any worse. She'd just come back from one of the worst 'successful' missions she'd ever been on, then walked in on Rhys flirting with another woman-Cat still wanted to rip Tania's fingers off, but she couldn't because teammates didn't do that to teammates' lovers-and now her ex whatever-he-was was stopping her from getting home to her couch and TV.

"You won't be getting an apology from me, Liam. I suggest you head home and sleep off those drinks you had."

"You know I've been waiting at this bar every night for you."

"Now that's a bit creepy, even for you. It's time you left."

He took a deep breath and drew himself upright, as if bracing himself for something. Or getting ready to attack.

She almost rolled her eyes. *So not my night.*

Liam took a step toward her, his hands clenched into fists.

Someone came out of the bar. Someone tall, with sandy hair and eyes that widened.

Dammit. Why does he have to see all of my humiliating moments?

"Don't do whatever it is you're planning, Liam," she said. "You won't like the results and they'll be much worse than last time. There are no witnesses now."

"You fucking bitch," he said, raising his fist. "I—"

She slammed her fist into his gut and his alcoholic breath whooshed out of him. The next punch struck his throat and he dropped to his knees gasping like a trout on dry land. "That is the second time tonight someone has called me that, and it's the last," Cat said quietly. "Don't come near me again or I will put you in the hospital."

Rhys came to stand behind her. "And again you're being too lenient," he said with false cheer. He put his face close to Liam's. "Go near her again, asshole, and I will bury you." He straightened. "Alive."

"Now get the fuck out of here," Cat said. "And don't come back to this place. My friends and I come here."

Liam scuttled off, wheezing.

What the hell had she seen in him? Cat shook her head, trying not to laugh. She looked at the anger etched onto Rhys's face and that opened the dam. Giggles bubbled out.

Rhys frowned at her. "Are you okay?"

She clutched her sides and nodded, now unable to stop. How could she explain that she was laughing at her own love life? That bit of embarrassment only made the laughter come louder.

Rhys slowly smiled, as if unable to stop himself. "What is so funny?"

She shook her head as her laughter died down. "My life. Between him and Steve, I really couldn't pick any worse losers to date."

Rhys didn't smile like she expected. He looked away. She almost sighed. Now she'd embarrassed him with talk of her love life. "Look," she said, hoping to make him feel more comfortable. "It's not a big deal. I'm not looking for sympathy or anything. I just thought it was funny."

His gaze caught hers. "You deserve so much better than those losers. I just don't know why you can't see that."

She didn't say anything. She couldn't. Her throat had

tightened with his words. What did he want from her? Was he saying this as a friend?

The door to Chien Noir opened. Marc and Zach stood there. "Hey, Cat," Zach said. "You good? We saw that guy follow you out."

"I'm all good," Cat said, moving away from Rhys and breathing a bit easier. "He just had a few complaints about my behavior that I had to take care of."

"All cleared up?" Zach said. Marc stood silent, but he watched Rhys with narrowed eyes.

"Yes, but if you see him around here again, you can tell him that you're friends of mine and I said you could have fun with him."

"Excellent," Zach said. "Well, I'm going back in. There's a pretty brunette that wants to practice her massage technique on my aching shoulders."

"Go," Cat said, laughing. "See you Monday."

Marc let him pass, his eyes still on Rhys. "You coming, Rhys?"

Rhys's jaw tightened. "I'm done for the night."

"Okay, *teammate*."

Rhys nodded. Marc said goodnight to her and then went inside.

She put her hands on her hips. "Are you going to tell me what that little bit of testosterone mudslinging was for?"

"He thinks I want to be more than friends with you," Rhys said in a low voice, his eyes on hers, wishing he could just take this woman to bed again and get her out of his system.

She took a step back. "But you don't."

He snorted. "Of co—"

She held up her hand to stop him. "You can't. There can be nothing between us."

That made him scowl. "But there is something. You feel it just as much as I do."

"It doesn't matter. We're teammates. And maybe friends. But that's it," Cat said. "So there's no problem, is there?"

"Nope," he said with gritted teeth. "No problem." Besides the fact that he wanted to strip her naked and have mad monkey sex with her, there was no problem. This woman was going to drive him insane.

She frowned a little, almost as if she'd expected him to protest, but he wouldn't. Not until she did, anyway.

Hmmm. Could he somehow get her to compromise? Maybe they could be friends with benefits?

"What is that sneaky smile for?" she asked him.

"I'm thinking of ways to make you let me walk you home."

She waved a hand. "I don't need you to protect me."

"I know that, chère," he said laying on the drawl. "But my grand-mère would roll over in her grave if she knew I'd let a lady walk home alone."

Cat snorted. "Have you used that line on a lot of women?"

He shrugged. "A few. That doesn't make it any less true."

She lifted her chin, a dangerous sparkle in her blue eyes enticing him closer. "Okay," she said. "But you have to answer some of my questions."

He smiled and started to speak, but she cut him off with a wave of her hand. "And you'll give me serious, truthful responses. Deal?" She stared at him, a small smile on her lips, obviously confident he wouldn't take her deal.

"Deal," he said, and almost laughed at the look of consternation on her face before she smoothed it away. "Lead on, oh fearless leader."

The humor drained from her face. "Don't call me that."

"Why not?"

"I think I proved on the mission that I'm neither fearless nor a real leader."

"Are you serious?" He shook his head. "What would— no, what *could* you have done differently? We had a mission to complete. You completed it with no loss of life."

Her voice was low and bitter when she spoke. "So you think it was a success?"

He sighed and started walking. After a moment she caught up to him. "To our superiors it was a success, Cat. You know we can't save everyone."

"Dammit, Rhys. I know that." She strode ahead, setting a fast pace. It was at least a minute before she spoke. "This was different, though."

"I know," Rhys said. And he did.

They walked in silence, each lost in their thoughts. Rhys wanted to lift the darkness from Cat's eyes. Being in command weighed heavy on a person, and he could see how this last mission affected her.

He needed to distract her, and he had a few ideas about how to do that. Unfortunately, she'd already vetoed the way he'd have chosen. So they'd have to talk.

"Are you going to ask your questions?" he finally said.

She startled slightly and then looked at him, not slowing her pace. "Fine. Why did your grandmother raise you?"

"Whoa, pulling out the big guns right away," he said. He hated talking about his past, but if that's what it took to get her out of her own head, then he'd lay his miserable life story before her.

"I'm okay to walk by myself if you don't feel like answering," she said.

So that's how she wanted to play it: she was trying to drive him away. Well, he always liked a challenge. So let's see how little Miss Perfect Family dealt with this.

"My mother was a crack whore," he said. He ignored Cat's quick gasp and plowed on with his story. "She didn't know who my father was. My grand-mère raised me from the time I was a baby. My mother would only come around when she needed something. Usually money."

"Damn," she whispered. "Is she still alive?"

He shrugged, knowing it looked callous but unable to dig much deeper into that scarred area of his soul. "I tried to find her after grand-mère died, but I couldn't."

"Why did you end up on the street?"

Her steps had slowed and he matched them, but he didn't look at her. He didn't want or need her pity. "The foster system couldn't find me a family and wanted to ship me off to some dinky town. So I left."

"That must have been hard."

"The hardest part?" he said staring at the cement sidewalk. "Was watching another family move into my home."

"I'm sorry."

"Don't be sorry," he said. "You wanted the truth."

"Yes, but I didn't mean to drag you down into my depression."

"Don't worry about me. Besides, I have family now." When she raised her eyebrows in question he continued. "The military is my family. Has been since I joined when I was seventeen."

Her brows drew together in a slight frown, as if this wasn't a good answer for her. But what did she expect? Besides, the guys on his team were his brothers—she'd said it herself. Why did he need anyone else?

They kept walking, but the silence was no longer comfortable, more like a heavy weight to be endured. It bowed their shoulders and kept their eyes down.

Hell, she felt sorry for him now. That hadn't been his intention. He never should have opened up to her and dragged her into his issues. He was supposed to be cheering her up. He stretched his legs, lengthening his pace, forcing her to keep up. This wasn't how he'd seen the night going.

Cat stopped. He debated for a half second whether to just keep walking. Maybe he should go back to the Chien Noir and find Tania. He could lose himself in mindless sex for a night.

He stopped and looked back at the woman who plagued his thoughts. He could still see the blue of her eyes in the streetlights, which glinted off her white-blonde hair. There was no way Tania could compare to her. He was fooling himself—and not very well.

Cat pursed her lips. "Well, we're gloomy tonight," she said.

He sighed. "Maybe I should head home." He didn't want to, but he'd respect her wishes.

She gave a little shake of her head. "That would probably be the smart thing to do," she muttered. Had he heard her right? He stepped closer.

"Time to live a little," she said softly, and this time he definitely heard her. She looked up at him and smiled. His heart skipped a beat at the reckless look in her eye.

"I've got something that will cheer us up," she said. "You up for it?"

Rhys's pulse jacked up a notch. Visions of her naked immediately dispelled his black mood. "They call me Lucky, remember? I'm up for anything."

Cat sucked in a breath. Rhys's eyes glowed golden with heat as he watched her. She'd better nip that in the bud before the heat grew as wild as Rhys himself. That brought thoughts of their one night together, and the explosive kiss they'd shared in Niger. Her heart sped up.

Calm down, Cat.

She held up her hands as if to hold Rhys back. "Get a grip on those thoughts, Lucky," she said, deliberately using his nickname to put some emotional distance between them.

"What thoughts?" he said in a low voice, even as he stepped closer to her.

She wanted to close the distance between them. She knew how good it would feel to lose herself in his strength for just one night, but she couldn't. He was like a drug for her—the more she had him, the more she seemed to want him.

But we can be friends.

She had the discipline to make it through special operations training. She sure as hell could deal with a hands-off policy with Rhys Lafayette. Failure wasn't an option.

She stepped back and smiled like a friend would. A friend who didn't want to strip him naked and lick her way down his body.

Stop that, Cat.

"We need to laugh," she said. "And I have the perfect thing to help us."

His face scrunched up like he'd found a Brussels sprout

in his beer. "Laugh?"

Her grin widened. "Yes. You're coming to my apartment."

"Now you're talking," he said quietly.

"As my *friend*."

"I'm really beginning to hate that word."

Cat laughed and he smiled at her, his hand reaching up to brush a piece of her hair behind her ear. "It's good to hear you laugh," he said.

Emotion welled in her with his simple statement, but she refused to name it, let alone give in to it. "Come on," she said. "We're almost there."

"I know," he said, still in the low voice that set the butterflies in her stomach whirling.

Three words described her apartment. Basic, cozy, and colorful. A one bedroom that took ten steps to cross, it had a galley kitchen, an alcove for a dining room, and a tiny living room with an overstuffed couch, a TV, and a small, blue painted desk with her personal laptop. The personality came from the electric blue couch and the purple and green pillows on it. Her brother always said it looked like someone had stuffed a peacock and turned it into a couch, but she liked it. The rest of the place followed the theme. Colorful art, pillows, and a plush throw rug. Heaven. Her bedroom was done in oranges, pinks, and reds.

The elevator let them off at her floor. As she put her key in the lock, memories of the first time Rhys had come to her place raced through her mind. He'd called her apartment fun and exotic. Her lips twisted as she realized Rhys was the only man she'd brought home to her apartment in the last six months.

Now that was just sad. True, she'd been insanely busy with missions, but to be celibate for half a year? Maybe her mom was right—maybe she really did need to meet a man.

She glanced at Rhys.

Some other man. And she wasn't going to sleep with Rhys just to satisfy some itch.

Her inner voice protested that it wasn't just an itch, but she ignored it.

"So what are you going to show me?" Rhys said, startling her from her thoughts.

She grabbed the distraction with both hands. "A movie," she said brightly. "We need to laugh and relax. What better way than to watch a funny movie?"

"Please tell me you're not going to make me watch some romantic comedy."

"Not tonight," she said. "Though I know you secretly wish you could."

He snorted.

"Beer's in the fridge. I'll set up a selection of movies I have and you can pick."

She went to her laptop and brought up her movie file. "Okay, *Hot Fuzz, Shaun of the Dead, Tropic Thunder, Galaxy Quest,* or *Bridesmaids.*"

Rhys came over and handed her a cold beer, the top already twisted off, and started to peruse her files. "You've got quite an eclectic taste in films, Valkyrie."

She shrugged, and unstrapped the holster that kept her backup Browning 9mm hidden at the small of her back, under her t-shirt. She placed it on her dining table and plopped onto her couch, leaving Rhys lots of space on the other side, and went through her takeout menus.

"I've heard *Bridesmaids* is hilarious," he said.

"Let's do it," she said.

They decided on Thai food and ordered too much, chatting about their favorite movies until the food showed. With open boxes of noodles and various stir-frys set up on her coffee table, they started the movie.

The opening was an awkward five-minute-long sex scene where the woman was obviously not enjoying herself and trying very hard to. Rhys didn't say a word. Cat looked over at him and his face had the same expression he'd had earlier on the street. The Brussels-sprout-in-his-beer look.

She started to giggle.

His gaze snapped to her, his eyes wide. Her giggles turned to outright laughter. And then he joined in, his laughter loose and loud. By the time the couple on the screen finished, Cat had tears running down her face from laughter.

"Okay," Rhys said. "I needed that. This might have been a good idea."

"When are you going to trust that I am full of good ideas?"

"Woman, I've trusted you since I met you on that mountaintop and you told me to get my ass on your bird,"

Rhys said.

Cat smiled. "We work well together."

Rhys nodded. Without saying another word, they enjoyed their beers and the food, and watched the movie.

When it was over, it was only ten o'clock. Too early to call it a night even though she was bone tired, because she knew she'd only toss and turn if she tried to sleep. She looked at Rhys and he seemed to be having the same thoughts.

"Another one?" she asked.

"It was definitely a two-movie mission," he said.

She tried to smile, but couldn't. "Definitely." She stood up and stretched. "But I've forgotten the best part."

Rhys's eyebrows raised. "Really?" His eyes skimmed down her body, which heated under his gaze. "What would that be?"

"Stop that," Cat said with a smile. "Friends, remember?"

"Fine," he said, grumpily. "What'd you forget?"

"Popcorn. I'll be back." Cat threw a package of popcorn in the microwave and then changed out of her jeans and into a loose comfy t-shirt and yoga pants. Definitely not something she'd ever wear in front of a guy she wanted to sleep with, but totally okay to wear in front of a *friend*. Zach had seen her in this same outfit many times. So Rhys could, too.

She grabbed two blankets, as well. When she went back to the couch with the blankets and popcorn, Rhys had cleared their plates off the coffee table while she'd been gone, and now his feet rested on the table while his SIG

Sauer P226 and holster lay on the floor near him. His eyes were closed.

She watched him for a minute. His breathing was deep and even. She knew he could wake in an instant and this was only combat sleep, but he obviously needed it.

And so did she, but dreams would come tonight and she didn't want them. She needed more of a distraction before she'd find sleep.

She carefully put the bowl down and then shook out one of the blankets. She draped it over Rhys, knowing it would wake him, so she spoke softly at the same time. "It's just Cat, Rhys," she said. "I'm covering you with a blanket. You're safe. Go back to sleep."

He didn't move, but his face relaxed and his breathing deepened. Good. She should probably kick him out, but she suspected he too wouldn't be able to sleep on his own tonight.

It's not like anything was going to happen between them.

She sat down on the couch, got cozy with her blanket and popcorn, and then took the remote. She glanced at Rhys.

Yup, still sleeping. But was it a deep enough sleep?

She decided it was and then started pressing the buttons on her remote that would bring up her guilty pleasure.

She'd missed at least four episodes of *The Bachelor*, but she had them recorded. She loved the first episodes the best, when all the women were together in the house. Seeing all of them gossiping and fighting over one man was like a car

178 · Trish Loye

crash she couldn't not watch. This was something not even Zach or her family knew she watched.

She pressed play.

Five minutes into the show, Rhys spoke. "Tell me you're not making me watch this."

Cat jumped. Rhys still lay in the same position with his eyes closed. She held back her laughter. "You're not watching it. Your eyes are closed."

And with that she felt him relax. It wasn't that she was touching him, but she could almost sense the energy radiating from him dim a bit. His muscles eased into the couch and she suspected he was really letting sleep take him now. Almost as if she'd given him permission to stay.

And if she was honest with herself, she had.

CHAPTER 15

A click sounded in the silence. Rhys opened his eyes. Morning light snuck in past the blinds lighting the dim room. He'd turned the TV off at three in the morning, when an infomercial of some kind had woken him. Cat had been curled up asleep on the other end of the couch. He'd tucked the blanket in around her and then settled himself back to sleep. He'd spent the night in much worse places than a couch.

Cat was no longer on the other end of the couch—she was draped over his chest. He could feel her soft breasts against his chest, and his hand lay on the curve of her hip. He turned his head to look down at her.

Her brilliant blue eyes were open and staring at him. Desire stirred as he looked at her sleep-tousled hair and parted lips. His hand tightened on her hip.

Another click. Someone was trying to get in the front door.

Cat tensed, her sleepiness cast aside, her eyes wide and alert.

"You expecting anyone?" he whispered by her ear.

She shook her head no, even as she eased off him. She grabbed her gun from the dining table while he picked his up from the floor. They positioned themselves beside the door. Rhys put his weapon back in the holster, handed it to Cat, and readied himself to grab the guy. Cat still had her weapon trained on the door. She'd be his backup. Rhys raised his brows when he looked at Cat.

She nodded back. Ready.

They really did work well together.

No more time to think. The handle turned and the door started to open. Rhys stepped forward, yanked the door open, and dragged the man standing there into the apartment. The man fought back, twisting in a way that let Rhys know he was a trained fighter. Rhys grunted when he took a powerful hit to his stomach. He blocked the next attack before striking the man hard on his chin and using the split second of the guy's shock to get behind him with an arm around his neck. He ducked his head to keep the man's fingers out of his eyes and applied pressure. In seconds the guy would pass out.

"Stop!" Cat yelled. "Rhys! Dylan! Both of you stop!"

Rhys stepped out of the guy's reach with his guard still

up.

"Cat?" the man said, slowly straightening from his fighting crouch. "Who is this nut job?" He stood a bit taller than six feet, with the same wheat-blond hair and brilliant blue eyes that Cat had.

"Let me guess," Rhys said. "Brother?"

Cat nodded. "Older, but not wiser. This is Dylan."

Rhys stuck out his hand. "I'm Rhys."

Dylan took his hand and they played the not-so-subtle game of who could squeeze the hardest.

"Nice to meet you, Rhys," Dylan said with a grin and a last bone-crunching squeeze. If he hadn't done the same thing back, his hand might have been sore. As it was, Dylan's grin just got wider and he nodded. "That's a helluva grip. Tell me you're not a paper pusher like my sis?"

Rhys snorted at the thought. "I work at E.D.G.E. Securities. I'm an account manager there," Rhys said, sticking with his cover story. He took his weapon and holster back from Cat and strapped it on.

"So." Dylan looked at Cat's gun, still in her hand, and then at Rhys's. "What kind of clients do you have that you need to carry?"

"Dylan," Cat said, putting her weapon on the dining table, "what are you doing here?"

"I've got a couple days leave and I thought I'd visit you," he said. Even Rhys didn't buy the innocent look on his face.

Cat's eyes narrowed and she stared hard at her brother. It looked like some kind of sibling telepathy was at play.

"Did Mom put you up to this?"

"I think I need to hear more about E.D.G.E.," he said in response. "What did you say it stood for again?"

Rhys stepped around Cat and moved into the tiny kitchen while the siblings avoided each other's questions like two circling cats.

He found a frying pan, eggs, mushrooms, peppers, and cheese. He started coffee and began chopping while he listened.

"I already told you," Cat said. "It's a security company. Elite Digital and Global Enforcement."

"Really? Because I never did buy you leaving the military to join a security company to guard rich companies' oil assets."

"You're avoiding the question of why you're here," Cat said. She moved into the kitchen, grabbed another knife, and started slicing mushrooms. She and Rhys stood side by side and worked in tandem as if they'd been doing it for years.

"Fine," Dylan conceded. "Mom sent me. I *am* on leave, and she convinced me to come down here. I haven't seen you in a year, so here I am. Mom wants to know who you're dating and what he's like. What would you like me to tell her?"

"To mind her own business?" Cat muttered.

Rhys laughed. Cat added the sliced mushrooms to the frying pan. He wondered how she was going to answer this question, especially since he was staying for breakfast. The smell of frying mushrooms and peppers made his stomach growl.

Both men waited for Cat's answer. "Tell her that I'm not dating anyone." Cat looked at Rhys as if defying him to say something. "I'm not," she said again.

He nodded, knowing that's what she'd say, but disappointment still ran through him. He turned back to the frying pan and added the eggs, no longer hungry.

No one said anything until breakfast was ready. He slid eggs onto two plates and handed them to Cat and her brother.

"You're not staying?" Cat asked.

He'd planned on it, but now he just wanted to go punch something. He shook his head. "I told Jake I'd meet him at the gym. I'll just grab something there. You two enjoy."

He left before she could protest. He'd had enough of being her friend right now—he just needed a little space to make sure she stayed in that category.

He made it to the street and zipped up his leather jacket against the brisk morning air. Striding down the street, he dialed one of his buddies from his old SEAL team. This was something he'd decided on last night, to wipe the shadows out of Cat's eyes.

"Scattalone," he spoke into his cell. "I know it's early, but I've got a favor to ask."

It was three hours earlier in San Diego than Montreal.

"Damn, Rhys. It's six a.m. on my day off," Scat grumbled. "Fine. I'm up. What do you need?"

"I need an off-the-books team for a mission."

"What and where?" Instantly, Scat's voice lost all trace of grogginess. Rhys smiled. He knew his buddies would back him up on anything.

"Northeast Nigeria. We've found some of those missing schoolgirls."

"E.D.G.E. found them?"

"My team did. But we don't have permission yet to go back. I'm afraid by the time we do, the girls will be gone."

"Give me the details and I'll see who and what I can come up with."

Ten minutes later, Rhys got off the phone feeling confident that within days he and his old team would be tracking those girls down. He could get the call from Scat to go at any time, so he needed to enjoy this break with Cat while he could.

Should he tell Cat of his plans? He knew she was more than capable of handling herself, but his team knew him. How would they handle a woman in their mix?

He sighed. He had at least another day to make the call of whether to include Cat. Did he dare ask her to go against the rules? She could be discharged from E.D.G.E.—and even from the military. After just a few minutes of thought he realized he couldn't ask her, not after she'd spent her career proving she belonged. He'd hate himself if this mission took that away from her.

Even so, he knew she felt a duty to those girls.

He called her number and she answered on the first

ring. "Hey," he said. "I was wondering if you wanted to get dinner tonight. I've got something we should talk about."

Her long hesitation made him speak again. "Just a dinner as friends. I promise," he said.

"Okay," she said. "Text me the details."

He smiled at that. "Is your brother still there?"

"Yes, and listening as hard as he can."

"Well, you pick the place since you know the city. How about seven?"

"Good. I'll see you then."

Rhys hung up and let his smile widen. He was going to get those girls out, and he would convince Cat to break some rules and come along.

And maybe afterwards, he could convince her they should be a team outside of work, as well.

Rhys went to the Combat Sports Gym near E.D.G.E. HQ with Jake later that morning. They sparred in the center ring after having lifted weights for a while.

Rhys walked right into a strike Jake threw and grunted.

Jake stepped back. "Lucky, your head isn't in the game, and you're gonna lose it if you don't focus."

Rhys rolled his shoulders and then nodded. "Focused."

Jake stepped closer, and Rhys knew he'd lead with a punch. They'd been sparring together for years and Rhys knew how Jake fought. Jake had a bit more power, but Rhys had more speed and reach. It was usually an even match, but not today.

After Rhys took a hit to the kidneys, Jake pulled back again.

"What is it?" he asked.

Rhys shook his head.

"Mission failure?" Jake asked.

"No. It was a success," he said in a flat voice. He slid through the ring's ropes and jumped to the floor.

"Ah, one of those," Jake said. "Wanna grab a drink later?"

"Can't. Got some things to take care of." He didn't want to tell Jake about what he'd planned. He hated to pull his buddy in on an off-the-books mission. Jake had found happiness with Dani, and Rhys didn't want to screw that up by landing the guy in jail—or worse.

Jake grabbed his arm. "Buddy, I know that look. What are you planning?"

"Nothing, dude. I've just got things on my mind."

Jake stepped in front of him, blocking his way to the locker room. "You're telling me what's going on."

Rhys crossed his arms. Maybe he could divert Jake's attention with a fight. "Who's going to make me?"

Jake rolled his eyes. "What are we, ten? Give it up, Lucky. You know you're going to tell me eventually."

That was true, but Rhys would tell him after the mission was complete. "Look, man, I just don't want to mess up what you've got going here."

All humor left Jake's face. "This isn't an E.D.G.E. op?"

Rhys kept his face still, neither confirming nor denying.

"Rhys, I'm your brother. Tell me. Because I swear to god if you go somewhere unsanctioned and get your ass killed, I will murder you myself."

Rhys looked away, thinking it through. He, Scat, and the guys could do this together–they were hardened SEALs. His old team could kick anyone's ass.

Not one of them was Jake, though. There was no one he trusted more in the thick of it. And Rhys knew that on a mission like this, to rescue those schoolgirls, he needed the best. He needed Jake. And even if he didn't, there was no way in hell Jake was letting him out of this gym without getting the whole story.

Rhys sighed. "I'm gonna go save some little girls," he said finally.

"Where?"

"Nigeria. It's not sanctioned. But Scattalone and Roddy are with me."

"It's important?"

Rhys nodded.

"Then I'm in."

CHAPTER 16

C at left her brother at her apartment and went in to work. She decided to work out first and headed to the subbasement fitness level of E.D.G.E. HQ, where the Beast was. Marc and Zach were already there, lifting weights.

"Hey, Cat," Zach said.

She grabbed a skipping rope and began to warm up. "How was the rest of your night?" she asked.

"Zach drank too much and is now engaged to a hooker. You know…the usual," Marc said.

Zach punched him in the shoulder. "I'll have you know, Cat, I was very good. Unlike this guy. Two women!"

"The ladies like me," Marc said. "They'd like you too, if you'd shower more."

"Ha!"

Marc and Zach continued to rib each other while Cat moved through her routine, not really listening to them. Pushups, pull-ups, and core exercises to warm up her upper body, then onto a bit of stretching. She had a lot of energy to work off, or rather emotion, and knew she'd be going hard through the Beast. No sense pulling something.

"So what happened with you and Rhys last night?" Marc asked.

Cat straightened from her lunge, her gaze snapping to the guys as they both worked on their pull-ups.

"What do you mean?" she asked.

Zach looked at Marc and then focused on a spot above her head as he counted off reps.

Marc had no problem replying. "I mean he went after you like a *knight-in-shining-armor*, to save you from your ex. Isn't that what all women want?"

The question stung her, and she narrowed her gaze. "I don't need a knight—or anyone—to rescue me. I think I've proven that."

Marc dropped to the ground and held up his hands. "Easy, Valkyrie. I know that. Zach knows that." He shrugged. "I'm not sure Rhys does, though. And if he thinks you need to be rescued then maybe…maybe he's not the best choice for the team."

Zach let go and landed beside Marc. "I hate to say this, but I agree. I like Rhys and I think he's a good operator, but if he can't trust your abilities then maybe he's not right for us."

Cat ran a hand through her hair. "Where is this coming from? Is this just because of last night?"

Marc held up his hand and ticked his points off on his fingers. "He let an asset get killed trying to protect you. He wanted to interfere in your fight at the airbase. And he went running off after you last night."

Cat tilted her head as she studied Marc, trying to figure out his real point. This didn't seem to be about Rhys's ability. "He performed well on the mission."

Marc sighed. "You know I think of you like a sister."

Zach elbowed him. "A sister who could actually kill you if you give her this advice."

Marc glared at Zach. "You agreed. Now shut it." He turned to Cat. "We've seen how Rhys looks at you." His lips compressed, as if he didn't want to say the next part. But trust Marc to never back down. "And how you look at him. We don't know what happened between you last night." He held up his hand to forestall Cat's protest, so she crossed her arms and waited, anger brewing. "And we don't care. But we do care if what's between you interferes with either of your judgment on a mission."

Cat didn't move or say anything, she just stared at her two friends, her teammates, her brothers-in-arms. Her anger boiled over, and she couldn't stop her words.

"Have I *ever* let my feelings interfere with my judgment or a mission before?" she snapped.

"No, but—" Zach said.

"Then take your advice and shove it. I don't need or want

it. Are we clear?"

"Clear," they chorused.

She strode to the Beast, needing to move. *How dare they?* She didn't even pause before starting her run to the ten-foot wall.

Anger gave her excess energy, but made her sloppy. She cursed herself, Marc, Zach, and then finally Rhys, who seemed to be at the root of her problems.

By the time she hit the tunnel, she was cursing the Boko Haram and the political dickheads who said they couldn't go back. The dark water closed over her head and she'd been so preoccupied cursing everyone that she hadn't steeled herself against her memories.

The cold water, the blindness, and the confinement brought the memories of the accident rushing back. She'd been sawing frantically at the jammed seatbelt of her teammate, her lungs burning. Wanting, needing a sip of air, her throat aching with it. Her heartbeat pounded in her ears, the only sound in that horrible silence under the water. Her inner voice screaming, *Leave him! Leave him!*

She opened her mouth and water rushed in, almost choking her. Her mind snapped out of the old memory and she pulled herself through the rest of the tunnel. Her lungs were past the burning stage and the ache diminished. A bad sign. How long had she been under? She needed air *now*.

A part of her just wanted to drift, but she made herself swim to the end. She hauled herself out, gasping for air.

Two pairs of legs stood in front of her.

"Thought we were going to have to come in after you," Zach said in a calm voice.

"What the fuck, Cat?" Marc sounded anything but calm. "You trying to scare us or something?"

She shook her head and coughed up the water she'd swallowed. How to explain? She couldn't. "I'm good."

"You don't look good," Zach said, crouching by her. "What happened under there?"

She looked up into Zach's compassionate gaze and her breathing steadied. "I'm good, seriously. I just let some old memories sidetrack me."

Marc reached a hand down and lifted her easily out of the water. "Don't pull that shit again," he said roughly. She smiled at him. He may be the most cantankerous man at E.D.G.E., but she knew it was because he cared so much.

"I'm good." She waved them off. "Go back to your workout."

"And what are you going to do?" Zach asked.

"You already know. I'm going to run the Beast again and make sure I can do it without freezing."

Marc nodded as if he'd expected no less. "Don't make me get wet saving your ass."

She laughed as she walked to the wall to run the course again. This time and the next when she ran it, she stayed focused, not letting her thoughts stray from the task at hand. Once she had her mind under control, she ran it once more just to prove she could.

She was toweling off when Marc and Zach approached her again. She held up her hands. "No more advice, guys."

"No advice," Zach said. "Just wanted to let you know that if you decide to go back, we're with you."

She nodded. She didn't tell them they didn't have the go-ahead. They had faith in her. They expected her to get them back there to do their duty. And she would…somehow.

"But…," Zach continued, rubbing the back of his neck.

"But?" she asked, her eyes narrowing.

"But we don't think Rhys should come," Marc said.

"That is not your call," Cat said calmly, but her voice held an edge.

"Easy, Cat," Zach said. "We don't want Rhys off the team entirely."

"Yet," Marc said.

Zach punched him in the arm and continued. "We think he needs more training with us before he's allowed on another mission. He needs more time getting used to you."

Cat almost growled. She hated that anyone needed to *get used to her*, but they had a point. "I'll take it under advisement."

She left the guys racing each other on the Beast. Zach and Marc only wanted what was best for the team and the mission. And that's what she needed to concentrate on, too.

Running the Beast over and over had cleared her head. By the time she'd changed, she felt focused and resolved once again. Cat went upstairs to Blackwell's office and knocked on his door.

"Enter," he called.

Sarah, the petite ex-CIA agent, sat across from Blackwell. Quiet to the point of fading from a room, which Cat suspected was exactly how she liked it, Sarah used her stillness as a weapon. It's why everyone called her Ghost. Cat didn't know her well, but she knew she could talk in front of her.

"Sir, I'd like to put together a team to go to Nigeria and get those girls out," she said.

Blackwell pinched the bridge of his nose for a moment before looking up at her. "I thought we'd discussed this, Valkyrie. We do not have approval for such a mission. Commander Knight is working on it."

Cat shook her head. "Sir, those girls are moved all the time. We need to go in now. Ask forgiveness rather than permission."

"Isn't that what you're doing now?" Blackwell said. "Asking for permission?" He continued, "I have already sent the requests up the chain of command. We've been told to wait out. My hands are tied. If anyone decides to go in and disaster strikes, then they risk losing not just their position with E.D.G.E., but they will most likely be court-martialed and discharged."

Cat clenched her fists. She couldn't leave this alone. This wasn't what she'd trained for. She needed to do something, and it needed to be soon.

Blackwell stood up. "Did you need anything else, Valkyrie?"

She stared at Blackwell, not sure she could continue to work at a place that would leave innocent girls to be raped, tortured, and killed at the hands of mad men just because it was inconvenient to their superiors.

"Valkyrie?" Blackwell stared hard at her. "I cannot sanction a mission. You will be on your own if something happens. We won't be able to come after you. Understood, soldier?"

The light finally dawned. He was telling her that she could go and he wouldn't stop her, but she wouldn't have help and this wasn't on-book. "Understood, sir."

She left the room and went to her office. She needed to think. She plopped into her seat and pulled up a map of the area. For a second, she considered calling Rhys to let him know what she was planning, but she stopped herself before she punched in the numbers.

She needed Marc and Zach on this mission, and knew she could force the issue and have Rhys come help, but it would cause strife. She needed everyone on the team to trust each other implicitly. And that wouldn't happen if Marc and Zach kept waiting for Rhys to pull some kind of protective macho bullshit.

To be fair, she wasn't sure he would anymore. But Zach and Marc needed proof. She rubbed the back of her neck, trying to ease the tight muscles there.

Rhys had told her last night that the military was his only family. If he joined her on an unsanctioned mission, he could be dishonorably discharged from the only family he had left.

She couldn't do that to him. Her gut churned, but realistically their chances of success weren't great. They had to move twenty girls past two hundred men and not get caught. She bit her lip. Who could she get to come with her?

Either way, she had to tell Rhys what the team was doing. But later. After the plans were made.

Coward, her inner voice taunted.

At least I'm going to tell him. Eventually.

Cat looked up. Sarah had stepped into her office at some point and stood watching her. The woman was as silent as her call sign suggested.

Cat was in no mood for someone to get the drop on her. "What do you want?"

"I can help," Sarah said. "Blackwell filled me in. I have contacts."

Cat tilted her head, wondering how this seeming mouse of a woman could help on a mission like this. "Why?"

"I heard about the girls," she said. "And I... I can't just walk away knowing they're in that situation."

Cat understood that. "Grab a seat. What can you do for me?"

"I know of a flight we can get on to get to the insertion point."

Getting to Nigeria and out again without using commercial air travel was one of Cat's big headaches. If Sarah could solve that then she was halfway there.

Sarah laid out her plan to get in country. Cat listened intently, pointing out potential flaws that could land them in trouble. To her relief, it seemed Sarah had already thought of every one of them.

"So," Sarah finally prompted, after nearly an hour of discussion. "What do you think? Am I in?"

Cat hesitated, but only for a second. "Honestly? I don't think I could do this without you."

Sarah nodded. "Who else is coming?"

Cat took a deep breath. "Marc and Zach have already said they're in. The rest… I'm about to find out. Either way, I want to be on that plane tonight."

"I'll be ready," Sarah said.

CHAPTER 17

C at left Sarah making plans and then ran down the back stairs to IT. Dani was in and typing furiously while staring at a string of numbers and code streaming down her holographic screen. It looked like something from *The Matrix*.

"You busy?" Cat asked.

Dani didn't look over. "Just trying to get ahead of this cyberstalker who's after a governor's daughter. Give me a few minutes."

Cat paced back and forth twice before Dani stopped typing. A countdown began in the corner of her screen. "You have ninety seconds before I need to be back online," she said.

"I need satellite imagery of the northeastern part of

Nigeria for the last twenty-four hours."

Dani pushed her wheeled chair across the room to another desk. She tapped the console box on the desktop and the holographic screen there came to life. Dani was already wearing the thin gloves that let her manipulate the data, and she flicked her fingers through images so fast that Cat had a hard time keeping up with her.

"Okay, I've got it. Sending the images to your inbox now," Dani said. "Are you going back there?"

Cat nodded. She wasn't sure how much to tell her friend. "Another rescue mission."

Dani nodded, but studied her face. "What's different this time?" she asked.

Cat bit her lip. The woman was too perceptive—probably all that time living with criminals who might kill you. She'd learned to read people well.

Cat decided to distract her.

"Have you met Q yet?"

"Q? As in the tech guy from James Bond?"

"Well, her name isn't Q, that's just her call sign. Her name is Charlotte Singh. Charlie. But she is our resident genius. Well, her and Gears."

"Gears?" Dani looked over at her program and then back at Cat. "This I gotta see." She slid her chair back to the original holograph image and started typing madly again. "I'm going to attach a cyber-tracer to the creep's subroutine signature. It probably won't work, but it'll lull him into thinking I'm stupid and then his guard will be down and

I'll snag him next time."

"You sure?" Cat said. "I can introduce you another time."

"Nah. This is a good plan. Believe me. I've only been chasing this guy for a couple of days. He doesn't know what I can do yet."

"How do you know he's a guy?"

"His arrogance," Dani said.

Cat laughed. "Fair enough."

Cat led Dani to the operator's elevators, but with a quick pit stop to her office to snag a small bag of candy she kept for emergencies just like these.

"What are those?" Dani asked, pointing at them.

"Swedish Berries," she said. "And my bribe."

She pushed the number for the top floor of the building. Dani frowned.

"E.D.G.E. keeps their lab separate from everything else," Cat said, "in case something goes wrong. No sense in having the lab blow up the armory or anyone else."

"That's…"

"Pragmatic," Cat said. When the doors slid open, they faced a small bare alcove with a steel door and a console beside it. Cat placed her hand on the console and waited while it scanned. The door slid open.

Inside, a wall of windows let in the afternoon light as they stepped into a large white-walled room.

"Watch out," a feminine voice shrieked.

What looked like a metallic Frisbee flew toward them. They ducked and it pinged off the wall behind them, sparks flying before it gained velocity and headed back into the lab. It careened over a long table covered in wires and metal bits, flying toward a slender woman with light brown skin and dark hair pulled back in a loose braid. She stood in front of a clear wall, behind which someone in a biohazard suit bent over a microscope.

The woman waved her arms at the miniature flying saucer. It zoomed right for her and she ducked behind a table. A tall, spare man stood in another corner, a remote control device in his hand, his fingers rapidly punching buttons.

"Need help?" Cat called.

"Yes!" the woman shouted. "Harold has lost control. It detects motion. But be careful. It has a bomb on board."

"A bomb?" Dani squeaked.

"Don't move," Cat said.

Cat looked around the room, ran to one of the tables along a wall, and grabbed a fire extinguisher. She jumped onto the table in the middle of the room. The saucer zoomed straight for her. She sprayed the sucker as soon as it entered her range. It wobbled in the air and then the woman was there and snatched it when it dropped.

"Brilliant, Cat! Why didn't I think of that?" she said, pushing a button on the device's side. "Any time you want a job, you're hired."

"Good to see you, Q," Cat said. "And I think I have enough excitement in my normal job that I don't need to work in here."

Charlie laughed and turned to Dani. "I'm Charlie, though everyone calls me Q—though I'm not sure why, because Q wasn't actually smart, he just handed out the toys to James Bond. I, on the other hand, am a certifiable genius, but don't let that intimidate you. I'm actually a really nice person."

Cat laid a hand on Charlie's arm. "Easy, sister," she whispered. "Take a breath. Don't scare her off."

Charlie bit her lip, looked at Cat, and then back at Dani. "I'm talking too much, aren't I?" She shrugged. "I tend to do that when I'm nervous."

Dani frowned. "Why are you nervous?"

"I'm…not really good with new people."

Cat decided to save her. She looked at Harold and lowered her voice. "Where's Gears?"

Charlie grimaced. "I probably wouldn't have had the flying bomb issue if he hadn't decided to go on a mission. I mean trip. He went on a trip."

Cat smiled and then handed her the candy. "I brought you a present."

Charlie popped two of the gummy berries in her mouth. "You want something, don't you?" She took her saucer and walked to the worktable in the middle of the room.

"Come on, Q," Cat said. "Don't be like that."

"You haven't come to visit me in ages."

"I haven't been home in ages," Cat chided. "You know that. You know all the missions."

Charlie gave a huge sigh. "I just wish I could go on a

mission."

Cat ran a hand through her hair. "Look, when I get back we'll all go for a movie or something." She looked at Dani, who nodded. "A girl's night."

Charlie turned around, her smile back. "A girl's night? I've never been on one of those."

"Neither have I," Cat muttered.

Dani laughed. "Don't worry, I'll organize it."

"Thank you," Cat whispered to her. Then to Charlie, "I'm going to Nigeria. I—"

"You're going to rescue those girls, aren't you?" Charlie said.

Even Cat was taken aback. Charlie shrugged. "I read all the reports. I don't actually need much sleep and I have a photographic memory, though I don't need it to remember your report. It sounded horrible, Cat. I'm so—"

"Q!" Cat said, stopping the woman's verbal vomit. "That report was classified. Were you supposed to read it?"

"I have the highest security clearance," she said. "Besides, I don't leave a trace when I read them. Just like Danielle."

Cat looked at Dani, whose face was red.

Cat shook her head. "You two will get on great. Let's forget the report, though. I need something that will help me. I need an edge for the mission to succeed."

Charlie stuck both her index fingers into the air. "I have just the things. Can you say *micro-explosives*?"

Hours later, Cat already had Zach, Marc, and Sarah on board with her plan. They were in the equipment room packing their rucksacks with all the kit they'd need. They had a bird ready to transport them to their military flight in an hour. Cat had outlined her plan to the guys. After they packed, they would go over it one more time. Her mind focused on all the hypotheticals of the situation. She kept her map out so she could memorize it as she packed.

Cat's phone dinged. It was a text from Rhys.

Still on for dinner?

Dammit. She'd forgotten dinner. She looked at her pack. Should she answer?

"Everything good?" Zach asked.

"Yup," she said, still eyeing the phone.

"Is it Rhys?" Marc said.

Her gaze snapped to him. "Why do you say that?"

His lips twisted into a cynical smile. "Because I've only ever seen you flustered around him."

That stopped her. Was that true? She racked her brain, trying to think back over her actions since Rhys had come to E.D.G.E. Was she *flustered* around him? It made her sound like a schoolgirl with a crush, and that annoyed her. She needed to start acting like a team leader around him.

Her phone dinged again.

Jake and Dani asked me to cook for them again tonight. Bring your brother.

Crap. Her fingers hovered over the keys. What should she tell him?

I'm busy at the moment. I'll call later.

Now she felt cowardly for putting off the conversation, but she wasn't going to talk to him in front of the others.

"What are we doing about a pilot?" Marc asked. "We can't do this without one. And while I'm sure we've all had the basics trained into us, I'd really prefer to have someone with a bit more experience in combat."

Cat heaved her ruck onto the trolley for loading later. A wild idea came to her and she smiled. At least something would go right for her. "Don't worry. I've got it covered."

Zach followed from the elevator to her apartment door. "I don't get it," he said. "You've got an E.D.G.E. pilot hidden in your apartment?"

"No, not an E.D.G.E. pilot."

"Seriously," he said. "What are we doing here? We need to be finalizing our plan and getting on that plane."

"I need your help."

"You said that already."

She opened her door and swung it wide. "Dylan, look who I brought for a visit."

Dylan padded to the door barefoot. He rubbed a hand over his buzz cut and then yawned. "Zach? What are you doing here?"

Zach looked at Cat. "Seriously? Your brother?"

"Why not?" Cat said. "He's CSOR and he's a tac hel pilot."

Zach stared at her. "You know why. Blackwell will crucify

you."

"Well, he should have sanctioned the freaking mission then. I'm doing the best I can. Do you have any better ideas?"

"What mission?" Dylan said. "Cat, what's going on?"

Cat looked at Zach, waiting. If he wasn't behind her on this then she'd do something else, but she believed her brother could do it. He could be their pilot.

"He's good," she told Zach. "You know that, you've flown with him."

"He'll have to be read in," Zach said with a sigh.

"Don't worry, my brother won't breathe a word of it to anyone, will you, Dylan?"

Her brother crossed his arms. "If someone doesn't tell me what's going on, I'm going to start breaking things."

Zach laughed. "Spoken like someone from the regiment."

Dylan's eyes narrowed. "Just because I didn't try out for JTF2 like you doesn't mean I can't kick your ass." Then he looked back and forth between Cat and Zach. "But something tells me you're not working for JTF2 anymore. Are you a civilian too?"

Zach snorted. "Never. I work at E.D.G.E."

"The *civilian* company that employs my sister?"

Cat shook her head, finally resolved. She'd been struggling with this for so long now, but it seemed like the decision had been made for her. She couldn't do this without a pilot. Dylan was a pilot–and a good one, at that. A pilot she knew would have her team's back. It felt like fate had intervened.

"No, the secret government organization that we both work for doing black ops. And we need your help."

Dylan started to laugh. Cat just waited him out. Finally he stopped, then frowned at her. "What? You're shitting me. I thought that kind of thing only happened in movies."

"No, Cowboy, it's real," Zach said, calling her brother by his nickname. "And we need a shit-hot pilot to fly our bird."

"Wait. You work for a secret organization doing black ops and you guys don't have a pilot? What kind of chintzy organization is it?"

"We have pilots," Cat said. "We just don't have one for this particular mission."

Dylan's eyes narrowed as he stared at his sister. "I can always tell when you're keeping something back."

Zach snorted but stayed silent. Cat put her hands on her hips. "This mission isn't sanctioned."

Her brother raised his eyebrows like he always did when he didn't believe her. "You want me to go AWOL for a black ops mission that even a secret government organization won't sanction? You *are* crazy. Next you'll be telling me the fate of the world rests on us."

Zach laughed. "You've definitely been watching too many movies, Cowboy."

Cat didn't laugh, she just held her brother's gaze. "Not the world," she said. "Just twenty innocent girls."

I'm busy at the moment. I'll call later.

Rhys rubbed the back of his neck and scowled as he read the text from Cat for the third time. When was later? Was she brushing him off?

It was probably for the best—he was getting too attached to Cat, anyway. He put his phone away and knocked on Jake's apartment door. He'd moved in with Dani before Rhys had come back from being deployed. They seemed like a good fit for each other. Rhys was happy for Jake, but not sure if he could handle the happy couple at the moment.

Jake pulled open the door, his smile dimming when he saw Rhys's face. "What's wrong, Lucky?"

Rhys put on his carefree smile. He suspected by the way Jake's eyes narrowed that he could see past it, though he didn't call him on it.

"Nothing," Rhys said. "I'm here to save your stomachs and make you dinner."

"I bought groceries," Dani called from the kitchen. "Are you making gumbo again?"

Rhys wandered into the kitchen to see Dani already chopping green pepper and celery. "Looks like I am."

Dani looked beyond him. "Cat's not with you?"

"No." He could feel his face tighten as the sting of it hit him again.

"Did they leave early, then?"

"Leave?"

Dani turned to him. "For Nigeria. Cat's going to get those girls."

Rhys felt like he'd been sucker punched. His fists clenched, and he fixed Dani with a hard stare. "Tell me everything."

CHAPTER 18

C at strapped herself in for the landing at the
Niger airbase. Sarah had used her CIA contacts
to get them on the provisions flight for the
base. The cargo plane had fold-down seats attached to the
walls, and crates of food stacked and strapped down in the
middle.

Cat checked her phone one more time. No messages.
She'd phoned Rhys late last night, but he hadn't answered
and she'd left him a short voicemail telling him the team
had left and it had been her decision to leave him behind.

She hadn't wanted to tell Rhys of Marc or Zach's
concerns, knowing it could compromise their ability to
work together down the road. As team leader, it was up to
her to take the blame on this–regardless of what it might

mean for her and Rhys. She'd said she would explain when she got back.

If they got back.

Marc sauntered over and sat in the jump seat beside her.

"So...your brother?" he said over the headset. The interior of the plane was too loud for a normal conversation.

"We've been over this, Marc. Deal."

"Have you thought that even if this mission is a success, Blackwell might bury you just because you broke protocol?"

She stared at her weapons case and ruck piled with the others near the food crates. "You have a point to make?"

Marc shook his head. "The minute your brother gets off this plane and the personnel on the base see him, then Blackwell and Knight will know that he knows everything about us. There'll be no turning back. You'll have blown E.D.G.E.'s cover. The best-case scenario is you'll be fired. The worst is you'll see prison time."

"Seriously, Marc? It's my brother and he's already in special ops. They won't send me to jail."

"You two do know that you're not on a private channel, right?" Zach's voice came over their headsets.

"Yes," Cat said with gritted teeth.

"Cat, you're a good leader," Marc continued on as if Zach hadn't spoken. "I don't want to see you punted from E.D.G.E."

Cat laughed. "You think they'll punt me for bringing along my brother and not for organizing an unsanctioned mission?"

Marc didn't react to her humor, his eyes serious. "I think they'll use whatever excuse they can, even if this mission is successful."

Cat sat back and studied Marc. "You don't trust Blackwell and Knight to have our backs, do you?"

He didn't say anything, but he didn't break eye contact either.

"Do you trust me?" This was something she needed for the mission. If he didn't trust her implicitly then he'd question her orders and that couldn't happen.

He hesitated and then gave a short, sharp nod.

"Then trust me on this," Cat said. "This mission is worth whatever fallout blows our way. We need Dylan to complete it. Blackwell, however uptight he might be, will understand that. Now let's drop this and focus."

Marc nodded. "Wilco, Valkyrie." He sat back, put his chin to his chest, and closed his eyes for a combat nap.

The plane's landing gear dropped and thunked into place, reverberating through the plane and the bones of her chest. Marc's words of warning tumbled though her head, but she shoved them aside. She had to do this mission. She'd never forgive herself if she didn't do something to help those girls, no matter the risk. Not many people could pull off what she could—which was why she had to be the one to do it.

The plane hit the tarmac and thundered to a halt. She unbuckled and grabbed her gear, ready to deplane the moment the back hatch opened. Her team followed her onto the tarmac and across to the tower, where an armed squad of soldiers trotted out to meet them.

She halted and felt her team do the same. She drew in a deep breath while the soldiers approached them. At least they weren't pointing their weapons yet.

"You've made an unauthorized landing," the man in front said. "Who's in charge here?"

She placed her weapons case carefully on the tarmac and held her hands out to the sides. She couldn't look completely harmless with her sidearm strapped to her leg and her knife in her webbing, but she tried. She even pasted a smile on her face. By the way the soldiers adjusted their grips on their M4 assault rifles, the smile had been too much.

A quick glance behind showed her team all staring with cold, hard eyes at the squad. Nope. A smile would never be enough. Her team stood casually, hands nowhere near weapons, but that didn't fool these soldiers. Time to reign this in.

"Sergeant," she said to the man. "I need to speak with Major Steve Dougall."

The sergeant shook his head. "I'm sorry..." His eyes flicked to her collar and over her chest to look for her rank. But E.D.G.E. never wore it. "Ma'am," he finally said. "I need your unit and your reason for deployment here. We have no record of any personnel scheduled for today."

Cat had known this was coming. "Of course not, Sergeant. If you'll show my team to a shaded waiting area,

I'll be pleased to accompany you to your commander, Major Dougall."

The sergeant stared at her a moment. Of course it wasn't protocol for her to jump the chain of command like this, but it was obvious they weren't an ordinary unit. The sergeant nodded and ordered his men to accompany hers.

"I'll join up with you when I'm done," Cat said to Zach, her second-in-command for the operation. "Until then, get some rest."

She followed the sergeant into the hangar and waited while he called in. He turned to her. "Can I give him a name, ma'am?"

This sergeant had obviously dealt with spec ops before. She nodded. "Tell him Valkyrie is here."

"Valkyrie? You're the one who busted Corporal Anderson up?"

She hesitated only a moment before nodding.

The man smiled. "Nicely done, ma'am."

It was only a few minutes before Steve strode up to her, his shoulders back and his chin high. He nodded at the sergeant. "You can return to your duties."

The sergeant saluted and left them to talk.

"What are you doing here, Cat?" he said. "There's nothing on the books."

"This mission won't be on any books."

"Black ops?" he whispered.

This was the tricky part. A black ops mission could be denied by the government if found out, but usually had support going in. It would be too easy to lie and say yes. Steve, who so desperately wanted to be part of special ops, would bend over backwards to give her everything she needed if she let him get involved.

She shook her head.

Steve frowned. "What are you doing, Cat? I can't sanction a rogue mission."

"I'm not asking you to sanction it. I'm asking you to let us use the airbase as our base of operations."

"Shouldn't you be asking the base CO this?"

Her lips twisted. "You know Colonel Harris dislikes me and anything to do with me. If he hears I'm here again, then the mission won't get off the ground."

Steve sighed. "And what do you expect me to do for you?"

"I need med support for casualties and any fresh intel you have on the Boko Haram's encampment. I'd also like a squad of men. The best you have."

His eyes narrowed as he studied her. "What are you planning, Cat? If you want intel then so do I." He held up his hand to forestall her protest. "This mission isn't sanctioned. I need to know what I'm signing my men on for."

He didn't need to know, but if she told him then she might get more help from him. It was a gamble she was willing to take. "We're going to rescue those girls."

He stared at her, then looked beyond her to her team lazing in the shade of a plane. "You're joking. I grant that you're good—"

"I made it into CSOR and you didn't," Cat said.

His jaw tensed and he shook his head. "Why are you risking this? For a bunch of girls the world has forgotten?"

That question reinforced her belief that she'd done the right thing leaving Steve. All at once, she thought again of Rhys, and his reaction when she'd made the impossible decision to leave the schoolgirls behind. Of anyone, Rhys understood her need to save those girls–she knew he felt the same way she did. It was going to kill him that she'd left him behind.

Damn—she needed to stay focused. Rhys was a distraction even when he wasn't with her.

"I want your cooperation, but I don't need it," she said. "This mission will go forward with or without your help."

His lips firmed and she knew she had him. He couldn't arrest her because they technically hadn't done anything yet. The special ops community protected and punished their own. If he ended up complaining she was on base, he'd be seen as a troublemaker by those who decided the postings. His career would be in jeopardy of stalling out worse than it had.

"What do I get out of it?" he finally said.

And again he showed his true colors. Her voice carried a hard edge. "What do you want?"

His gaze went down to her boots and back up.

She cocked her eyebrow in response, refusing to let him faze her. "Try again."

"Relax, Cat." He huffed a small laugh. "I'd never want

that again. I want a favor. I want you to recommend me to your superiors."

Insult upon insult. What the hell had she seen in this guy? Had she been that desperate for a relationship? Again, she couldn't help comparing him to Rhys. She shoved those thoughts aside.

"You want to be in the regiment?" she asked, referring to CSOR. "You've already tried twice. They won't ask you back again, no matter what I say."

He scowled and crossed his arms. "No. I'm done with that. I want to work where you do. I don't know what unit you're in, but if you want help from my men then you'll get me off this fucking base."

What the hell was she going to do with this loser? "I can't get you into my unit. It's not my call, you know that."

"Then get me off this nowhere airbase and doing something real."

She ran a hand through her short hair. Sweat ran down her back from the heat. "Fine. I might be able to whisper into the right ears about getting you back to Canada."

He shook his head. "Not good enough."

"That is all that's going to happen," she snapped. "Why don't you just do the best you can and then earn a better position? I can think of a lot worse ones than this."

"You don't get it, Cat. You never did. It's easy for you—"

"Are you fucking kidding me?" Cat laughed. "It's pricks like you that have made my life tougher than it should have been. I'm a damn good soldier—a better soldier than you.

My team is going to rescue those girls with or without you. You want to do something real? Then help me."

She could see him calculate her odds of success in his head, which weren't good. So she sweetened the pot.

"If we're successful, you can take the credit."

His eyes lit with avarice. That was why he would never be in special ops-he wanted others to know what he did and how good he was. Being in spec ops meant never getting recognition, but that's not why they did it. At least for her, she did it to help others and to help her country. She didn't do it for praise.

Steve nodded. "I'm in. Tell me your plans and I'll see what my men can do."

She shook her head. "Not gonna happen. Like I said, lend me a squad of your best men. Your best. And I'll see they get commendation for what they do."

His eyes lit up when she said commendation. "Fine. I'll lead them myself."

That was going to be trouble. "You need to stay here and make sure no one asks questions about us."

He drew himself up and put his hands on his hips. She almost snorted. Did he think she found him intimidating?

"I'm coming," he said. "Or my men aren't."

She considered all the cons of taking him. She wanted his men as a distraction far away from the actual Boko Haram encampment—which would hopefully be far enough away that Steve wouldn't be able to screw up her mission.

"Okay," she said. "But I'm in charge. In fact, anyone on

my team has the authority to tell you what to do."

His jaw tightened. "Fine."

"We'll leave tonight," she said. "Briefing at 1600 hours. Get some rest."

She left him and strode back to her team. Her gut twisted with the thought of Steve on her mission. She prayed she'd made the right decision.

CHAPTER 19

Eight hardened men sat at the table in front of Cat alongside her team. She pointed at a position on the map. "This is where I want your men, Major."

"Hold on," Steve said. "That's not what we signed up for."

"You signed on to follow my orders. You and your men will take position to the east of the encampment. When I give the signal, you will begin a false attack just as morning prayers end. Lead them on a chase."

She pointed to a bridge further down from the one she planned to use. "I'd advise you to withdraw here. Don't let them cut you off. Head across this bridge. The Niger Army patrol here. They should be able to assist you if you get into trouble."

"Do they know we're coming, ma'am?" one of the

sergeants asked.

"They will. The major and I will let them know to expect you." She pointed to the bridge they'd used originally to get to the encampment, and then to the infiltration site. "This is where we'll set the Black Hawk down."

"Who's flying?" Steve asked, staring at Dylan. There was no love lost there.

"The best pilot here," Dylan answered. "Got a problem?"

"Enough, gentlemen," Cat said. "Major, we'll need your Chinook with your best pilot on standby to transport those girls when we get them out." She went over details of call signs and timings next. "Any questions?" she asked.

"What about the rest of the plan?" Steve asked.

"Need-to-know only," Cat said.

"That's bullshit."

To their credit, Steve's men shifted uncomfortably in their seats to hear their CO address the mission leader in such a way.

"Be ready for 2200," she said to his men. "Dismissed."

She turned to Steve. "Major? We need to talk." She left the briefing room and strode down the hall to another empty room. It held two desks and filing cabinets, the admin domain.

Steve stomped into the room after her. "Don't think you can boss me around. I'm a higher rank than you."

Cat let him ramble on while she shut the door carefully and then crossed her arms. She didn't have time for this crap, and she let him see that on her face.

"Are you done?" she asked when he'd finally stopped ranting.

His eyes narrowed. "I won't be sidelined."

"And I won't have you hampering my mission. You will do what I say, when I say it. Are we clear?"

"I'm not—"

"Are we clear?"

Steve looked like he'd just stepped in something nasty. "Yes," he finally said.

"Be ready for 2200 hours or be left behind." She went back to finalize the real mission with her team.

In the briefing room, Dylan stood waiting for her, his arms crossed. "I can't believe you're letting that asshole come on the mission. He'll fuck everything up."

"Without him, we don't have air support or the extra men."

"We can do this without him," Dylan said.

Sarah stepped into their field of vision. "You're called Cowboy, right?"

Dylan nodded.

"That tells me that you're impulsive and probably a bit of a showoff."

Cat bit the inside of her cheek so she wouldn't smile. Dylan scowled. "Or it could mean I'm from Calgary. Cowboy country."

Sarah shrugged. "It could, but I don't think so."

"What's the point of this?" Dylan turned back to Cat, but Sarah's next words stopped him.

"The point is that you're impulsive. You aren't thinking this through. Of course we need air support. How did you plan to get twenty young girls back over fifty miles to this base?" Now Sarah crossed her arms and a coldness filled her voice, telling them that this woman, no matter how petite, had seen her share of dangerous situations. "That impulsiveness needs to be checked. Now. I won't have you endangering me or the team."

Cat stepped in. She couldn't let Steve's negativity influence any of them. They needed to trust each other. "Easy, Ghost. Dylan may be my brother, but he's also one of the best damn helicopter pilots I've ever flown with. If you trust me, then trust him."

After a moment of cold scrutiny, Sarah nodded. "I trust you."

Cat had a feeling that Sarah didn't speak those words often. It was time to get down to business.

Rhys liked being back with his old team again. He sat in the back of a C-130 heading to Niamey, the capital of Niger, for a fueling stop before heading to the remote base where Cat's team would have already landed.

He'd had a friend in Navy intelligence track their movements. It hadn't been easy, since they'd gone undercover and stowed themselves on civilian and transport flights. According to his friend, they'd arrive approximately eighteen hours before Rhys's team.

Rhys turned up the classic rock on his iPod, something he always listened to before a mission. He pulled out his deck of cards and began shuffling. He flicked card after card through his fingers. Ace of hearts, seven of spades, queen of diamonds. He wanted to throw the cards like knives, but didn't think the air crew would appreciate that.

Shuffling the cards was repetitive and usually relaxed him. This time, the tension didn't leave him. He hadn't been able to relax since Dani had told him of Cat's plans.

Why the hell didn't she ask me to come?

He'd listened a dozen times to the voicemail she'd left him, but he'd gotten no answers there.

He thought he'd proven himself to her. Didn't she trust his skills? Or was it him she didn't trust? Either way, he was going to get to the bottom of this and figure out where they stood. No way was he going to let her play hot and cold with him.

He needed to make sure she was okay. He knew she had skills, but this was almost a suicide mission. There were two hundred men in that camp and she wanted to evac twenty hurt and frightened girls?

Why didn't she ask me?

A hand gripped his shoulder. Jake stood in front of him. Rhys pulled his ear buds out.

"Your head on straight?" Jake asked.

Rhys let the cards play through his fingers. Two, jack, nine. "Five by five."

Jake sat next to him. "We're gonna catch up to her. She's

not stupid and won't rush in without a plan."

He nodded. Two, eight, king.

"We'll find her, Lucky."

He clenched his jaw and kept flipping over cards. Red four. Black nine. He paused. Queen of spades.

The Black Hawk touched down, the wind from its rotors flattening the tall grass. The half-moon gave off just enough light for Cat to see the empty clearing where they'd landed before. She grabbed her ruck before the blades had started to slow and jumped off. Her team followed. They had a lot of work to do before dawn.

She and the others kitted up while Dylan lifted his NVGs and spoke to his copilot and aircrew before jogging to catch up to them. They'd leave them behind to guard the bird. Cat took a quick GPS reading and did a final check of the mag on her rifle.

"Locked and loaded?" she said.

"Roger," came the replies.

"Move out."

The rotors hadn't fully stopped before they left, jogging into the darkness. Their fifth-gen NVGs had been developed by Q and Gears, and were less cumbersome than most goggles. Cat could see everything clearly with a slight green cast, including the aardvark sitting under a leafy bush about ten meters away. Its pig-like snout sniffed the air as it watched them walk by.

They reached the bridge over the Yobe River within thirty minutes. Sweat ran down her back. The humidity of the air made it thick and almost tangible. The wet season meant days that started bright and sunny and ended in torrential downpours.

One guard sat on the other side of the bridge, leaning against a stunted palm tree, smoking. From the way he held his breath when inhaling, she suspected it was ganja, the local marijuana.

They hunkered down into the grass, easily hidden from the guard's sight. He had no NVGs and looked like he was almost asleep.

Cat signaled to the others and they drew close. "I'm going under to set the charges. Zach, keep sights on the guard. Marc, you're with me. Sarah, you're overwatch."

"Copy that," they said.

She slithered through the grass to the edge of the bridge. The guard's eyes closed and his hands lay slack on his rifle, his ganja cigarette forgotten beside him.

She nodded to Marc and then slid down the slope to the river below. The bank was muddy and slick from the rains. Its dark waters rushed and covered any noises they made. Cat took off her ruck and slid out the small pack of specially designed explosives that Q had given her. She tucked it into her webbing, slung her rifle over her back, and then gripped the beams underneath the bridge. She swung out and worked her way across the water. Near the far side she hooked her legs over a beam and used that to steady herself while she set her charges.

Q had taken typical C-4 and mixed it with an explosive accelerant to create a malleable agent, safe to transport, but ten times more combustible than normal C-4 once detonated—meaning Cat didn't have to carry pounds of it to demolish a single bridge. She hung upside down under the bridge, hidden from the guard but also from her team, except for Marc. The river raged beneath her. She focused on her task, refusing to dwell on what waited below.

Damn, she hated dark water.

She peeled off the packaging from the explosive and then pulled bits apart and molded them into the shapes she needed. She used the adhesive to stick them to the joints and trusses of the bridge. Next she placed the radio-controlled detonators into the plastique. The controller was tucked safe into her webbing. She took a last survey and nodded.

This would go boom very nicely.

She made her way to the far side of the bridge and up to the sleeping guard. He snored and she ignored him, scanning the tall grasses and stubby trees beyond, her rifle up and ready.

She made a hand signal and her team came across the bridge. Marc handed Cat her rucksack. They made their way silently past the sleeping guard and toward the Boko Haram encampment.

At their running pace, it only took them about an hour to reach it.

It was about three-thirty in the morning local time. Dawn was just over an hour away. They needed to work quickly.

Thankfully, the encampment was quiet. Some men slept sprawled in the dirt by a dying fire. Three men stood at different points on the perimeter, but their rifles were slung, not at the ready. One smoked, and Cat knew the flaring of the cigarette would wreck his night vision. The other swayed where he stood, either close to sleep or under the influence of drugs.

She signaled Sarah to move to the high ground on the north side to be their overwatch. Sarah would be their spotter with binoculars and let them know via their secure comms the movements of the enemy.

Even though she only had one more team member than before, their mission directive was different. Now it was the girls they had to rescue. They no longer had an American civilian as the highest priority, and Cat had come prepared to blow the shit out of everything.

With that thought in mind, she and Zach snuck into the encampment, easily avoiding the guards. Marc and Dylan covered them from the stubby trees just outside the perimeter. Zach had become a demolitions expert from his time in JTF2, making him her perfect partner. They separated once inside the perimeter and slunk through the shadows of snoring men and cement buildings.

From their previous mission, they knew the layout of the buildings. She crept to the armory she'd found with

Rhys previously. She set her explosives so the building would implode. Zach did the same with the barracks. Next, she crept to the building where the girls slept. The main room had its window open but lay dark. She moved quietly along the outside to the next room. The window to the girls' sleeping room had another lock on it. She placed a tiny bit of plastique on the back of the lock and a small detonator that Q had given her for this situation. She hoped to be able to get the girls out the door, but it was always best to be prepared.

Once they had the explosives in place, she and Zach made their way back to Marc and Dylan. They all had their game faces on, their eyes serious and focused. This was a Hail Mary plan with the ability to SNAFU at any moment. Had she been right to drag them into this, because of her need to do the right thing? What if her brother was killed because of this mission?

She breathed deep to calm her nerves, so her team wouldn't see her worry.

"Dawn in thirty minutes. Take cover. Minimal radio contact."

"Copy that." Marc and Zach moved off, but Dylan gripped her arm and squeezed. "Don't worry, sis. We'll do this."

She squeezed his arm back. Her brother could always tell when something was up with her. She didn't bother denying her anxiousness. "Stay safe."

She crept to her position at the northern compass point.

The rest of them took up observation posts at the other compass points around the encampment. They settled in for the rest of the night and the long hours ahead. She wanted as much intel as possible before they went ahead with their plan.

She knelt in a good position, on a slight hill where she could see most of the encampment, and took precious minutes to dig a narrow trench about six inches deep. The ground was soft because of the rains. She burrowed in and pulled her ghillie suit over her, the suit more of a net with a hood made of a burlap-like material. Before they'd headed out, she'd covered it in some of the native grasses so she could blend in better. Last, she set her rifle sights for the targets below.

Sarah was somewhere to her left. The woman had had more time to dig in and Cat couldn't see her position. With her NVGs she could see Marc farting around near a small bush, spreading the dirt he'd dug. Zach had taken position far from the road and trucks, so no one would run over him, but close enough that he could see that side of the camp. She couldn't see Dylan at all, but trusted him to be in position.

"Spooky," she said in a low voice. "Get in position. The sun is coming up."

"Trying. Damn aardvarks," he said. "My first position was compromised by one."

A snort came over the line. "Did the little animal scare you?" Zach said.

"Fuck off." Marc finally lay down in his position. Within a minute, he disappeared to the naked eye under his camouflage.

"Everyone settle. Stay alert. Eyes on. Ghost is overwatch," she said.

And now they waited.

CHAPTER 20

C at lay still in the dirt as the two men approached her position. The sun was hidden by thick clouds, but she knew it was past the zenith. Sweat dripped down her face, but she didn't move to swipe it. They were fifteen feet away.

"Valkyrie, two tangos in my sight." Sarah's voice whispered in her ear over her comm, letting Cat know she had the men targeted.

Cat didn't reply, but held still as the men kept walking toward her. Ten feet now. They seemed to be early twenties. One wore blue jeans and a camouflage vest, while the other wore camouflage pants and a bright red t-shirt. Their turbans hung askew and both cradled assault rifles.

Cat tensed but held still. They obviously hadn't seen her

yet by the way they joked with each other, pushing one another and laughing. The men came closer still, chatting in Hausa. They stopped about five feet away. She could see the way their pupils were dilated. They'd probably taken tramol, the popular opiate of the area.

A scarab beetle about three centimeters long crawled over her hand and then inched under her shirt sleeve. She could feel its legs like a feather touching her skin. She'd been trained better than to move because of a simple insect, but the bug crawling up her arm made her grit her teeth.

The men slung their rifles over their shoulders and unzipped their pants. They urinated while laughing about something. She picked out the words *kill*, *infidel*, and *face*. She thought they referenced someone they'd already murdered.

The men finally finished their business and wandered back to the encampment.

"Close call," Sarah said.

Cat had pinpointed her location about an hour after dawn. She'd finally seen a slight hump that must have been Sarah's helmet.

"Copy that," Cat said. The acrid scent of the urine was still strong. She shifted her arm and pressed it into the ground, crushing the annoying beetle. "I'm radioing the major. The tangos have started to party. It's time."

Once she contacted Steve, it was just a matter of waiting.

They watched the camp. The only women were the girls they'd come for. All wore hijabs, probably having been forcibly converted to Islam. Cat only counted five of them. Two tended a large fire where they stirred a pot of clothes boiling in water. Three had gone into the building that Cat assumed must serve as the DFAC–she could still smell pungent herbs and spices from dinner. All five girls had bruises covering them. The rest of the girls hadn't emerged from their building, though man after man entered and then, after long minutes passed, left again. Cat's rage simmered with each male visitor to that building.

She would rescue these girls or die trying.

Men began to scurry and shout to each other. Most had wrapped the ends of their turbans across their faces, leaving only their crazed eyes showing. They loaded up on weapons, their shouts becoming louder and more strident. The girls rushed back into their building.

Good, that would make things easier.

One man emerged from the armories building wearing full camouflage, and crossed belts of GPMG ammo strapped across his chest. He waved his rifle and shouted in Hausa, but she could understand "Death to America." The men gathered around him. He gave a speech she couldn't hear, which was probably good since she knew it would only piss her off. The men raised their rifles as they cheered and shouted when the speaker was done.

This was obviously the leader of this sect of the Boko Haram. Cat put him in her sights. She hated these crazed fanatics and how they used religion as an excuse for their violence and bloodlust. A single shot and she could end him. She could save lives.

She narrowed her eyes, studying the man. The girls were her mission, not wiping out this insanity. Her mission couldn't change.

It wasn't long before engines roared to life and men leapt onto the backs of the pickups, flatbed trucks, and jeeps. Weapons fired into the air, accompanying the shouts and war cries that echoed across the encampment.

The trucks rumbled down the road. They'd left a single decrepit pickup behind. That could be useful. Cat did a scan of the area. Only about twenty to twenty-five men left in camp. The men left behind fired their weapons in encouragement before turning away. A few were already lighting up ganja and heading to the girls' building.

"Head count," she ordered.

"Twenty-two," Dylan said.

"Twenty-three," Sarah countered. "There's one on the north side of the DFAC jerking off."

Cat rolled her eyes. "Anyone spot any stragglers?"

"I get twenty-two," Marc said. "Though I can't see jerkoff."

Zach snorted again over the comms. "How do you want to play it, Cat?"

"Sarah, stay overwatch. Control our movements. Steve and his men will buy us an hour, maybe two. We've got to get those girls out and get them the ten miles to the bridge in that time." She raised her rifle. "Sarah, jam their radio signals so they can't call for help. Everyone else, fire when you've got a tango targeted. Headshots, people. Make them count. Weapons free."

She sighted her rifle on a man about to enter the girls' building. She breathed evenly. After she'd exhaled but before drawing in the next breath, she pulled the trigger.

The man fell and lay immobile. The snapping cracks of her team's rifles sounded. She sighted two more tangos and fired. Two more down. Another by the cooking fire, his gun raised and spraying bullets outside the perimeter. Her round took him between the eyes.

Sarah's voice, calm and measured, sounded in her ear. "Doc, tango running east to the remaining truck."

A rifle crack. "Tango down," Zach said.

"Cowboy," Sarah said. "Tango running east of the armory will come into your zone."

"Got him," Dylan said.

They picked off the men one by one, until only five remained, holed up in their barracks.

"Cowboy and Spooky," Cat said. "Throw a grenade in that building and take care of them. Doc, meet me at the entrance to the girls' building."

She raised up from her position, shedding the ghillie net and racing into the encampment, her muscles protesting the hours of inactivity. She forced them to move and move hard. Now was not the time to groan.

She met Doc at the door. He nodded and she ducked into the building, rifle up, scanning the room. Doc rolled in behind her, watching the other side of the room.

"Clear," she said.

"Clear," he said.

They moved as a unit to the far door. Sniffles and whimpers as well as shushing noises came from behind it. A loud boom and screams accompanied gunfire outside. Marc and Dylan were taking care of the rest of the soldiers.

"Spooky, sitrep," Cat said.

"Clear," Marc said. "Five tangos down. Coming to you."

"Valkyrie," Sarah's voice sounded urgent in her ear. "We have company. One truck coming. Two miles out."

Cat swore. "Spooky, Cowboy, greet those guys when they come." She turned to Zach. "Doc, let's get these girls out of here."

She opened the door to the girls' sleeping room and pasted a smile on her face, though she felt like doing anything but smiling. The girls huddled in one corner together, hugging each other.

"Come," Cat said in Hausa. "We're friends. We're here to help you get back home."

Cat didn't speak Hausa well, but when she said the word home, the girls all started repeating it. Their eyes welling with tears, they reached out to her.

Doc stepped into the room behind her. One of the girls gasped and the others retreated, huddling tighter than before. Cat cursed again, inwardly this time. Of course they'd be scared of Zach—a large, muscled black man, a bigger and scarier-looking version of the men who had been raping them for months.

She held up her hands. "It's okay. He's a friend. A friend."

The girls shook their heads and whimpered, their eyes wide with fear.

"Doc, go change places with Ghost." She keyed her mic. "Ghost, get your ass down here now. I need you."

Zach took off at a run and the girls visibly relaxed and started asking questions. Their voices were soft at first, then became shrill as they crowded around her. "Wait," Cat said, then into her mic, "Ghost. I need you."

Sarah finally arrived. The girls seemed taken aback by her sudden appearance. She slung her rifle over her shoulder and started speaking Hausa to the girls.

"Get them outside," Cat said to Sarah. "We need them calm and able to move fast. This is going to be tight."

"Valkyrie," Sarah said softly and pointed.

One girl lay on a pallet. Blood seeped through her dress, staining it from between her legs. She looked at them with feverish but hopeful eyes. The enormity of what they wanted to accomplish pressed down on Cat. Men were coming and more would be on the way soon. These girls limped and some couldn't walk.

What the hell was she going to do? Why had she thought she could pull off this mission? Had she just doomed her team as well as these girls?

"Valkyrie?" Sarah asked. "Cat?"

Cat blinked. She focused on Sarah's questioning face. She could do this. She *had* to do this. She keyed her mic. "Spooky, Cowboy, secure the truck. Doc, sitrep."

"Not in position yet," Doc said.

"Roger," Cat said. She slung her rifle and then bent down to pick up the girl lying on the pallet. She hoisted her in her arms. The girl couldn't weigh more than eighty pounds, though she looked to be a teenager. Anger swelled in Cat again and the girl in her arms tensed.

"Shhhh," Cat said, trying to relax her face.

The girl attempted a small smile. "Home?"

Cat nodded. "Home."

While Sarah organized the other girls, Cat strode to the door with the frail girl in her arms. She stepped outside and froze. The girl in her arms shrank further into them, giving a shrill scream.

A Boko Haram soldier stood before her, his eyes wild, his assault rifle aimed at her chest.

The sun was high overhead. Rhys sat on the outside bench of the MH-6 Little Bird as it hovered over the same infil site where the Black Hawk rested. Rhys, Jake, Scat, and Roddy fast-roped to the ground. The aircrew of the Black Hawk met them, but Rhys had already gotten the sitrep in the air. No one had heard from Cat or her team.

Rhys waved off the aircrew and began to run. He had no idea of Cat's plan, and he didn't want any delays before he reached her. Her team would already be at the Boko Haram base by now. And the thought terrified him.

She's smart.

Not just smart, but incredibly tough. She wouldn't take on an enemy camp of two hundred men without a plan. She had a good team backing her up. She would be okay.

She had to be okay.

Clouds roiled in the sky, blocking the fierce sun, but sweat still drenched them in the heat. It must be over one hundred degrees Fahrenheit. Rhys and his team ran silently through the tall grass. When they could see the bridge in the distance, Rhys held up a fist. The team halted.

"Scat. Tango on the far side."

Scattalone unslung his sniper rifle and knelt, bracing his elbow on his knee. Normally he'd lay prone, but the shot wasn't more than four hundred yards away. "Seen," Scattalone said. "Yellow."

They waited until Scattalone could get a clear headshot.

"Green," he said a moment later.

"Fire," Rhys said.

Scattalone pulled the trigger. The crack of the shot seemed muffled in the thick air. The guard toppled and fell face first.

"Let's move," Rhys said.

The team ran behind him. They crossed the bridge and continued on to the encampment. He'd briefed the others about the layout, but he had no idea what to expect when they got there. Were they running toward a firefight? Would they wreck whatever plans Cat had? Or had her team already been massacred?

No. His woman was smart. He had to remember that.

His woman.

And she was his—his to protect and to help. How dare she leave him behind when she needed him? They would have words when this was over. His jaw clenched as he ran.

She was smart.

His boots pounded into the dirt. He pushed himself to go faster. The others kept up.

She was smart. She was okay.

They drew close to the encampment and had to slow. Most of the trucks seemed to be gone. In the distance, he could see a dust trail where one drove back to the camp.

A loud boom sounded from one of the buildings.

"That was a grenade," Roddy said.

Rhys saw Zach running as if hell were on his heels, toward the perimeter.

"College, head off that incoming truck. Roddy, go south. Scat, you're with me." He started running to the center of camp.

A shrill, high scream stopped his heart.

CHAPTER 21

The scream still echoed as Rhys raced through the camp, passing sprawled bodies of Boko Haram soldiers on his way. He tracked movement but didn't see Cat anywhere. Jake moved to the truck parked on the east side of the compound. Roddy ran to the south perimeter while Scat stayed by Rhys's side.

He ran to the girls' building, knowing that's where Cat would be. It came into view and fear clamped his chest like a vise. Cat stood with a small girl in her arms, unable to defend herself as a man in a turban raised a rifle to shoot her.

A cold and calculating calmness overtook him, focusing his every sense on the scene in front of him. He didn't say a word, but stopped, raised his rifle, and took the headshot.

The man dropped and didn't move.

He caught Cat's gaze then. It was like a wall broke open. Emotion rushed through him, anger and fear swamping him. He strode to this woman who drove him insane, not knowing what he was going to do. She still clutched the child to her chest, her eyes wide and lips parted.

He wanted to kiss her. He wanted to strangle her.

He shook his head, trying to sort himself out. "We are going to talk when we get out of this."

Her mouth opened, but the other schoolgirls and another operator came out of the building, interrupting her.

He turned away, scanning the encampment for any further hostiles. "Save it," he said. "We need to get these girls out of here."

She nodded, but as she passed him she whispered, "Thank you."

His grip tightened on his rifle at the thought of how close he'd come to losing Cat before he even really had her.

He ground his teeth together. Now was not the time. He had a mission.

Cat carried the girl to the last truck in the encampment. Marc stood guard while Dylan sat behind the wheel, the truck idling.

"Doc, how close is that returning truck?" she asked Zach, who stood overwatch on the hill.

"Two minutes out," Zach replied. "We could lose some girls if it turns into a gun fight while driving."

Zach was right. If they all got on the truck and the other soldiers chased them, firing into the open bed, then they'd end up with casualties. She caught sight of Jake running toward them with two more hard-faced men flanking him. Rhys must have brought his old SEAL team. A plan ticked into place and she keyed her comms.

"Doc, get to the vehicle. You're in charge of the team. Drive those girls to the exfil and call for a medevac to meet you there."

"What about you, Valkyrie?"

"I'm staying behind with Lucky and his team. We'll take care of these tangos and then follow in their vehicle."

"Roger," Zach said.

Cat helped the girls load onto the truck bed. Marc and Zach hopped on as well. Sarah jumped in the front beside Dylan.

"Don't take too long," Zach told Cat.

She smiled. "We'll probably beat you there. My brother drives like a grampa."

They tore off, headed for the bridge and safety. Cat turned to see Rhys standing tall beside her, his gaze on the approaching truck. "Let's go," he said. "Roddy and Scat have taken position on a rooftop and Jake's behind the barracks." He started to run to the nearest building, the armory, and she followed. "We need cover now."

They slid behind the building's corner just as the truck

full of men, shouting and firing weapons, skidded to a stop. Men piled out like ants from a hill, rushing into the encampment. They didn't run straight at them, so Cat reasoned that the tangos probably didn't know where they were.

Behind the building, Cat knelt while Rhys stood over her. Both had their rifles trained on the incoming enemy.

"Fire," Rhys said over the comms.

The team's rifle shots mixed in with the Boko Haram soldiers' weapons fire, so the soldiers didn't notice anything wrong until their men started falling. They looked around wildly. Some ran back to the truck; some ran to the buildings.

Cat sighted and fired, sighted and fired. She kept it up until she couldn't find any more easy targets. She felt no remorse about killing these men who had raped and murdered countless children.

"Next move?" she asked Rhys as they scanned the area.

"We need that truck," Rhys said. "Change your comms to channel 356."

She did so and the team's voices filled her ears.

"—can lure them away," Jake said.

"No, College. There's two of us. Valkyrie and I will do it."

"You sure?" Jake asked.

"He's sure," Cat said. She didn't know the plan, but trusted Rhys's instincts.

Rhys looked down at her and his eyes glowed almost golden with emotion. Then he went back to scanning the encampment. "Give us thirty seconds to get into position and then go for the truck." He nodded at her. "Let's go, we're the distraction now."

They ran to the girls' building. Rhys fired random shots at nothing, blatantly giving away their position. She followed him into the building. "Aren't we cornering ourselves in here?"

"We'll go out the window in the girls' room. I'm assuming you took care of it?"

She grinned. "It's set to blow. Just give me the signal."

He didn't grin back and she deflated slightly. "I'm still pissed at you," he said. "Now tell me what else you've set to blow."

She told him where the rest of the bombs were while he stood near the door. "They're coming," he said.

She peeked out and saw about a dozen men creeping toward their position. The men fired at them. She raised her rifle and shot two, while Rhys took out another two before the soldiers scrambled for safety.

"We've got the truck," Jake said over the comms. "Haul ass."

"There's going to be a boom," Rhys replied before he nodded at her. "Do your thing."

Cat already had her remote in hand. She blew the armory building. The explosion shook the walls of their building and thudded through her chest. That was powerful explosive Q had given her.

She blew the little charge on the window lock in the girls'

room next. She left Rhys firing at the tangos and ran to it, slamming the shutters open. "Clear," she called.

Rhys ran into the room and leapt through the window. She jumped after him, but not before she'd left a present for the tangos. She and Rhys raced to the truck where the rest of the team waited. While she ran, she counted down in her head.

Five. Four. Three. Two. One.

Thunder and a concussive force jolted her forward. A single man screamed in agony.

"What the hell kind of grenade was that?" Rhys shouted to her, keeping pace beside her.

"You know me," she said. "I only use the best."

A few men who hadn't gone into the girls' building followed them as they ran, so Cat blew the other structures. She heard more screams, but didn't look back. The truck had already started moving when she jumped into the back. Jake and Scattalone crouched there, rifles up and ready while Roddy drove.

They'd done it. She grinned, not caring that Rhys was pissed at her. He was here. They'd saved the girls together. She faced him, and saw the start of a smile on his face. Her heart lightened. Then, something behind him caught her eye. Clouds of dust rose from the road in the distance.

"Shit," she cursed.

Rhys looked behind him, while Jake nodded. "We've got more company."

"Just get to the bridge," she said. "I've rigged it too."

Jake grinned, his teeth showing white against the grime and camouflage smearing his face. "I like this woman, Lucky. She's a keeper."

Rhys didn't say anything, just glowered and turned to face the approaching trucks. Jake arched a brow at her, but she didn't answer his unspoken question. How could she, when she didn't know if what she'd done could be repaired?

They jolted over bumps as Roddy drove them fast to the bridge. Jake thumped the back window into the cab. "They're gaining."

"I'm pushing it as hard as I can. This clunker can't give us more."

"They're going to catch up to us," Rhys said. "We need to be ready."

"We'll be ready," Cat said, changing out the magazine on her rifle, her hands steady no matter the bashing of the rough ride. "We can handle a truck full of these bastards."

"Copy that," Rhys said. He still didn't look at her and she lifted her chin, focusing on the hostiles closing the distance. She couldn't be distracted by Rhys, but she wasn't going to let him shut her out when this was over. She'd only tried to do what was best for the mission–and for him.

The other truck was only five hundred meters away, but with all the jolting and swaying it was doing, there was no way they could pull off any kind of decent shot. Instead, they conserved their ammo and waited.

Five hundred meters.

Two hundred meters.

Without speaking, they all raised their rifles and fired at the truck behind them. Men crowded the back of the pickup, and it wasn't hard to just fire into their midst. Even with her rifle bouncing from the ride, she could hit enough of them that the truck skewed off the road. It roared back seconds later. Gaining still.

Cat chanced a glance ahead. She could see the bridge. "Bridge ETA three minutes," she called out as she turned back.

Something punched her chest twice, then her arm. The force slammed her back into the bed of the truck.

"Cat!" Rhys yelled. And then he was there, his hands pressing her to lay back, his fingers probing the wound in her left arm.

"Shit," she said, batting at his hands, gasping for air, trying to get her wind back. "Stop it... I'm fine."

The truck swerved and Rhys dropped a hand beside her head to steady himself and leaned in close. His gaze seared her. "You've been shot," he said. "Now lie still."

Her body armor had saved her life, but it still felt like someone had struck her with a sledgehammer to the sternum, twice. Besides gasping like a fish, her upper arm throbbed and burned where a bullet had ripped through it. She steeled herself not to flinch while he finished his examination.

"Sitrep?" Jake asked.

"Her chest armor stopped two. Upper arm is a deep graze," Rhys replied, before Cat could say anything.

Bullets dinged off the side of the truck. "They're trying to pull up alongside." Jake said. "Time to fire back, boys and girls."

She struggled to sit up and pulled her arm from Rhys's hand. "We'll wrap it later."

He nodded. "We're going to do a lot of things later."

She wasn't sure how to take that. Even though she hurt, her mind jumped to something hot that required little clothing, though she knew that's not what he meant. Still, a girl could hope.

She lifted her rifle with a grunt and started firing back. Each recoil of the rifle sent a shock of pain through her. She ignored it and soon was swept back up in the fight for their lives. The closer the truck came, the easier it was to shoot the soldiers—which they found out when Rhys killed the driver. Their truck careened off course.

"Nice shot," Cat said.

"Won't be long before they're on us again," he said.

Sure enough, Cat saw them open the driver's door and a body fell to the ground. The truck straightened its path and headed for them again, like a dog with a scent.

"Almost to the bridge," Rhys said, now crouched by her side. "Can you run?"

She scowled. "It was my arm that was hit, not my legs."

He laughed. "I forgot who I was talking to."

Trees brushed either side of the truck as it neared the river. They skidded to a stop in front of the bridge, right beside the pickup they'd sent the girls in. Roddy parked the truck so it became cover for them as they crossed.

They grabbed their gear and hopped out. Cat grit her teeth when she landed. Jake and the other two men ran across the bridge. Rhys took up position behind the truck and started shooting at the fast-approaching soldiers.

He glanced back at her. "This is where you run," he said, firing again. "I cover you. You cover me when I run. Remember basic training?"

"Not funny, Lucky. Just don't be slow."

She raced across the bridge. The pounding of her feet set off a teeth-clenching throb in her arm. The rest of the SEAL team had already found firing positions on the far side.

"Move it, Lucky," Jake's voice ordered over the comms.

Cat made it to the far side, her heart thumping hard. Jake motioned her over. "Get ready to blow the bridge."

She nodded and reached to the webbing pocket where she'd put the detonator. Her fingers touched shredded material and her eyes widened. There was a hole in her webbing and a quarter-sized dent in her body armor near her shoulder.

She pulled out the transmitter and swore. It had been smashed. Jake looked at it. "That can't be good."

"It's not," she said.

Without the transmitter, there was no way to blow the bridge from this side of the river.

"We can hold them off until the Chinook picks up the girls," Jake said.

But that didn't leave any way for them to escape. She

pressed her lips together. There was only one thing to do.

"I don't like that look on your face," Jake said.

"Get those girls to safety." She took off back across the bridge, passing Rhys as he ran the other way.

CHAPTER 22

Cat raced past Rhys, going the wrong way.

What the fuck is she doing?

"Cat!" Rhys yelled. He turned and chased after her, back to the wrong side of the bridge. He held up his rifle and fired at the tangos, who were way too close for comfort now. Their truck stopped and tangos piled out even as Cat reached the end of the bridge. She immediately slid down the bank.

He knew then that something had to be wrong with the explosives—or else she'd totally lost her mind in the heat of battle. He ran after her, but stopped before sliding down the bank. He hunkered down and spread cover fire. "Talk to me, Valkyrie," he said over his comm.

"Get across the bridge, Lucky."

Rhys couldn't look at Cat, since he was too busy picking off the crazed soldiers trying to surround them. "Not without you."

"Get over the bridge, Rhys. Please."

"What the hell, Cat? I came here for you. I'm not leaving without you."

She swore.

"Whatever you're doing, Valkyrie, do it now," Jake said over the comms. "More trucks full of tangos. ETA one minute."

The tangos had obviously gotten in touch with their buddies, who had come roaring to their aid.

Rhys slid down the bank and changed his mag when he had cover. Cat hung by her legs from under the bridge, fiddling with the blasting caps and detonator in the explosive. Blood drenched her left sleeve.

"The transmitter's gone," she said without looking up from her work.

"Are you putting in a new detonator?"

"No time." She grabbed hold of the bars and swung her legs down. "You're a crack shot right?"

"Shooting C-4 won't detonate it."

"That's why we have to shoot the blasting cap." She jumped down beside him and unslung her rifle. "Last chance to run."

He looked into her face, smudged with dirt and camouflage paint that made her blue eyes brilliant, while determination set her jaw. There was no way he was leaving her.

His woman.

"Stop asking me to run. You've already pissed me off, chère. Don't keep adding to the list you have to answer for."

Her eyes widened, but she nodded and then pointed behind him into the trees. "If we find cover in there we should have a clean line of sight for the shot."

Gunfire ripped into the bridge, showering them with splinters. They both leaned against the bank and fired back at the encroaching tangos. "We're on the wrong side when the bridge goes boom," Rhys said between shots.

"I need the explosive in those joints in order to make it fall. Our only visual is from this side. Besides, there's another bridge twenty klicks away."

"There's another way to cross the river." He hated to do this, but she had to realize what needed to be done. He glanced at the raging water behind him, one of the only things he knew the woman beside him feared. He'd do anything to save her from that. "You know I can take this shot myself. You can still make it across the bridge."

She shook her head. "The tangos are too close. Besides, who's gonna provide covering fire for you if I leave you behind?"

He didn't say anything, but watched her for a few seconds. Her eyes narrowed as she sighted down her scope, pulling her trigger. She was solid. It was always better to have a partner in a mess like this. Time to get to work.

"College," Rhys said over the comms. "Give us covering fire. We're getting into position to blow this sucker."

"You coming back?" Jake asked.

"Negative. Blowing it from this side."

"Evac plan?"

"Run and then swim."

"Copy. Don't make us wait too long."

"Wilco. Lucky out."

The SEALs increased their rate of fire, letting their weapons run full auto, making a thunderous sound. The tangos ducked behind their truck.

"Now," Rhys said.

They scrambled up the bank and sprinted the short distance to the trees, not stopping until they were about twenty yards in. He glanced back. He could only barely see where the shot would be. He steered their run alongside the river. The view opened enough.

He stopped and ducked behind a tree, pulling Cat with him. She wobbled and his hand came away wet with her blood. Shit. He'd forgotten she was bleeding. He should have made her run to safety.

He dropped down and steadied his breathing as he sighted the small bit of white plastique he could see. Looking through the scope, the brass blasting cap was just visible.

Bark sprayed above him. "Covering fire," he said.

"On it." Cat lifted her rifle, her face tense with strain. He knew her arm had to be killing her, but she didn't say a word. She opened fire.

He sighted the blasting cap again. They were only about

one hundred yards away at this point, an easy shot normally, but the target was less than half an inch wide.

He slowed his breathing and focused on the shot, shutting out all sounds.

He pulled the trigger.

The blast of light was instantaneous. He ducked his head against the booming shock of sound and force that followed. Fuck, that had been a bigger explosion than he'd expected.

"What the hell was that stuff?"

But Cat didn't answer. She was on her knees, shaking her head, her helmet askew. He tackled her to the ground where she wouldn't be an easy target.

"Cat, can you hear me?"

She frowned and nodded. "Warn me next time. I think some shrapnel hit my helmet."

Cat's helmet had a crack in it. His fingers traced it. Thank God E.D.G.E. used the best and lightest armor there was.

The gunfight started up again.

"Sitrep, Lucky." It was Jake's voice over the comms.

"Five by five, College."

"You've got tangos running through the woods to your location."

"Copy that."

He stood up, making sure he was covered by a tree. He changed his mag and noticed Cat's hands shake just a little as she did hers. Her face was paler than normal. She'd lost too much blood already, but he had to push her or they weren't going to get out of this.

"Come on, Valkyrie. It's time to run." He held out his hand. It told him how hurt she was that she took it. "Don't quit on me now."

She bared her teeth and her eyes blazed. "Never." She turned and ran.

He followed, jumping logs and racing through the squat trees, promising himself that at the first opportunity he was going to convince this woman she belonged with him.

Cat's arm had numbed, and she knew her senses had too. She'd managed a rough bandage a while back, but the wound needed something more. Her head and arm pounded in time with her heart. She panted more than she should, but didn't complain and kept focused on the situation. Rhys needed a partner at his back, not a liability, if they were going to get out of this.

They'd run probably only five kilometers, but it felt like a marathon. It was late afternoon, the heat pressed in on them and the sky getting steadily darker with thunderclouds. The darkness within the trees had grown, which gave them an advantage, but the number of Boko Haram soldiers chasing them seemed to grow along with it.

Their progress slowed. More trucks had come, disgorging more soldiers to comb through these scant trees for them. The tangos had been driving her and Rhys away from the river. They'd been able to stay within the cover of the trees and brush that grew on either side of the Yobe River, but it had been a close call at times.

A rolling thunder broke through the shouts and calls of the soldiers chasing them. It would rain soon. Rhys halted and held up a fist. She stopped behind him, gaze scanning for movement as she listened intently.

Rhys knelt by a fallen, hollowed-out log. It looked like termites had eaten through it. He pulled at the bark near the bottom and dug under the log.

"What're you doing?" she whispered.

"They're herding us. We need a hiding place so they'll go by."

She didn't offer to help him dig, but instead kept watch. They didn't have much time, but she didn't urge him on. He knew as well as she did that the soldiers were almost on them.

After long tense minutes he finally said, "Done. Get in."

Rhys had dug a six-inch-deep, narrow trench beside and under the log. It would allow them to use the top part of the log as cover while they nestled in the dirt under it.

She shook off her webbing, stored it near where her head would be, and then dropped and rolled into the trench. Rhys had scattered the dirt he'd dug while she settled. He dropped in beside her and used leaves and branches to cover them.

It was dark, and a tight fit. They didn't move and barely breathed. She prayed for the rain, which would make it more difficult to find them and would cover any noises they made. Her throat was dry, though the rest of her body was damp with sweat. She swallowed, wishing she'd thought to have a drink before holing up.

Voices speaking in Hausa made her still. She forgot her discomfort, her throbbing arm, her thirst and fatigue. She breathed silently, her rifle gripped loosely in her hands. She could only see Rhys's broad back in front of her.

The voices yelled, blaming each other for losing the fucking Americans. One man stood right near the log. She craned her head and could see his boots out the far end. Rustling noises sounded and then the scratch of a lighter. Moments later, the thick scent of marijuana entered their hiding place.

They could not be caught by these men. They wouldn't just be killed, but the Boko Haram had a reputation for torture unlike any other. She would be raped repeatedly during it all, before she and Rhys were both eventually beheaded. She would not go out like that.

She wouldn't let Rhys die like that, either. He'd gotten into this mess because of her. She'd make sure he got out of it.

The soldier continued to smoke. Another one joined him. She gripped the handle of her knife. Should they kill them now, before more joined them? She reached up and squeezed Rhys's shoulder. He shook his head slightly. He had a better view and obviously knew what she was asking.

She trusted his judgment and settled back, still holding the handle of her knife. Sweat rolled into her eye, stinging it and making her blink. A termite of some kind crawled on Rhys's back. She tapped it off silently, wishing she could do that to whatever was traveling up her leg.

Gunshots cracked the relative calm of the moment. A man shouted at the two smoking to move it or he'd kill them. The marijuana butt dropped in front of the log and the men ran off, shouting threats to Americans. The third man cursed, fired shots, and went running off.

She let out a long breath that she hadn't known she'd been holding. She squeezed Rhys's shoulder again, but otherwise didn't move. They weren't out of danger yet.

They waited. The patter of rain on the log started. The rain would help hide them from the searching men, but it would also hinder their hearing when they finally started to move.

Three times men ran past their hiding spot, but none stopped. The rain continued to fall gently, making their hideout damp as well as hot. Her arm ached and she had the urge to sneeze.

It had been about thirty minutes since they'd last heard shouting.

"Time to move," Rhys said quietly, rolling out of position.

Cat followed, wanting to groan, but instead focusing on being thankful the soldiers had missed them. "They'll come back with another sweep."

"I know," Rhys said. "We've got to hit the river while we can. But first…" He dumped his helmet, pulled out his med kit, and tore the wrapper off a bandage. "Let me see that arm."

She held up her arm and he used his knife to slice the sleeve open so he could see the wound. She'd managed to shove a quick bandage against it earlier and tie it off, but her sleeve and the bandage were soaked with blood.

"We need to do this properly, or you'll lose too much blood to make the swim." Rhys threw the old bandage in the log and then pressed a clean one to the wound. "Hold this," he said. He unwrapped a long bandage and started to wrap that around her arm again and again.

The rain came down harder. Cat pulled off her helmet, closed her eyes, and let the rain sluice down her face, the coolness a welcome relief.

Rhys tugged the bandage tight. "You're set."

She opened her eyes and stared into his. He hadn't moved back. His hair lay plastered to his head and raindrops hugged his eyelashes. She sucked in a breath at the heat and determination in his eyes.

"We're going to make it," he said. His hand went to the back of her head and pulled her in for a short, hard kiss.

"Damn right," she whispered, but he'd already turned away, putting his gear on and changing his mag. She did the same.

"We do a straight run at the river," he said. "No stopping, no thinking, just jump in and swim. It's dark enough that if no one's around we should be fine." He looked at her. "You can do this."

She nodded and knew she could. She'd trained exactly for situations like this. She ran toward the river with Rhys keeping pace.

As they ran closer to the river, they could make out shouts coming from somewhere near them. The rain screwed up her hearing and she couldn't locate the source. Were there soldiers standing on the riverbank?

She glanced back at Rhys, but he motioned straight ahead. She could make out the river through the trees. It seemed darker and more turbulent than before. A single soldier stood by the bank. Without hesitation, she shot him in the head. He fell into the water and was swallowed by the churning river.

She slung her rifle across her body as she ran, not wanting it to be swept away from her. She leapt bushes and rocks, her heart thundering not from exertion, but from fear of the dark current that could so easily choke the life from her.

"You can do this," Rhys said again, as he pulled up beside her.

"I know," Cat said.

Their feet pounded the earth together. The river loomed before them. Memories of that failed mission tried to surface, clawing at her insides, but she refused to acknowledge them and ran harder.

"Stay with me," Rhys said as he ran down the bank and plunged into the water.

Gunfire and shouts ripped the air behind her. The bullets impacted the water, making small fountains where they hit. She didn't look back. The water pushed her legs as she ran in, making her slip on the rocks beneath the surface. She dove after Rhys.

She swam under the surface, but not too deep. She let the current carry her down, trying to spot Rhys in the murky water. She couldn't see him. She lifted her head and gasped in air. Shouts muffled by the rain made her duck under again, just as bullets zipped around her. She let the current carry her downstream before surfacing again.

Where was Rhys? He'd said he'd stay by her.

She dove again, fighting the current and the burning of her lungs, her arms sweeping through the darkness, searching, before popping up to the surface and dragging in another breath. She no longer heard shouts or gunfire.

"Rhys," she screamed. "Rhys!"

She dove again. Where was he? Where was he?

This couldn't be happening. She had to find him. She dove deeper, swimming against the current as much as she could, but it dragged at her, sucking her down further. It was almost completely dark this deep.

Her leg hit a jagged rock and the pain focused her.

Something had happened to Rhys. The only way he wouldn't come to the surface was if he was trapped by something or he was unconscious. She doubted anything could trap a Navy SEAL in water, so he must be unconscious.

She stopped fighting the current and began to swim with it. She rose once for another breath of air and dove again. Her limbs were heavy in the water, tired from supporting her and the extra weight of her kit and weapons. Her wounded arm ached from use, and from the driving water that tore at the bandage and her flesh.

The rushing water and her heartbeat filled her ears, creating a cacophony that drowned out reason. She swept her arms again and again in front of her. Where was he? Had she guessed wrong? SEALs were trained to swim without air longer than normal people. But even so, he didn't have much time left. Her lungs squeezed tight with her need to breathe, making her want to claw her own throat, but she stayed under, going deeper.

She wouldn't lose him this way. She wouldn't. She kept swimming, the need for air dissipating as a sense of calm washed over her. She knew logically that this was a danger sign. She was close to blacking out. Lethargy overtook her and her body demanded that she just float. Close her eyes. Open her mouth for air and let go. Forget Rhys.

She closed her eyes.

Rhys.

Something drifted into her leg. She jerked in the water and grabbed.

An arm.

It was like she'd been tasered; she jolted to life. Holding tight to the arm, she swam for the surface, dragging the body with her.

Please God, let it be Rhys and not that soldier she'd shot.

She broke the surface, gasping and coughing, hauling the person up with her.

"Rhys!" she screamed. His head hung limp, his helmet

gone. She strained to keep them both afloat. Blood poured down his face, too fast for even the rain to wash away. The wound was high on his forehead. A bullet must have grazed him and knocked him out.

She couldn't see anyone on either side of the bank, so she stayed on the surface and made her way to the other side, no longer fighting the current, just trying to make it across as fast as possible. She swam on her back, Rhys's head on her chest, her arm supporting him.

"Rhys," she said. "Wake up. I need you."

She continued to talk to him as she worked her way to shore. She had no idea if Rhys was breathing or not. Panic ate her reason as she swam, using the last of her energy.

Her arm hit a rock and she turned to look. She could stand. Slipping and wobbling, she dragged Rhys onto the muddy bank. Kneeling beside him, she felt for breath as she radioed Jake.

"College, this is Valkyrie, over."

She tilted Rhys's head back and opened his mouth, blowing her breath into him. "Come on, Rhys. Breathe, dammit."

"College," she said into her mic. "Do you read me? Over."

She blew again. "Rhys, you bastard, wake up."

"Valkyrie, this is College. Sitrep."

She blew once more into Rhys's mouth. "We're on your side of the river. Downstream…" She looked around. "Downstream maybe eight kilometers from the bridge. Lucky's down."

"Stay put, Valkyrie, we're almost at your position."

She didn't reply but blew another breath while she put her fingers on Rhys's carotid artery, feeling for a pulse.

Faint, erratic. Hope bloomed. She breathed for Rhys again.

And again.

And again.

He began to choke. She rolled him to his side and he vomited river water onto the bank.

"Damn," he whispered when he was done. "What happened?"

"You were shot in the head," she said, sitting back on her heels, the words catching in her throat. She'd almost lost him. She stared at the river, blinking fast.

"Chère?" His voice cracked. "You saved me? Hey. Are you okay?" His hand reached for her arm. She moved away and didn't answer, feeling like one touch would shatter her.

They were alone in the mud and rain. They'd rescued the girls, blown up a bridge, taken out dozens of the Boko Haram, and survived the river. And all she wanted to do was cry. She swallowed her emotions and scanned the far bank for tangos. They weren't out of the woods yet. Now was not the time to lose it.

"Can you walk?" she asked, her throat still thick.

"Yeah," Rhys said. He stood and swayed slightly.

She grabbed him and put his arm over her shoulder. "Did I mention you were shot in the head?"

His smile was crooked. "We did it, chère. We saved those

girls."

She managed a smile. "We did. And now it's time to face the firing squad for it."

CHAPTER 23

"I was already checked out both in Niger and in Germany," Cat said, as the doctor waved a pen light in her eyes.

"Knight wants me to examine you," the gray-haired doctor said gruffly. "So that's what I'm doing."

Cat's left arm ached and the stitches pulled and itched. She sat on an exam table in jeans and a tank top. She had purple bruises the size of saucers on her sternum and near her shoulder where the bullets had struck her. Thankfully, the bullets hadn't cracked her ribs, just left her with a soreness that demanded she go have a hot bath as soon as possible.

"I'm going to recommend you stay overnight for observation," he said.

"Sorry, Doc, but that's not going to happen. My bed is way more comfortable than the cots here. Don't worry, I know how to take care of myself."

The doctor huffed. "Of course. But I still have to recommend it."

The door to the room opened and Blackwell and Knight entered. Cat tried to stand up, but the doctor just pushed her back onto the exam table. "Don't move." He poked at the stitches in her upper arm, tsking.

Blackwell scowled at her. "You appropriated government vehicles and weapons for an unsanctioned mission."

"Yes, sir." She had wondered when the brass would find her. Commander Knight stood silent behind Blackwell, letting him take the lead. She knew they would dress her down, but would they kick her off the team as well?

"You misled government officials and military officers," Blackwell continued, the edge in his voice growing sharper.

At that moment the door opened again. Rhys, a bandage on his forehead, entered followed by Jake, Sarah, Marc, Zach, and her brother.

"Excuse us, sir," Rhys said, his voice demanding attention.

"What is it?" Blackwell barked.

"I was the other team leader for this mission. I'll share whatever bullshit you're going to dish out."

Blackwell raised one eyebrow as he regarded Rhys.

Jake and Sarah moved to stand beside Rhys. The rest of the team crowded in.

Knight put his hands on his hips. "Enough, Blackwell.

Time to ease off."

Blackwell's eyes glittered and his lips quirked in a small smile. "But I haven't gotten to the good part yet, where I slam my fist on the table."

Knight laughed and clapped Blackwell on the shoulder. "They don't understand your humor, Derrick." He gazed at the men and women around the room. "We have been told to sanction the people who conducted the unauthorized mission so no one else decides to go rogue."

He stood there a moment, eyeing them all. "Consider yourselves sanctioned," Knight said.

Rhys grinned. "And now can we go have a drink to celebrate?"

Knight nodded. "Twenty young girls are back with their families today because of what you did. I am proud to have you all working for me." He smiled. "First round is on E.D.G.E."

Everyone shuffled out of the room after that. Blackwell and Knight waited while the doctor helped Cat into a sling for her arm. She tried not to grimace at the doctor's efficient movements.

Rhys waited by the door.

They hadn't spoken alone since coming back from the mission. They'd spent a day getting checked out at the U.S. military hospital in Germany before being flown back to Montreal, where black-windowed SUVs picked them up. Cat had chosen to sit in one with Jake, Sarah, and her brother. She'd purposely been avoiding being close to Rhys since they'd made it back to the airbase in Niger. She'd just been too tired to deal with the chaotic emotions being around him brought up.

The room cleared out.

Blackwell stared at Rhys. "Did you have a question, Lafayette?"

"No sir, just waiting for Valkyrie."

Knight raised his eyebrows, and a blush heated Cat's face. Damn. She was acting like a schoolgirl. She had to be professional.

"I'll be done in a minute," she told Rhys with no emotion in her voice. "Meet me in my office and we'll go over the reports."

Rhys clenched his jaw, knowing when he'd been dismissed. He waited outside the room, determined to speak with the woman currently driving him insane. Moments later she opened the door, her head down. He touched her good arm before she walked into him. "Are you okay? What'd they say?"

She lifted her head. A smile blossomed on her face and lit her impossibly blue eyes. "The team is mine. Permanently."

"It's the only thing they could do," he replied. Damn, he wanted this woman, especially when she smiled at him like that.

Her face dimmed and she glanced back at Knight and Blackwell, who still spoke quietly inside the room. She moved away and tried to sidle around him.

"Where're you going, chère?" he asked quietly. "You know we need to talk."

She straightened her shoulders and looked him straight in the eye. "No," she said. "There's nothing we need to talk about. You are now officially a member of my team. We have leave for a week. Go rest and recover."

He tilted his head as he regarded her. "Are you blowing me off?"

She shook her head, looked back at Knight and Blackwell, and then motioned for him to follow her.

He obliged and she led him to her office, but she stopped in the doorway—not letting him into the room.

"This thing between us is over," she said. "I can't be involved with someone I work with. If you have a problem with that, then I'll need you to request a transfer to another team."

He stepped closer. "And what reason should I give them?"

She tilted her chin up. "Tell them whatever you want. I'm sorry, but I won't have anything that could potentially jeopardize my team or my future missions."

"We worked well together in Nigeria. Why would that jeopardize the team?"

She sighed. "Others have seen the way you look at me-"

"And the way you look at me," he said.

"You're not listening, Rhys. The rest of the team doubts us. They doubt we can focus on the mission."

"It doesn't matter what they think. Unless you doubt us?"

"I'm sorry, Rhys." She stepped back. "I have a report to write." She closed the door in his face.

He clenched his fists and stared at the door for a moment. No way was he letting her shut him out. He'd let her have this moment, but this conversation wasn't over.

I'll see you soon, chère.

Cat lifted her head at the sharp rap on her office door. Had she really expected Rhys to leave so easily?

She yanked it open. "Rhys, I mean—"

Her brother stood there, a half-smile on his face. "Hey, sis."

Her shoulders slumped slightly. She assured herself she was relieved it wasn't Rhys–but if that was true, why did she feel slightly lost inside?

"Hey." She waved her brother inside. "You heading back to Petawawa?"

He nodded. "Colonel Blackwell is going to smooth things over with my CO. He also said that E.D.G.E. might need a helicopter pilot in the future."

She hugged her brother. "That would be amazing."

"Well, I'm not finished with CSOR yet," he said. He shrugged and then blew out a long breath. "Look, I just wanted to say that…I'm sorry for being disappointed in you before." He shook his head and pointed around him.

"I had no idea what you were really doing. I just thought you'd…"

"Given up?"

He nodded. "I'm glad to see you didn't."

"I only wish Dad knew, too."

"Don't worry about him," Dylan said. "He's proud no matter what you do, even if it's some fancy-schmancy marketing job that's too complicated to explain."

She laughed. "When will I see you again?"

"Maybe sooner than you think." He gave her another hug and went to the door. "And hey, I think Mom would approve of Rhys."

"Don't you start too," she said.

"He's not Steve."

"Doesn't matter."

"Your call," he said.

And it was, dammit. She waved goodbye to her brother and then leaned back against her desk. She was doing the right thing where Rhys was concerned.

She grabbed her coat and slid one arm into it, pulling it over her hurt shoulder, letting the sleeve flop over her sling. She just wanted to go home, but decided she should pop into the Chien Noir for a celebratory drink with her team.

Marc and Zach stood with Dylan, Sarah, and Jake.

"Nice timing, Cat," Marc said. "Jake here was just about to buy another round."

"Me?" he said. "My team saved your asses. I think you need to buy the round."

Marc snorted. "Can't argue with that." He motioned to Cat to follow him to the bar. "Where's Rhys? I figured he'd be here for sure."

She shrugged. "I haven't seen him."

"Huh," Marc said. "I thought he'd be right by your side."

"Why would you think that?"

"Seriously?" He ordered the beers before turning back to her. "Anyway, I wanted to apologize to both of you."

"We both do," Zach said, having come up behind her. "We underestimated you both. You're both good operators. Whatever you do on your own time is your business. Not ours."

Her mouth dropped open.

"I'm not apologizing twice," Marc said. "So you can just pass it along when you see him next."

"Technically," Zach said, "you haven't actually apologized yet." The two of them carried the beers back to the table, ribbing each other as they went.

She swallowed a gulp of icy beer and closed her eyes for a moment. Her team accepted her and Rhys. She almost laughed. Now that there was nothing to accept. She opened her eyes.

The whole relationship had added too much stress to her life and the missions. She couldn't afford to let herself be so distracted. It didn't matter what her team thought. It only mattered what she chose.

And she chose her career.

Cat slid the faded t-shirt over her head and pulled on her flannel pajama pants. She towel dried her hair one-handed from the hot bath she'd had, before slipping her sling back on.

She hadn't stayed long at the Chien Noir, not even finishing her beer. It had worried her that Rhys hadn't joined them, but she was also secretly relieved that she hadn't had to face him. The tension between them was daunting. He was a good operator, but if they couldn't come to terms about this thing between them, she'd have to transfer him to another team herself. Nothing was going to distract her from her job.

She'd realized when she'd pulled him from the river just how much she was coming to care for Rhys. She hadn't brought him on the mission because she was worried about how their interaction would affect the team, and then when he'd almost drowned, she'd lost sight of the mission entirely. She couldn't work with that kind of stress, and knew that she had to put a stop to anything between them. Her insides ached at the thought. But it was just added to the list of her already-hurting body.

She went into the living room and plopped on her couch. Her stomach grumbled, and she wondered if popcorn was considered a healthy dinner. She turned on her TV and started scrolling through her list of movies to watch on Netflix. She flicked through the romantic comedies. An image of a happy couple chasing their overly large dog centered on her screen and caught her eye. She wanted—no, needed—a happy ending right now.

Someone knocked on her apartment door.

She froze, knowing in her core who it was. She wished for a moment that she was the type of person who could pretend she wasn't home. She didn't want conflict tonight. She just wanted... She looked at the image of the couple again. She flicked off the TV. That wasn't the life she'd chosen. It wasn't an option.

Why not?

Because they worked together. It wasn't professional.

Dani and Jake work together.

Because he would betray her once they'd had their fun, or once he got tired of taking her orders.

He isn't Steve.

She stood up, tired of arguing with herself, and went to the door just as he knocked again.

"Open up, Cat." Rhys's voice carried through the door. "I know you're in there."

She opened the door. His hair was damp, but his face was scruffy from not shaving for three days. The bandage seemed stark white against his tanned forehead. His t-shirt molded to his broad chest and his jeans hung low on his hips. He looked delicious.

He held his leather jacket in one hand and a bag from her favorite Thai restaurant in the other. He held up the bag. "I brought dinner."

She suddenly felt frumpy in her pajamas. Her stomach rumbled and her face heated. She grabbed the bag. "We're not having sex."

"Woman, my head aches and I'm exhausted. I didn't come here for sex," he said, grabbing the bag back and walking in. "I came to eat and to talk."

He went to her small dining table and started pulling out tinfoil boxes of food. "It occurred to me to check the regs regarding fraternization. Can you guess what I found?"

She didn't say anything, but her face stayed heated.

"That's right," Rhys nodded at her guilty expression. "Nothing. I asked Jake and even Commander Knight."

"You didn't!"

"I did," he said, starting to peel off the lids to noodle and spicy chicken dishes. "Can you grab some plates?

Her mouth dropped open. "You—"

"Want plates. Yes."

She rolled her eyes, but went to grab some, along with some utensils. "I can't believe you spoke to Knight about this."

"You didn't leave me any choice," he said quietly.

She whirled to confront him, plates in hand, but he continued to speak.

"It's fascinating, actually," he said. "As E.D.G.E. operators, we are outside both military and even most government jurisdictions. We have no fraternization rule. And then that made me wonder, chère. Can you guess what I wondered?" His Louisiana accent thickened.

She hovered, plates in hand, a few feet away from the table where he now sat, the food laid out before him like a king before a feast.

"Come sit down, chère. I can hear your stomach grumbling from here."

She slowly walked to the table and sat down, passing him a plate. He began to pile food on it before handing it to her and then piling food on the other plate. He pointed at her plate with his fork. "Eat."

The aromas scenting the air made her mouth water, but her muscles tensed like she was crossing a minefield. She wasn't sure where to step next.

She started to eat. If he'd brought her food, then she could listen to whatever theory he'd concocted. It wouldn't change her mind.

She noticed he wasn't eating. He watched her instead.

"Did you poison the food or something?" she joked.

He didn't smile. "Would you like to hear what I wondered?"

"Not really," she said, shoving a forkful of spicy chicken into her mouth.

"I wondered if you knew about this rule. And then I realized that of course you did. That's why it was okay in your mind to jump me six months ago and give me one of the best nights of my life."

"I didn't jump you."

He grinned and finally began to eat. "I beg to differ. But that's not the point here. You knew there was no rule and yet you led me to believe tonight that this *thing* between us, as you called it, was against the rules. When really, you just didn't want to pursue it."

She swallowed the food in her mouth and sat back. No longer hungry. "What do you want, Rhys?"

"I want to know two things," he said. His voice carried a lethal edge. "Number one, why did you leave me behind for this mission?"

She didn't answer, not sure she should answer it honestly.

His gaze bore into her and his voice harshened. "Did you think I wasn't good enough?"

"No," she said quickly. She couldn't have him thinking that. "No. I think you're more than capable as an operator."

His head tilted and his gaze narrowed as he studied her. "Then you don't trust me."

"No," she said. "I trust you." It surprised her how true those words were.

"Then why?"

She sighed. "You distract me. I distract you. We hadn't worked out the kinks of the chemistry between us. I was afraid it would hinder the mission." She didn't need or want to mention that Marc and Zach had felt the same. Just like she wasn't going to mention they'd now given their stamp of approval.

He set his fork down and leaned back, no hint of softness anywhere in his face. "And now?"

She knew what he wanted to hear. And she had to tell the truth. "I think we can work together."

"Think?" he almost growled. "I am a Navy SEAL with years of training. Do you think I can't put my feelings aside for the good of the mission? Do you think I need to be handheld like a child?"

She looked away from his eyes, which almost glowed with outrage. His well-muscled chest and arms spoke of a disciplined man who protected others. That was his job. He would never back down from a fight and he'd never shy from doing the right thing, even if it cost him his life. Cat hadn't known him long, but she already knew this about him.

"I'm sorry," she said. "I trust you as an operator. And *I know* we can work together. I won't leave you behind again."

He let out a long breath. "Good. Now we have matter number one settled."

"Number one?"

"There is something else we need to discuss, chère." He smiled slowly. "But it can wait until we're both feeling better."

Cat frowned. "I'm not sure I like the sound of that."

He stood up, picked up his plate, and moved to her couch. "I'm not watching *The Bachelor* again, just so you know."

The feeling of being in the minefield came back. She followed him to the couch with her food.

He waved his chopsticks for her to sit down. "Nothing but friends tonight, Cat," he said. "We're both too battered for anything else."

Something inside her eased. She sat on the couch and let her muscles relax. "Have you heard of *Outlander*?"

CHAPTER 24

It had been a quiet week since they'd gotten back from Nigeria. Quiet, but satisfying. She'd spent most of it with Rhys, just watching movies and exploring Montreal with him. She'd gotten him hooked on *Outlander* and he'd shown her how to make gumbo.

Each night he'd gone back to his hotel room. They'd fallen into an easy friendship–and if her gaze sometimes lingered on his sleek muscles, she tried not to let him know.

Today was the first day she'd felt like herself. She'd left off her sling for most of the day, as they'd gone to see different apartments for Rhys to rent. Her arm ached a little, but she knew it wouldn't be long before she was back to full strength. Maybe tomorrow she'd try going for a run.

A knock sounded. She opened the door, a smile on her

face. "What are we doing for dinner tonight?"

Rhys stood there, his face serious, his eyes somber.

She stepped back. "What's wrong?"

"We need to discuss the second issue." He moved into her place and took off his leather jacket. His broad shoulders filled out his t-shirt.

She brought her gaze back to his face before it could go any lower. "Second issue?"

He smiled slowly. Knowingly. "After the mission I said I had two things I needed to discuss with you."

She swallowed. "I don't think we need to talk about anything else."

"The second issue," he said distinctly. "You care about me."

She frowned, spun away from him, and ended up on the far side of the room. "Of course I do. You're a soldier under my command. Don't read anything more into it."

He crossed his arms and arched a brow. "I'm going to call your bluff, you know."

"There's not going to be anything between us," she said.

He stalked closer, his gaze warming. "Why not?" His voice was almost a growl.

"I can't have a one-night stand with a soldier on my team. I won't."

He smiled in satisfaction and her stomach tumbled at the look in his eyes. "Who said anything about just one night?"

She stepped back and waved him away when he moved

toward her again. "Okay, I admit we are great in bed, but what happens when that burns out? We're left feeling awkward around each other? Or worse, you start to resent me for being team leader and telling you what to do."

He frowned. "I'm not Major Asshole. I don't kiss and tell and I'd only resent your leadership if you left me behind again."

She sat on her couch and put her head in her hands. "I'm sorry, Rhys. I've learned the hard way that this type of thing won't work."

"So you're just going to give up? That doesn't sound like the Valkyrie I met on that mountaintop in Afghanistan. That doesn't sound like the woman I came to E.D.G.E. to find."

She raised her head. "You came to E.D.G.E. to find me?"

He shrugged as if it didn't matter, but she could see the uncertainty in his eyes. "You intrigued me. The first time at E.D.G.E. I tagged along with Jake to see what the unit was about, but I came here for you." He smiled. "And then I found you. Did you think I would walk away after we had a night like that?" He shook his head at her. "Woman, we are good together. Not only that, but I trust you. You've saved my life and I've saved yours. We owe it to each other to give this *thing* between us a chance."

She stared at him. "Define chance."

He moved closer and took her hands in his, pulling her to her feet. She stood so close that a deep breath would have their chests touching.

"We date," he said simply. "We can take it as slow as you'd like. Though I'd really like to see you naked soon." His hand brushed down the side of her face and cupped her cheek. His smile was sweet. "My cards are down, Cat, and I'm all in. Just let me know what I can do to convince you I'm serious."

Cat stared into his eyes. She trusted this man, more than she'd trusted anyone before. It had felt wrong to leave him behind before. And it felt wrong to send him away now.

It was time to throw reason out the window and follow her heart. No more running from her past mistakes—she would take this chance. She ran a finger over his bottom lip and he nipped it, his eyes darkening with need.

"Can we skip the first date and go right to bed?" she asked. "I'm not much for slow."

Rhys's heartbeat accelerated with Cat's words and the desire in her eyes. He didn't hesitate, not wanting her to change her mind. He held her head as he lowered his lips to her oh-so-soft ones. Sensation and heat washed over him. He pressed closer to her, backing her into the wall, needing to feel her against his chest.

One hand stroked down her body, to cup the swell of her breast. He rubbed his thumb over the tight nipple and she moaned into his mouth. The sound set him on fire and he repeated the motion, just to hear her once more. He trailed his mouth down her neck, the scent of vanilla and woman making him want more. He licked down her skin, pressing his hips into hers, before pulling her t-shirt off her, careful of her arm. He swallowed hard at the sight of all that golden skin begging for his touch. The fading bruises on her shoulder and chest didn't mar her perfection, just reinforced his belief that this dynamic, tough woman should be his.

He skimmed his hands down her body to her hips, grasping her pajama pants and pulling them down. She stood before him in only simple black bikini bottoms, her blue eyes blazing with need and her hands reaching for him.

He sucked in a breath against the tightness in his chest. "God, you're beautiful."

Her face twisted slightly at his words. He pulled back. "You don't believe me."

She shrugged and reached for him again. "It's not important."

He tilted his head as he studied her. Was it true? Had no one she trusted said that to her before? She blushed under his gaze. "You don't think you're beautiful."

Her lips pressed together and she reached for her top, now on the floor. He snagged her wrist before she could grab it. Then he snagged the other before she could grab him. He held her arms gently and he could see the temper flare in her eyes. Had no one seen her strength as beautiful?

"Chère, have you only ever dated idiots?"

"Rhys," she said.

He ignored the warning in her voice. "You are a beautiful woman, chère." He kissed her softly on her lips and then pulled back to look at her again.

"You don't—"

"You are an incredibly sexy woman." He leaned in to kiss just behind her ear, trailing his tongue down her neck. She moaned. He looked at her again, envisioning everything he wanted to do tonight.

Her one arm twisted in his grip. "Stop—"

"You're a stubborn, but sensual woman," Rhys said as he bent down and sucked a nipple into his mouth. Her back arched and her breathy gasp made his cock twitch in anticipation as he moved to her other breast.

When he pulled back this time, her eyes were heavy-lidded and she didn't say anything.

"And you're so responsive it makes me feel like an impatient teenager," he whispered as he went to his knees before her. He still lightly held her wrists by her sides, not wanting any interference as he licked and nipped his way down her belly. But then he released them so he could pull her panties down her long sleek legs. "Ah, Jesus."

He licked her then, tasting her, and she cried out his name. He did it again and again, finally holding her hips while she squirmed.

"I could do this all night," he said.

She tugged his hair, tilting his face up. "Now, Rhys. Don't make me beg."

He inhaled sharply. What a sight that would be. He

pictured her lying before him, writhing with pleasure and calling his name. Desire crashed over him and his cock hardened further, if that was even possible.

She tugged on his hair again. "Rhys!"

He smiled and knew it looked predatory. Next time. He couldn't wait right now. "As you wish, chère."

He stood up and captured her mouth with his, his need driving him. Cat dragged off his shirt, her hands spreading against his chest, stroking his stomach and then unbuttoning his jeans, pushing them and his underwear down. He snagged a condom out of his pocket before kicking them the rest of the way off. He ripped open the package, his hands shaking. Heat flared through him when she gripped his hard length to help roll on the rubber. He groaned.

"Now that's a good sound," she said in a husky voice.

Passion surged and he pushed her back against the wall, lifting her one leg up so he could guide himself in. He sank in to the hilt and ground himself against her even as he tried to get his control back. But he'd never had any with Cat.

She moved her hips and he was lost. He gripped her ass in his hands and lifted her up so her legs wrapped around his waist. He braced her back against the wall and used the power of his legs to sink into her over and over again. He couldn't slow or stop. Her nails raked his back and he trailed his teeth on her neck in retaliation. Her head dropped back, giving him more access. He'd never seen anything sexier than the look of abandon on her face.

"I'm not going to last, Cat."

Her gaze focused on him, those blue eyes captivating him while her hands gripped his hair. "I'm not asking you to."

His balls drew up tight as he plunged into her again and again, harder and harder. She gave a high cry and her insides rippled around him. He groaned and lost himself as the orgasm took him.

Cat shuddered against him as he tried to breathe again. Her lips were swollen from his kisses, her face flushed and her eyes bright. His heart skipped a beat. Fuck breathing. He kissed her and her arms wrapped tight around him.

He pulled back and grinned. "Told you we were good together."

Her blue eyes lit with mischief and challenge. "Is that all you've got, sailor?"

He could love this woman. He bent and swept her up in his arms. "Be careful what you ask for, chère."

CHAPTER 25

The alarm buzzed and Cat hit it to stop the noise. 5:30 a.m.

She pulled the covers over her head. Just one snooze. She snuggled further into the warmth, her hand reaching out for Rhys's hard body. It had been a month since they'd gotten back from Nigeria and they'd spent most of those nights together, either at her place or at his new apartment.

Her hand came up empty. She opened her eyes to see Rhys already in his running shorts and t-shirt. His long, muscled legs were almost as good to look at as his chest.

"Come on, sleepyhead," Rhys's warm drawl seemed to caress her. "If we don't go now, we won't have time."

She threw the covers back. "If I'd known how chipper

you were in the mornings, I'd have left you in Nigeria."

He threw her running gear at her. "Then you would have missed some of the best sex of your life."

She laughed. So true, but the man didn't need to know that.

Her phone beeped from the bedside table. Rhys's chimed from his pocket.

She snagged hers. "Blackwell's calling us in. Looks like another mission. Briefing in thirty minutes."

"I'll make coffee," Rhys said. "You grab the shower first."

They made it to the briefing with minutes to spare. She still held Rhys's hand when they walked in. She'd forgotten to let go. Her stomach clenched when she saw Marc and Zach already at the conference table. She let go of Rhys's hand, but it was too late. They'd seen.

She lifted her chin. She'd made the decision to be with Rhys, she just hadn't advertised it. It was time her team knew and came to terms with it. She sat down and waited for the ribbing to start.

"Any ideas what this is about?" Zach asked her.

She blinked. Then decided to lay all the cards on the table, as Rhys would say. "What? No jokes?"

Zach smiled at her and Marc quirked an eyebrow. "Did you think we didn't know?" Marc said. "You two have been walking around with freaking perma-grins on your faces all month. How could we not know?"

Zach rolled his eyes. "What Marc's trying to say is that we're good with it. We trust you both not to let it affect the team or a mission."

Her shoulders relaxed. It was good to have the truth out. Her team would function better for it. She smiled at Rhys and he squeezed her hand once under the table.

"Glad to hear it," she said to Zach and Marc.

Blackwell strode in at that moment. "We've had news. Al Shabah is rumored to be on the move."

Zach straightened, a fierce glint in his eye. "Do we know where he is?" Zach had been tracking the terrorist Al Shabah for months.

"Negative. But we believe he's heading for the States. As soon as we have confirmation we'll be sending Alpha team in."

Cat listened to the rest of the brief. She and her team would begin training scenarios related to this terrorist that favored bombings of civilian locations, as well as tracking him with all of E.D.G.E.'s significant resources.

"Valkyrie," Blackwell said. "I want a daily report. Al Shabah must be stopped."

"Yes, sir," she said.

They all stood when Blackwell left the room. Cat turned to Zach. "Doc, I want you to find Dani and have her help you track down Al Shabah. Marc, Rhys and I will brush up on our demolitions. We'll be ready for anything this asshole throws at us."

Marc and Zach agreed and left the room. Rhys stood quietly, watching her.

"What's wrong?" she asked.

"We're in this together," he said.

And she knew exactly what he was talking about. This was the first real mission since they'd rescued the girls. He was asking if she would doubt him.

She went to him and hugged him tight. His muscles tensed under her hands. She pulled back and looked into his eyes. "I trust your judgment and your skills as an operator. More, I trust you as the man who holds my heart. I will never leave you behind again."

He smiled and his arms came around her. "Good. I came to E.D.G.E. to find you. I won't let you push me aside again. You're stuck with me."

She kissed him, and the familiar liquid fire rolled through her. She hated having to pull away. "I wouldn't have it any other way. Now let's get to work. We've got a tango to catch."

AUTHOR'S NOTE

Thank you so much for reading **Edge of Reason**.
It means so much to an author to be able to share their
stories with others. If you enjoyed mine then I would
appreciate it if you would help others enjoy the book too.
You can do this by telling a friend, or writing a review
on either Amazon or Goodreads.

Unfortunately, the Boko Haram is very real and have
massacred 1000's of innocents. They use the guise of
religion to spread their hatred. I hope this story shows
that the people and the choices they make are the ones at
fault, not any religion they choose to hide behind. I also
want to reiterate, that while the Boko Haram is real, any
and all events and names in this story are purely fictitious.

Thank you for taking this journey with me.
I hope you'll enjoy the next story as well!

ABOUT THE AUTHOR

Trish writes about strong, kickass women who don't
need to be rescued and the heroic men who fall for them.
Before becoming an author Trish spent time as an officer
in the Canadian Army and then worked as a physicist.
Now, her career includes being a mother and an author.
She considers herself to be a geek and a nerd, though
knowing the difference really just makes her a dork.
Her addiction to reading rivals her addiction to tea.
She lives in Calgary, Alberta with her husband,
two girls and one house cat that thinks it's a tiger.
To find out more about Trish and her books,
visit her website.
www.trishloye.com

MORE BOOKS BY TRISH LOYE

E.D.G.E. SECURITY SERIES
Book 1: **Edge of Control**
Book 2: **Edge of Reason**
Book 3: **Edge of Danger**

COMING SOON!
Christmas Novella: **Edge of the Season** (Dec 2015)
Book 4: **Edge of Courage** (Winter 2016)

If you want to stay up to date on my newest releases
then be sure to sign up for my newsletter.
You can find out more about me and my newsletter at
www.trishloye.com.
I also love to hear from readers so please contact me at
trish@trishloye.com.

Keep reading for a sneak peak of

EDGE OF DANGER

BY
TRISH LOYE

The third book in the thrilling
E.D.G.E. SECURITY SERIES.

Now Available!

CHAPTER ONE

Detective Alyssa Harrison held her Glock 19 in her right hand as she ran up the stairs to the third floor of the dilapidated building. She kept her breathing even, and her mind focused on what waited for them. It was the rare moments like this when she finally felt alive again.

She keyed her radio. "Bravo team, report."

"Almost in position," Detective Riley Castor replied.

Alyssa checked behind her. Detective Drew Patton, her tall, lanky partner, his brown hair flopping in his eyes, ran behind her. Eight members of NYPD's Emergency Services Unit followed after him. Riley, an intense officer with a

Latino background, led a similar team on the opposite side of the building.

She wasn't taking any chances today.

At the door to the third-floor hallway she stopped, and keyed her mic twice in the predesignated signal to Riley's team. Drew opened the door and Alyssa swung into the hallway, her Glock up and pointed ahead. A woman standing in the corridor with a basket of laundry squeaked.

Alyssa used her left hand to point to her badge and then brought her finger to her lips. The woman's eyes widened, but she nodded. Drew shuffled her aside. Alyssa kept moving to apartment 314, while Riley and his team crept down the hall toward her from the other stairwell.

They met in the middle at a plain white door with gold metal numbers. Cigarette smoke made her nose itch and, from inside, a TV competed with music.

Someone was home.

Alyssa held up three fingers. An ESU officer stepped up to breach the door with a metal battering ram.

Two fingers.

One.

He struck the door just below the knob. Splinters flew and the door burst open. He stepped back. Alyssa entered the cramped apartment followed by Riley and Drew. She took it all in quickly as she moved past a small closet, the dirty gray carpet muffling her footsteps.

The galley kitchen held nothing but a few day's worth of dishes on its counters. In the main room, a skinny Asian man sat bolt upright on a saggy couch. He held a cigarette in one hand and a TV remote in the other. The TV blared a baseball game in front of him. A fire escape blocked the view of the open window behind the couch.

Alyssa stepped in front of the TV. The man dropped the cigarette and jumped up.

"NYPD. You're—"

He threw the remote at her and leapt for the window.

She dodged, lowered her weapon, and pulled her Taser. She aimed for his back and pulled the trigger before he'd even touched the window frame. The man jerked and a small whine came from him as the Taser snapped. By the time the five seconds were up, she'd holstered her gun and snagged a set of cuffs. She jerked his arms behind his back, cuffed him, and tossed him to the floor. She nodded at one of the ESU officers. "Frisk him and keep him quiet."

She pulled her weapon again and moved to the bedroom door. Drew and Riley met her there. A thumping bass beat escaped the room, but no other sounds could be heard.

"You ready to take down this asshole?" Alyssa asked.

"Let's do it," Drew said.

Riley nodded.

Alyssa studied the door. It had a lock. She stood in front of the door and shifted her weight.

"Seriously, Al?" Drew said. "Do you really need to—"

"Hell yes," she said, and slammed her foot into the door. It burst inwards with a satisfying crunch. She rushed in with Drew and Riley right behind her.

Screeching guitars assaulted her ears. A long-haired man worked over a table by the light of a desk lamp.

"NYPD! Hands up!" she shouted.

The man whirled, his eyes wide. He held a soldering iron in one hand and a circuit board in the other.

Four pressure cookers still in their boxes stood by the wall. Wires, blasting caps, and detonators littered the rest of the table. The smell of homemade black powder overwhelmed the cigarette smoke from the other room. The acrid mixture of sulfur, charcoal, and potassium nitrate smelled like a chemical solvent. Four large canisters of it sat by the table.

Her heartbeat sped up. A cold sweat broke out on her forehead as she imagined the damage this amount of black powder could do. Maybe as much as the bomb in the souq.

No. Don't think about that.

The iPod and speakers still blared music by the door. She kept her weapon on the man and signaled Drew. He shut off the music. The sudden silence was cutting.

She swallowed hard, wishing she'd let someone else take the lead. "Walter Pike?"

He shook his head. "My name is now Mujahid Nassar."

She raised her eyebrows as she looked at the underweight, pale-skinned man, whose sparse facial hair competed with his acne. She'd let the feds sort this one out.

"Walter Pike, you're under arrest for conspiring to use weapons of mass destruction. Put down the tools and stand up."

The acrid scent continued to bite the inside of her throat. She needed water. Dust seemed to coat the inside of her mouth and throat.

No. There was no dust. No heat. It wasn't real.

Dr. Martinez said she needed to focus on another sense. She could do this. She was here in the apartment with a scumbag who wanted to blow people up.

"Alyssa," Drew said in a low voice. "You with us?"

The gun grew heavy in her hand. A trickle of sweat rolled down her back. She fought to control her breathing. She couldn't let this happen. Not here. Not now.

She nodded. Pike held his now-empty hands above his head. Shit. She'd lost some time there. "Get some cuffs on him."

"Hey!" he said. "I didn't do anything. It ain't illegal to have any of this stuff."

Drew holstered his weapon while she and Riley kept a bead on him.

"What kind of fucking idiot are you?" Drew said. He wrenched the guy's arm down and spun him before slamming him onto the worktable. He ratcheted the handcuffs onto the suspect before handing him off to another officer.

"Aren't you supposed to read me my rights?" Pike asked.

"I don't have the stomach for it," Drew said, handing him off to a uniformed officer, who started to recite the Miranda warning before Pike could protest further.

Alyssa stared at the table's contents. Enough supplies to

double the damage of the Boston Marathon bombing. A hand appeared in her vision and forced her gun down. She blinked. Fuck. She hadn't lowered her weapon.

Riley watched her with his dark, intense gaze. "You okay, Al?"

No. She could hear echoes of screams in her head.

She took a deep breath. That was a mistake. She coughed out the sharp odor of black powder, but at least she snapped back to the present.

"I'm fine," she said. "I just need fresh air." She left the room. All the triumph of an investigation coming to a head had dissipated like smoke in the wind.

Drew followed her, of course. She holstered her gun and forced a smile. "We did it," she said.

He just stared at her. His brown eyes narrowed. "Want to talk about it?"

Fuck no. "Talk about what?" She wasn't sure if she was pulling off the innocent act.

"The way you froze in there."

Nope. Not pulling it off. Fuck it, then. She scowled. "I'm fine."

"You're not fine."

"Leave it alone, Drew."

He crossed his arms. "We all have our shit, Al. If you've got a trigger then you've got to tell us."

"I told you, I'm fine." Her radio beeped.

"Harrison," she answered.

"The captain wants your team for an urgent briefing,"

dispatch said. "Return to CTB. Briefing in thirty."

"Copy that," Alyssa said. She motioned to Drew and Riley. "ESU can take it from here. The captain wants us in."

"For what?" Drew asked.

"No idea," Alyssa said, making her way past the swarming ESU officers. "But it must be something big if we're being called off our case."

The three of them belonged to the Counterterrorism Bureau of the NYPD. They'd been working the Walter Pike case for two months, so for their captain to call them in at this moment meant something big was coming down the pike. It made her pick up the pace as they trotted down the stairs. Drew and Riley stayed right with her.

As she drove their car back to CTB headquarters far north of Central Park, they had time to rehash the case.

"Do you think the captain is calling us in to give us an award?" Drew asked.

Alyssa looked over at him in the passenger seat. "You're not serious."

Drew laughed. "Hell yeah. I freaking deserve a medal. We all do, for dealing with the scum of the earth every day."

Alyssa shook her head. "If you wanted recognition, you should have become an actor."

Riley snorted from the backseat. "He couldn't be an actor—he'd break the camera with his face."

Drew ignored him and continued. "I'm serious. The captain is making us all attend that ball that's coming up—"

"The Hero's Gala," Alyssa supplied.

"Yeah, that. I think he's going to award us a medal or something."

Riley cuffed the back of Drew's head. "You're out of your mind, man."

"Listen, asshole, no one's talking to you," Drew said. "So why don't you just sit there and look pretty."

Alyssa shook her head and tried not to smile. "The captain wants us to go because it's our unit's turn to show up and represent the NYPD. The gala is for the military guys and the vets. They get the medals. Sorry, Drew."

"I can buy you a medal if you want," Riley said from the back. "I'll even make sure it says Number One Cop."

They were still laughing when she parked in the lot next to a nondescript building. Looking around, it was a place no one would suspect of housing the elite counterterrorism unit. Inside, the officer guarding the entrance buzzed them through interior steel doors.

They headed for the large conference room, past the main cubicle area and down a short hall. Officers packed the room. She found a spot against the wall and waited for the captain.

Captain Marin charged into the room, officers giving way. Alyssa always got a mental picture of a grizzled pitbull defending its territory when she saw him. On the shorter side, he was dense with muscle. His buzz cut glinted more silver than brown in the overhead lights.

"Okay, people, a new message was sent out over the black net an hour ago."

Everyone quieted.

"The terrorist Al Shabah has surfaced again. It's been six months since we've seen any activity from him and he's come back with a vengeance."

Alyssa straightened, every muscle tensing in her body. He was back.

Captain Marin's gaze found hers. "Detective Harrison is our resident expert on Al Shabah, and will be leading the task force."

She took a step forward and all eyes turned to her. "What did the message say?"

"That Al Shabah is coming to the United States. I don't need to tell you that New York City is one of the prime targets for assholes like this. We need to be ready, people." He focused on Alyssa again. "Pick your task force." He let his gaze roam over the rest of the officers. "Everyone is to give Detective Harrison what she needs. This is our primary focus. Find Al Shabah and stop him."

Within fifteen minutes, Alyssa had a dozen men and women with her as they began to set up their strategy. This is what she'd trained and joined the department for. She'd sworn to hunt Al Shabah down and kill him for what he'd done.

And that's exactly what she was going to do.

Zach walked into the conference room now dubbed the war room by Dani, the newest IT tech at E.D.G.E. Security. He liked her snarky attitude, though he wasn't sure Colonel Blackwell, the head of E.D.G.E. operations, had yet come to terms with it.

He'd been called in for a mission brief by the colonel. His eyebrows rose when he saw both Alpha and Bravo teams there as well. This could be interesting.

He grabbed a seat just as Blackwell strode in carrying his ever-present laptop. "Okay, people. This takes top priority over any other training."

Everyone straightened and turned to Blackwell, who stood at the head of the long table. He tapped a few keys on his laptop and then activated the virtual screen. It came to life on the white wall behind him. He wore a special glove that allowed him to use hand movements to flick through the data onscreen.

A video began to play.

A man dressed in black from head to toe, his face wrapped to disguise his features, began speaking in Arabic.

"Soon all of America will know my name. I will no longer confine my war to the poor countries the West continues to invade time and again. Like the United States, I will take my own brand of terror to their streets, to their homes, to their children."

Zach stiffened, his hands clenching into fists. "Al Shabah."

Blackwell nodded. "He's taking his war to the United

States. The FBI are on full alert. All major cities are possible targets."

"What else do we know, sir?" Jake asked.

"Not much," Blackwell said. "CIA have their operatives in the Middle East on alert for any information. Sarah." Blackwell turned to the petite brunette with bronze skin. "We're sending you back to Iraq. Gather whatever intel you can."

"Copy that, sir," she said.

"We have a team covering the West Coast already. Cat and Rhys, you'll go to Washington to coordinate with the FBI agent in charge there. Zach and Marc, you've got—"

"New York," Zach said.

Blackwell's eyebrows raised, but he nodded. "You've got a theory?"

"Hitting the White House or the Pentagon would be ideal for Al Shabah, but it has too much risk of failure. Too much security. He'll want to go for New York. Something he can show the world: No matter how much America rebuilds itself, he'll be there to tear it back down."

"Those are my thoughts too," Blackwell nodded. "Bravo team will back you up from here. They'll be on call to deploy as soon as you have something. You'll be coordinating the search with Special Agent Masters. He's due to arrive in theatre tomorrow."

Rhys leaned his long frame back in his chair and eyed the screen. "Can this Al Shabah even get into the States?"

Zach answered for Blackwell. "This guy has gotten

into numerous Western countries, even after he's given them warning. He was responsible for the bus bombing in Germany and the Underground one in the U.K. I don't know how he'll do it, but we've got to be prepared for him. He'll make it to North America."

"You're no closer to tracking down his identity?" Cat asked him.

Zach gave a sharp shake of his head. "No one is. This guy literally is his name. Al Shabah. The Ghost. He had small cells working with him in each country he struck, but none of them have ever actually seen him."

"How long have you been after him?" Jake asked Zach.

"Since the bombing that killed those soldiers in Iraq. Two years now." Zach shook his head. "We were so close last year. I will find this guy and bring him down."

"Don't worry, Doc," Marc said from the other end of the table, where he'd been sitting quiet. "If he comes to New York, we'll find him."

Blackwell closed his laptop. "You've each been given a copy of the file we have on Al Shabah. Most of that has been created by Zach. Because of that, he will be team lead for this op. Wheels up in two hours."

"Yes, sir," they all said together.

Zach stood with the others, already going over his list of what he'd need for a covert mission in a major city, when Jake stopped him.

"You know I'm from New York, right?" he said.

Zach nodded.

"My parents live upstate, but my sis is a cop with the NYPD Counterterrorism Bureau. Chances are you're going to run into her."

"Okay," he said. "I'll say hi for you."

"No," Jake said, shaking his head. "You don't get it. She's fanatical about Al Shabah. She knew some of the guys who were killed by one of his bombs. She's been hunting him ever since."

"I thought you said she was a cop. What was she doing over there?"

Jake sighed. "Military intelligence. She followed me into the service out of school." He ran a hand over his short hair. "God, I wish she hadn't."

"Why? What happened?"

Jake stepped back and his face went blank. "Nothing. Just... Watch out for her, okay?"

"Of course," he said. "You don't have to ask. Besides, she might not even be assigned to this."

Jake huffed a breath. "Oh, she'll be assigned to it. She'll demand to be on the task force."

"She sounds like a firecracker."

"You have no idea."